DOWNRIGHT DEAD

A Dr. Annabel Tilson Novel

Book 5

DOWNRIGHT DEAD

by Barbara Ebel, M.D.

A Dr. Annabel Tilson Novel

Book One: Dead Still
Book Two: Deadly Delusions
Book Three: Desperate to Die
Book Four: Death Grip
Book Five: Downright Dead
Book Six: Dangerous Doctor

Copyright © 2018 by Barbara Ebel, M.D.

Paperback ISBN-13: 978-1-7324466-0-1
eBook ISBN-13: 978-1-7324466-1-8

This book is a work of fiction. Names, characters, places and events are the product of the author's imagination or are used fictitiously. Any resemblance to actual events, persons, or locations is coincidental.

CHAPTER 1

"I don't know nothin' 'bout birthin' babies, Miss Scarlett!"

Sitting on her boyfriend's couch, Annabel Tilson leaned forward and laughed. The popcorn she was eating practically hurled from her mouth as she hit the pause button of the TV remote. *Gone with the Wind* stopped.

"Can you believe it? she asked. "That's exactly how I feel. Just like Scarlett O'Hara's otherwise helpful maid, I don't know squat about obstetrics and gynecology."

"Tomorrow that will begin to change," her boyfriend, Dustin, said. "In four weeks, you'll be able to deliver a baby better than I can." He inched closer and rubbed her shoulder.

She glanced abruptly at him. "I'm only a third-year medical student. The residents will be catching the babies. I'll be observing, studying, and doing the scut work."

"Being privy to some of your prior medical cases that ended up in the police department, you've been doing more than that."

"Yeah, well, whatever." She leaned back into the upholstery and gave him a hard stare. "Do you mean you're one of those policemen who have escorted a pregnant woman in labor, ready to pop, in his patrol car?"

A sly smile crossed his lips, highlighting the dimple in his chin.

"Want to hear about it? I can give you the details back there." He pointed to his bedroom and his grin grew wider.

"Dustin Lowe! Don't tempt me. Can I take a rain check? I'd better head home and get ready for my first day on OB."

He moved the bowl of popcorn between them to the cocktail table. "I understand. New subject matter to ingest in only four weeks and your normal composure is turning into the jitters. Anything I can do to help?"

"No. You're empathetic about my studies already, which may stem from your own nerve-racking career. Actually, it was wonderful having these two days off after finishing my internal medicine rotation on Friday. Thanks for a nice day and a great wrap-up to the weekend."

Their knees touched and Dustin put his hand on her leg. The other one went around her neck and they closed the gap for a tender kiss.

1

She rose and toyed with her silky long hair. "We'll finish the movie next time. We have to. Atlanta is in flames and Scarlett's friend is about to give birth."

Dustin's yellow-naped Amazon parrot, Solar, flicked his head from his perch. "About to give birth," he quipped.

Annabel twisted her mouth at him. "Nobody asked for your two cents."

"What's your problem?" he countered.

She knew that was his favorite line, so Annabel threw up her arms. "Take care of Dustin and I'll see you next time."

She grabbed her purse and car keys while Dustin joined her at the door.

"Lucky you," he said. "He didn't give you any more back talk." He perched his elbow on the door frame and brought his hand to her hair.

"Don't look at me that way."

"What way?"

"You know what way." She gave him a quick kiss and tapped her finger in his dimple. "See you soon."

"Likewise. Go crush your OB/GYN rotation."

Annabel thanked the Uber driver, walked in the hospital entrance, and eyed the coffee stand. She veered right; she had a few extra minutes and couldn't resist.

"You're back," said one of the baristas.

Annabel chuckled. "Yes, back at the University Hospital. I'm starting OB/GYN and the VA Hospital doesn't exactly specialize in that patient population."

"I should say not. What can I make for you?"

She ordered and left with a mocha cappuccino. The team was supposed to meet and gather on the obstetric side of the fourth floor, so she punched the elevator button and rode up while sipping her hot beverage. The doors opened and the signs hanging in the peaceful lounge in front of her designated all of obstetrics to the right and gynecology to the left.

Annabel took a big sigh as she walked. After rotating in surgery, psychiatry, and internal medicine, she still did not know for sure what specialty she wanted to go into. She wondered if this rotation would pique her curiosity enough to treat more pregnant ladies and gynecology patients in the future.

Doors to the unoccupied labor and delivery rooms stood open. She poked her head in one of them. They looked more like hotel lodging than typical hospital rooms.

Annabel proceeded down the squeaky-clean hallway and a door flew open; a long-coated male doctor stuck his head out and looked toward the counter at the end where several people were milling about.

"I need help in here!" he shouted.

A female, also wearing a long white coat, dashed down the corridor and disappeared inside.

Annabel hesitated, wondering if she qualified as "help." Probably not. Less than twelve hours ago, she had mimicked the words that she knew "nothin' 'bout birthin' babies." Besides, medical students were often in the way when a real crisis was taking place.

The male physician swung the door open again and shouted as a nurse came rushing his way.

"Call anesthesia."

"He's putting in an epidural right now."

"Try and get another anesthesiologist from the main OR."

"It may take a while, Dr. Gash."

"Fetch another cart. I need more Pitocin and call the blood bank to send us two units of blood."

She peeled away and his eyes fell on Annabel.

"You a new med student on the service?"

She nodded. "Annabel Tilson."

He jerked his head in the direction of the room and she followed.

"Sir, you need to leave," Dr. Gash said to a man inside. The man, who Annabel assumed to be the patient's partner, was near the door and she couldn't see past him. When he turned, he appeared to be in his twenties and wore casual clothes and sneakers. His face was pasty white, his eyes bulged, and he stuttered something undecipherable. A nurse was behind him in a flash. She manually swept him away, escorting him out the door.

The sights and sounds in the room hit her like a harsh wake-up call from a dead sleep.

CHAPTER 2

A young woman about Annabel's age was on a labor and delivery bed, which was broken down in the middle and functioned as her birthing bed; she still held on to the handles. Her legs were sprawled open in the lithotomy position, her feet in stirrups. The female doctor stood between them.

Blood cascaded from between the patient's legs. A blue drape wasn't holding the flow adequately and it began spilling on the wooden floor. A newborn was off to the side on a table with a nurse hovering above it as Dr. Gash evaluated its status and looked over at Annabel.

"Tell them to get a pediatrician for Ms. Barker's baby," he yelled. "Stat."

The distressed patient on the delivery table grimaced and contorted her face, but with the clue that her baby was also in trouble, she let out a soulful cry.

Annabel darted two quick steps and hollered towards the nurses' station. "They need a pediatrician."

She breathed deeply and spun around to go back inside. She had completed her surgery rotation and had seen trauma cases, but this was the first time she'd seen that much blood pouring out of someone. From childbirth? This was insane.

Within seconds of her being gone, the group in the room came to another decision.

"We can't contain this," the female physician declared. "Bonnie Barker, you're going to the OR."

Annabel realized the physician must be Ling Watson, her new team's chief resident. As she stepped back into the hallway, a strong-muscled orderly was backing an empty wheelchair out of a nearby room. "There's an emergency in here," she said. "Can you help them transport a patient to the OR?"

The man went inside, where Dr. Watson gritted her teeth and bimanually palpated the woman's abdomen as well as inside her vagina. Confusion swept over Annabel. Was this some kind of CPR on the woman's uterus after birth … something to help a bleeding situation like this one?

No further words were spoken as the bed flew down the corridor to swinging doors ... straight into the obstetric floor's own OR. Masks, bonnets, and shoe covers seemed to magically attach themselves to everyone going in. Annabel stopped short and busted into a women's locker room and threw on scrubs. After getting properly attired, she rushed into the OR where Bonnie Barker's life depended on the medical team.

The patient's vital signs were registered on the monitors and beeped from the head of the table, where the anesthesiologist had already arrived. He was stripping open an IV package and a tourniquet was wrapped on the patient's left arm. When he whipped it out, he expertly slid the large-bore IV into a vein. Annabel realized the patient needed a larger IV than she already had. Fast replacement blood was needed to substitute for what she was losing.

The monitors painted a gruesome picture. Ms. Barker's blood pressure sagged and her heart rate bounced higher and higher. Dr. Watson continued her bimanual compressions. The patient became more quiet.

Ling Watson's eyes met the doctor at the head of the table. "Pitocin?"

"I just gave another ten units slowly," he said.

As Annabel contemplated the drug, she remembered hearing that it was the same as oxytocin - a neurotransmitter in the brain. But why were they using it now? Meanwhile, someone thrust two units of blood through the door and wiggled them at her. She grabbed them and verbally cross-checked the bags with the blood bank slips with a nurse to make sure ... correct patient and correct blood.

The anesthesiologist pulled the tab from one of the units and stuck the blood bag into an IV fluid setup and into a pressure bag. After pumping it up, blood began streaming into the woman's vein.

"I'll get blood for labs," the anesthesiologist said.

"Yes, she could have a coagulopathy," Dr. Watson said.

The anesthesiologist drew blood from the patient's other arm. Soon an OR tech ran outside with the filled vials for the lab.

Dr. Watson slid her hand off of Bonnie Barker's abdomen and nodded at Dr. Gash to help her out.

Caleb Gash stood on the other side of the table and began palpating.

"What about a uterine laceration?"

Ling took her hand out of the woman's vagina. Blood clung to her glove and dripped down. She eyed the drapes, the floor, and back between Bonnie's legs. "Thank God," she mumbled.

"Slowing?" Caleb asked.

"Like someone has turned off the faucet."

The three senior doctors in the room made eye contact with each other, acknowledging silently that the life-and-death situation was turning around. The patient's uterus was clamping down; beginning to behave itself.

The anesthesiologist took down the empty unit of blood and hung the next one. Bonnie Barker's blood pressure and heart rate began reversing their deleterious directions. Her oxygen saturation stayed acceptable with the oxygen the anesthesiologist had placed over her face with a mask.

"Let me take a good look," Dr. Watson said. "Make sure I don't have to ligate any blood vessels. Get me a Foley catheter as well," she said to a nurse.

She leaned over Bonnie's abdomen as much as she could. "Ms. Barker, we thought the anesthesiologist was going to have to put you to sleep and I would need to do a surgical repair to stop the bleeding. However, it is slowing down. We're waiting on blood work, which will tell us more as well."

Annabel had her hand close to the patient; Bonnie's arm was stretched out on an arm board. The patient acknowledged Dr. Watson's words by giving Annabel's fingers a light squeeze.

The time remaining in the OR took longer than the emergent manner in which the doctors and nurses sped Ms. Barker from her room to the OR and palpated her uterine fundus and resuscitated her. When they finally steered her bed out of the OR, they brought her to the recovery room where they could watch her closely.

Dr. Watson and the anesthesiologist sidled next to each other.

"At least seven hundred cc's blood loss in the delivery room," she said.

"At least six hundred cc's blood loss in the OR," he said.

"A major postpartum hemorrhage is a hell of a way to start the day."

Caleb Gash and Annabel stood nearby. He gave her a small nod. "Welcome to OB."

CHAPTER 3

Annabel stood for the longest time while the senior physicians talked at Bonnie Barker's bedside and then backed up to a corner, where they discussed the case in almost a whisper. She shifted her weight from one foot to the other, watching the post anesthesia care unit or PACU nurse tend to her patient. From the doorway, the patient's partner stuck his head in and cleared his throat.

The PACU nurse waved at him. "Don't be shy. You can visit for a few minutes. Bonnie will most likely be ready to nap soon after all she's been through."

He nodded and stepped in, but stood closer to Annabel than the bed. "How's the baby?" he asked her.

"I don't know. You can probably find out from the staff in the nursery or the pediatrician in charge. I take it you're the dad?"

He looked at his sneakers and contemplated her question. "Yeah," he said, nodding towards Bonnie. "But she quit me after she got pregnant."

"Quit you?"

"She didn't want to see me much after that. Like some big feminist idea to raise the kid with or without me. Turned down getting married. I mean, I offered after she didn't want an abortion. I'm an accessory to her becoming a mother and this is only the beginning of this kid's life." He eyed Annabel. "What happened back in the room looked pretty scary. By the way, I'm Tony. How come there are so many of you doctors taking care of her? She won't be able to pay a humongous bill from each of you."

"I'm a third-year medical school student, not a full-fledged doctor yet like them over there." She pointed to the corner and finally sat on the edge of an empty stretcher. "In other words, I'm free of charge and I'm here to observe, learn, and gain experience."

"Low man on the totem pole. Figures. You have a glazed-over expression like you're clueless."

"It shows that much?"

Without a parting comment, and with a soft stride, he was alongside Bonnie, who made a poor attempt to acknowledge him. Annabel wondered if it was only because of weakness from her harrowing experience, loss of blood, and resuscitation. She frowned and glanced at the doctors huddled together in the corner. At the moment, Tony wasn't the only one being left out to dry.

The orderly who helped out earlier passed by in the hallway and stopped when he saw Annabel. "Time you learn where to hang out when you're not with a patient or doing scut work," he said. "I'm Emmett."

"I'm Annabel Tilson," she said as they went down the hall and behind the main desk of the labor and delivery wing. "I bet you are aware of everything that goes on around here."

His furry black eyebrows inched skyward and he laughed. "More than most." He pointed towards the spacious room. Each of his forearms had a tattoo, but they were difficult to appreciate due to his dark olive skin tone.

"Pick a spot," he said. "This is the lounge those docs back there use, but Dr. Fleming and Dr. Ridley, the anesthesia residents, are here more often. That's cuz they're posted here this month running ragged with what I call 'mother's pain.' There's no other pain like it in the whole world or the whole universe ... I'm sure of it. If I'd been born the unfortunate sex of a woman, I wouldn't be doing what other members of my sex do. No sir. No thank you. No spitting out babies for me. I'd make sure I stayed a childless woman, if you know what I mean."

The smile lines around his eyes disappeared as he spoke. When he finished, he added one more thing as he grabbed an empty wheelchair to transport back to the ER. "Dr. Fleming is at the white board in there." He leaned over. "She's the real deal."

Annabel thanked him. She sat inside at a round table while the anesthesia resident used an eraser to remove a name. The woman shot her a glance.

"You must be a new student. Welcome. I'm Kristin Fleming, a fourth-year resident; a third-year anesthesia resident."

"I'm Annabel, a third-year student. A fourth year in residency is a long way off for me."

"I hear you. You have a long haul, but you've done a lot already. The journey is what's important, Annabel, not the end result." She put the eraser down, and with a spring to her step, she pulled out a chair. Dark, wide-rimmed glasses sat on her broad nose and two sets of earrings made up for her otherwise lack of jewelry. She was flat-chested, tall, and extended her lanky upper limbs on the table.

"I missed the case that just came out of the OR," Kristin said, "because I was in a patient's room doing an epidural for a woman's labor. Did you go in?"

"I followed and stayed out of the way. I always hate the beginning of a new service because I feel so helpless."

"That'll change. You'll be doing scut work before you eat lunch. That, in and of itself, is useful to the team." She contracted her lips in a pucker like some people furrow their forehead in thought, and then mumbled under her breath, "If you can call them a team."

"So true about the scut work, but don't get me wrong. I'm not complaining. I make the most of my rotations and end up having the most memorable, off-the-graph experiences. I love medical school and wouldn't change what I'm doing for all the gold in Fort Knox."

"Awesome. You interested in OB/GYN?"

"I don't have a clue. My dad's a neurosurgeon and I have an uncle who's a paramedic, so I had little exposure to that type of specialty talk at home."

Kristin nodded as Dr. Watson and Dr. Gash strutted in. They went straight to the couch and sat cozily next to each other. Ling unfolded a sheet of paper, flattened it down on the short table, and then noticed Annabel. "You might as well join us," she said. "Are Barker's lab results back yet?"

"I don't know," Annabel said, hesitating to sit across from them.

Ling rolled her eyes like Annabel was a fly on the wall. "It's obvious you inherited her as a patient. All right then ... sit down. Now is as good a time as any to explain the rotation to you despite what you might have heard. Every medical school doles out their OB/GYN rotation the way they want, but this is how we do it here. Ours is short compared to surgery or internal medicine. Four weeks is all you have unless you become totally impressed and enraptured like I am with the last remaining natural God-given act on the planet – childbirth. If you are, then I'll see more of you in a few years when you do a residency.

"However, the four weeks are basically split up. Two weeks of obstetrics and two weeks of gynecology, except that clinic days will be a combination of both types of patients. There's only one test at the end of the four weeks, which obviously covers the whole kit and caboodle. This week you'll do OB during the day and next week, you'll be on the twelve-hour night shift. The other student, Stuart Schneider, will be alternating the days and nights with you. We don't care what twelve hours you're doing when bi-monthly grand rounds are scheduled. You must attend that lecture no matter what. You'll most often see our attending doctor in clinic."

Ling tilted her head at Caleb. "Anything else you want to tell her?"

"Sure. We discuss patients once in the morning and late in the afternoon, but that is not set in cement because there may be active patient care going on … like what happened this morning. Our course of action around here depends on what's going on with a parturient's uterus and vagina."

"Keep up with the status of the patients on the board and write a daily note on everyone," Ling added. "It's not uncommon to salvage some time to study during the day, so do it. Dr. Gash and I won't be holding your hand. Don't forget that around here we're not only taking care of this predominantly young female population, but the safe delivery of their infants rests with us. That is a huge responsibility so, most of the time, we're on auto-pilot and not paying attention to students."

Dr. Watson's pager buzzed. She got up, and disappeared out the door. Caleb leaned forward, ready to follow the chief resident. "Find out any updates on Bonnie Barker and her baby," he said.

"How unusual was that this morning?" Annabel asked quickly.

"Here's your fact for the day. Information to commit to memory. For a normal birth of a single baby in a vaginal delivery, Mom loses, on average, five-hundred milliliters. That equates to two full cups of blood. Our patient lost well over double that amount. As a matter of fact, she lost more than a fifth of her prepregnant entire blood volume."

Annabel shuddered. Caleb rose and stuffed a notepad in his pocket.

"What about a cesarean section? What's the normal blood loss for that?"

"An entire one-thousand milliliters and, it goes without saying, you better learn everything there is to learn about Pitocin."

Annabel pulled out her pocket-size handbook on obstetrics and gynecology, and when she glanced back up, Caleb was gone. She thumbed through the index, ready to get her facts straight. In the first two years of medical school, she'd heard more about oxytocin because it was a protein produced by the pituitary gland; a naturally occurring hormone of male and female mammals that increases the concentration of calcium inside muscle cells which, in turn, controls the contraction of the uterus. She read that the synthetic, man-made version of oxytocin, is Pitocin and, apparently, used in obstetrics all the time for stimulating uterine contraction.

A "pop" sounded from the round table where Kristin Fleming opened a soda can and began pouring. Annabel broke from her reading. It was time to do her patient's follow up.

"Pitocin comes in handy," Kristin said, peering over her glasses. "It can induce abortion and be life-saving to control bleeding after childbirth. And labor? They don't call it that for nothing. Damn hard on a woman. Exhausting and painful as hell."

"You must be the guardian angel in all of this ... providing their pain management."

"So true. However, labor, plain and simple, can wear a body out. No matter how much a woman tries, her body just can't or won't push that baby out. Pitocin can induce labor or strengthen the contractions of labor. Often, that synthetic drug is as valuable to them as an epidural. They just don't realize it."

Annabel nodded. It was the same old thing. Patients often didn't realize the intricacies of the medical care they were receiving. No different from customers understanding the minute details of a tax accountant working on their tax return or an architect trying to make a particular geographic landscape work with a certain house plan.

"Thanks, Dr. Fleming."

Kristin gestured with her glass. "You're welcome."

The newborn nursery and neonatal intensive care unit, or NICU, was on the same floor as obstetrics and gynecology, but straight forward off the central elevators.

The faces peering into the main nursery on the right were mostly lit up with smiles. Other individuals and family members giggled, pointed, and made funny faces at the swaddled infants in their bassinets. The scenario on the left, however, painted a different picture. The NICU housed the premature infants having difficulty or ones with congenital abnormalities needing specialized care, or pre or postop premies that were in dire straits … their battle to live begun way too prematurely without so much as taking their first steps on Mother Earth.

Standing to the side of visitors, Annabel scoured the names of the babies in the main nursery and saw a card for "Baby Girl Barker." She wondered how a mother could carry a baby for months and not have a name picked out. Even if the mother didn't know the sex by ultrasound, she figured a woman would at least have a name for a boy and a girl. But then again, maybe she was waiting to see what the baby would look like and a name would spring into mind. She wasn't that familiar with newborns, but her impression was that they weren't that distinctive. They had to grow into their facial and bodily features as well as their personalities. She shrugged her shoulders and stared at the female newborn who appeared scrawnier than the two babies on either side of her.

Annabel recognized the physician hurrying past her as the pediatrician who had showed up in Bonnie Barker's delivery room. He seemed to be giving another doctor information as they walked together and opened the door to the nursery. "Another thing," the pediatrician said. "The Barker baby's position at birth? Breech."

The two men clutched the rim of the basket. They talked with a seriousness that could only be construed as concerning. The pediatrician gently loosened the baby's blanket and allowed the other physician to perform a physical exam.

CHAPTER 4

The cafeteria of the University Hospital bustled with activity as Annabel slipped through the aisles and found an empty table. How disappointing to eat lunch alone, she thought. She didn't even see any medical students around from other rotations. Maybe she missed them all because she peeled away from the labor and delivery floor later than her growling stomach wanted to. She had spent time in the ER with a pregnant patient who ended up not being admitted, but they had not informed her of that. Time may fly, heal, or steal, but to a medical student, wasted time was worse than being on a ship lost at sea.

Annabel reached for the salt as long fingers gripped it before she could and handed it to her. Tony stood over the table looking as forlorn as an abandoned puppy. He pulled out a chair across from her and sat without a word.

She jiggled salt on her side dish of steamed vegetables, hoping he wouldn't be too chatty, especially if he wanted to discuss his girlfriend's condition. At this point, he would be better off scrolling through Safari on his iPhone rather than asking her any obstetric questions to do with Bonnie.

He broke out in a smile. "My little girl is tiny, but I can hardly wait. Although I only wiggled my way through high school, she's gonna go to college. And I swear, she's gonna be a super soccer player."

"You play?"

"Play?" He straightened his shoulders and beamed even more. "I'm a soccer coach."

"Nice. You must enjoy the kids."

"Yeah. That's me. I have five siblings, so I grew up with people around me. I am more excited about this new baby than I ever imagined. Damn. Bonnie needs to marry me. But no mind; I won't let the young one grow up without a father. As a matter of fact, this is so cool - I plan on giving her brothers and sisters too, like me ... even if they're half-brothers and sisters."

Annabel thought he was getting ahead of himself, but at least he didn't seem to be the type to shirk his responsibilities. She also wondered if there was a problem with the baby. Why had the pediatrician called in another apparent pediatrician? She stirred the straw in her iced tea. "Did you hold your new baby yet?"

He set his wide jawline in a stern scowl. "No. Not yet. They're busy tending to her. I didn't know that nowadays births are complicated by all this modern scientific mumbo jumbo. I mean, I bet my sneakers that nobody did genetic testing on me when I was born."

"Genetic testing?"

"Some doctor upstairs told me they are going to test Baby Barker."

After he left, Annabel finished her meal in silent contemplation. Her first OB patient had not only encountered a problem, but apparently her baby had too. Bonnie and Baby Barker were mired in bad luck today. To their better fortune, which Bonnie was ignoring, Tony was a young man on the sidelines who really seemed to care about their well-being.

Upstairs, after scrolling for the information on the computer, Annabel made a note of Bonnie's hemoglobin and hematocrit on the index card she wrote up for her patient. As with other rotations, she logged each of the patients she followed in such a manner and always had their pertinent information in her white jacket pocket. In her opinion, the young mother's red blood cell counts were now acceptable. Of course, Bonnie had been transfused … the purpose of which was to bring the levels up so she would not continue to demonstrate the effects of an acute anemia, like what had happened in the OR.

Based on the scant reading she did before the rotation, she already knew that anemia is a common complication in a pregnant woman – if there are not enough erythrocytes or red blood cells that can carry hemoglobin, the functional iron-carrying protein. That critical protein transports oxygen molecules to the body's tissues and organs. Too few blood cells and a body will be oxygen deprived … causing symptoms of fatigue, shortness of breath, dizziness, rapid heart rate, and impaired cognition.

She opened up her handbook and looked under the "physiology of pregnancy" and scanned several paragraphs. In the pregnant woman, it said, anemia was most often due to iron deficiency due to two reasons. The first reason may be due to decreased iron stores prior to pregnancy. Or, secondly, it may be due to increased demands for iron because of an increased need from the growing fetus and an expanded maternal blood volume.

She extended her legs under the desk of the computer station and thought back to her surgery rotation where she had observed trauma patients. That was where she witnessed more than ever the color coding of blood. Arterial blood filled with oxygen-laden hemoglobin was bright red, but after it returned to the lung without its oxygen, it would lose its brightness. That blood would become bluish and was more synonymous with venous blood.

Thinking back to Miss Barker's postpartum hemorrhage, she couldn't imagine a few hundred years ago when there was no such thing as large-bore intravenous catheters and packed red blood cells for transfusion. No wonder women quite often died during or after childbirth in those days. And that was without taking into account the other horrendous problems and complications of pregnancy and delivery.

In essence, she didn't have to mimic what the anesthesia resident or the orderly had said. She already made up her own mind that women, even if they didn't know it, took on a lot by becoming pregnant!

"Are you going to sit there all day?"

Ling Watson paused as she delivered her comment while Annabel glanced up at her senior resident, who wore all the right curves in all the right places. Her nails were manicured perfectly and her fingers looked exquisite. She wore a solid blue gemstone on her right ring finger. The time she must spend on her hands, Annabel thought, was short changed when it came to her hair. She was blessed with smooth, shiny, jet-black hair, which she easily wore in a pulled-back, tight ponytail.

Dr. Watson tore down the hallway and Annabel caught up.

"Bonnie Barker's H and H is 11 and 33," Annabel said.

"Those are decent numbers, considering."

"Yes, I read that anemia in a pregnant woman is considered to be a hemoglobin below 10. But did you know the pediatricians are doing some kind of a work-up on her baby?"

"I'm hard core about the fetuses of my pregnant patients, but I'm all too happy to turn the newborns over to pediatricians once they take that first breath of air, which, by the way, should be within the first ten seconds of delivery." She stopped short. "You can come downstairs and watch if you want. A new patient. You can write up an H&P afterwards. Also, it's a huge subject. Tomorrow, regurgitate to me the adaptations a newborn must make to extrauterine life."

Annabel fidgeted with her hair as she trailed Ling into the elevator. At least that topic had been brushed over in courses such as physiology and embryology, but it was a complex subject. Now, for today and tonight, specific reading awaited her. It was doubtful she would have the time to address the personal items on her agenda.

In the ER, Ling barely glanced at the board as she swiped a stack of papers from the counter and brought them with her. She knew exactly where she was going as she shoved curtains back and entered a cubicle. Other than her protruding belly, a woman before them in a hospital gown appeared to be more like a medical patient than an obstetric patient. She struggled with difficulty breathing. Her hand rested on her abdomen as her quick breaths and unfamiliar situation caused her big brown saucer eyes to glance at them with fear.

"I'm not galloping, but I feel like a race horse gulping for air," she said in a high-pitched voice. Annabel guessed her age to be nearly twenty, but her voice made her sound like a prepubertal teenager.

"How long has this been going on?" Ling asked.

"A few hours."

"How far along is your pregnancy?"

"Last week I was 28 weeks."

"You been coming to prenatal clinic?"

"Yeah."

"First pregnancy?"

"Yeah."

"Any medical problems?"

"No."

"Any problems during the pregnancy so far?"

"No," she whimpered.

"Annabel, go check if the clinic chart notes have been sent over or if the secretary has printed out those notes from the computer."

Annabel hated to miss out on watching her first full history and physical of a pregnant lady, but she did as she was told. She scurried out and put a name to a face by glancing at the ER board: Mary Chandler, eighteen years old. She was boldly designated on the board and chart as G1P0. The "G" stood for gravidity ... the patient's number of total pregnancies, including the current one. Had Ms. Chandler had any before, that number could have also included miscarriages and stillbirths. The "P" stood for parity, which was the number of pregnancies ending in a gestational age greater than twenty weeks. Miss Chandler's G1P0 correlated with her confirmation that the current pregnancy was her first one.

"What were you doing when you were eighteen years old?"

Annabel swung around where she stood. Emmett, the orderly from upstairs, frowned.

"Not having babies, that's for sure."

He nodded. "I think these young girls were deprived of love as youngsters and are still longing for it. They think that by having a baby themselves, they will make up for that deprivation. They believe they'll give and receive love to and from their offspring like it's a winning gamble." He sighed heavily, un-gripped the back end of a chair, and plopped himself down.

"It's like this," he added. "Going into their adulthood, they think they're giving their future a value right off the bat. They ante up the pot with a newborn. Or so they think. In reality, they make themselves a donkey player."

"A donkey player?"

"I forgot," he said and shook his head. "You medical students don't have time for anything else except medicine. I'm talking poker. These little girls deal themselves the worst hand. Like holding a 2 and 7 off suit."

"I see. I'd better run along, though."

She hadn't expected the orderly to render such an opinion, but, then again, he could be a multi-faceted individual and this could be a side job for him. He could have a master's degree in psychology and be a stellar card player for all that she knew. She grabbed a handful of the blue drape at Mary Chandler's cubicle, ready to step inside. In four weeks, however, she was sure there would be no questions on her test about poker games.

Ling took the clinic record from Annabel as soon as she entered. Mary Chandler swiped her hand along her belly like someone was ready to snatch her growing fetus away from her.

"You just did internal medicine," Dr. Watson said to Annabel, "where you followed patients with high blood pressure mostly stemming from their lifestyle choices. Here lies a different ball of wax. There are hypertensive disorders of pregnancy. The state of pregnancy can instigate hypertension!"

"She said my blood pressure is way too high," Mary said. She swiped at the side of her eye where moisture began accumulating, ready to slip down her cheek in the form of a tear.

Ling folded down the stretcher's white sheet on Mary's lower abdomen and applied gel to her skin. From the cart alongside the bed, she grabbed a hand-held electronic Doppler ultrasound device and smoothly glided it across her patient's abdominal skin to evaluate the fetus's heart rate. She took her time and finally nodded. Mary gripped the side of the stretcher in anticipation.

"You remember what they told you in clinic? What the normal baseline fetal heart rate is?"

"A little bit," Mary said. "They told me that theirs is way higher than us grown-up people. Is my baby okay?"

"A normal fetal heart rate is between 110 and 160 beats per minute, which correlates with a good assessment of fetal status and well-being. Your baby is beating smack in the upper middle of normal."

"Thank God! So I can go home?"

"No way," Ling said. "Your blood pressure is 154/106."

Dr. Watson pointed to the clinic chart, suggesting that Annabel take a look. Mary's vital signs at each clinic appointment were jotted down on the inside flap of the folder. Annabel noticed the normal numbers around 110/70 for weeks ... up until last week, when they registered a reading of 130/88.

"We need to check some labs, but it appears that you are preeclamptic," Ling said to Mary.

"Pre what?"

"Preeclampsia ... a hypertensive disorder of pregnancy. Right now, your diagnosis is very concerning. Good thing you came in, Ms. Chandler.

Let's get you upstairs. Stabilizing you and your baby is our highest priority at the moment."

Ling pushed back the chart and eyed the woman's cell phone nearby. "Make your calls. You won't be going home for dinner."

CHAPTER 5

After several years of working the same job, Emmett considered himself an expert in the particular specialty of transporting obstetric patients. Little by little, he'd seen it all, or at least all that could be gleaned by escorting wailing mothers from one area of the hospital to another. On the other hand, the patients sometimes displayed an opposite expression – one of sheer joy if their baby had been delivered and mother and baby had healthy results.

Emmett glanced around the cubicle to make sure all of Mary Chandler's personal possessions were stashed under the stretcher. He had all of her paperwork at the foot of the bed; not a problem since she was slightly elevated and she'd propped her knees up. He didn't want to dillydally. When he heard Ling Watson use the term "preeclampsia" at the ER desk, he knew the obstetric floor would be expecting the patient and one of the first things someone would do upstairs was to put oxygen back on her via a nasal cannula.

"I'm taking you on a short journey," Emmett said. "Out of the ER and on your way. You will like the obstetric rooms. Nice and comfy."

"When I get to feeling better," she said, "all I'll want is food. Forget about later … right now I could eat a horse. Dr. Watson made it clear I was barricaded from going home for dinner, but that doesn't mean I'm not eating here. With a lady doctor, she'll get this preeclamptic disease under control right away. Then someone can smuggle me in some kind of a Big Mac."

Emmett pushed the stretcher along and grinned. "Will anyone be coming by to keep you company?"

"I told my mom and dad. They live north of Columbus. My mom is taking off tomorrow and driving down."

They reached the staff elevators and he pushed his load inside. A few floors up, they bounced over the lip of the door and headed down the main corridor.

"No one's given me a bumpy ride in a long time," she said. "Not even in a car."

Emmett grew concerned and she smiled at him. "I'm just yanking your chain."

"I see. You know what they say about rides. If you plant your feet on the ground and stay put, life will be predictable. But if you take a ride, life will be a lot more interesting and nothing is guaranteed. Including the bumps."

"For sure," she said as an aide from the desk approached and waved them to an empty labor and delivery room. Emmett turned in.

"What's your name?" Mary decided to ask him.

"Emmett."

"Hmm. Your mother blessed you with an uncommon name."

"It's been around. Apparently, Emmett is the masculine form of the female name Emma and I believe both origins are German."

"I'm still wondering about baby names. Isn't that crazy?"

Emmett slid the stretcher next to the bed and locked the pedals. Mary began to creep over.

"Nope. Happens here more often that you would think. Every week, anywhere from one to a handful of mothers will pick out their baby's name at the last minute."

She stopped for a moment to gather her breath. "Emma or Emmett. Those names have a ring to them. I'm going to consider them."

"Be my guest," he said and helped her scoot over. The nurse's aide stood on the other side and spread the sheet up to Mary's chest.

"I'll be right back," Emmett said. "I'm going to first take the chart work to the desk. The nurse assigned to Ms. Chandler will be expecting it." He moved the stretcher to the side; he still needed to move Mary's belongings somewhere else but figured he would do that when he came back. First things first, he thought.

At the counter, an obstetric nurse stretched out her hands for the paperwork as soon as Emmett arrived. Ling scribbled their new patient's name on the OB board and came out of the room with Annabel trailing behind her.

"She's preeclamptic," Dr. Watson said, "bordering on having severe features. All of us need to start moving and put out this fire."

The RN, chief resident, and Annabel headed to the room. Emmett turned and followed the three of them. After going through the doorway, Ling continued her hectic pace, her eyes straight ahead at Mary Chandler. She mis-stepped and plunged straight into the stretcher.

Ling righted herself, grimaced, and massaged her hip. She spun around and glared at Emmett. "Why the hell did you leave this here? No … actually, there is no excuse for leaving an obstacle in a hospital where it shouldn't be." Her hands landed on her hips. "Idiot!"

Mary Chandler shrank further into her bed and massaged her belly. Emmett swallowed hard and held his tongue. The RN looked away. Annabel kept her mouth shut too. Despite what happened and despite whose fault it was, she thought Ling Watson should have spared the outburst in front of their patient.

Mary looked to the side while tampering with the pulse oximeter on her finger. The nasal cannula oxygen prongs were in her nostrils and the reading from the oximeter showed 96%. Annabel felt a wave of relief for the young woman. At least mother and baby were getting enough oxygen; if there was any further worsening of the situation, she knew her residents would move fast towards delivering the patient's fetus.

"Your white jacket is different from those other two," Mary said to Annabel.

"I'm sorry. I thought I blended into the background. I'm a medical student; the rotation just began for me, so I am naive yet useful. I learn fast, and believe it or not, many, many patients become imprinted into my memory bank. Almost every patient can demonstrate a lot to someone in training."

"I'm a guinea pig, aren't I?"

"More like a celebrity. For the rest of my career, I'll remember you as much or more than a favorite actor in a good movie scene."

"Wow. Then I came to the right place."

"Did they give you the antihypertensive medication yet through your IV?"

"Yes, and Dr. Watson and Dr. Gash said they were … 'cautiously optimistic' that they wouldn't have to get my baby out soon."

Annabel checked the pulse oximeter reading again and then glanced at the continuous electronic fetal heart monitoring. Mary did the same. The ultrasound transducer placed on her abdomen conducted the sounds of her fetus's heart; the rate and pattern of the fetal heartbeat were displayed on a computer screen and printed onto a special graph paper.

"It looks like Greek to me," Mary said.

Annabel leaned closer to the bed. "Don't tell anybody, but right now, it looks that way to me too."

Mary's tense shoulders relaxed. "You ever get pregnant and give birth?"

"No. Not yet. I would be anxious just like you. Try to keep calm and brave for your unborn child."

"I'll try. I'll feel better when my mom gets here tomorrow. My parents were furious with me when I got pregnant, but they've accepted it. My mother more than my father. My mother finally told me … everyone makes mistakes and they must learn to live with whatever it is. Mine was bigger than most and it will leave a footprint on the rest of my life, but I must make it a huge growing experience. I will be thrust into the immediate demands of taking care of another human being and adult priorities will take root."

"Sounds to me like you're maturing already."

Mary smiled and patted her belly like her unborn fetus had taken his or her first step.

Caleb Gash poked his head in the door while calling Annabel by name. "Better hunt down Ms. Chandler's chest X-ray and bring it up here … the one they did before she left the ER. There's a lot riding on that."

"I'm on my way." She passed Caleb while realizing she still needed to write up her H&P on Mary. It would have to wait.

In the radiology department, Annabel did what she often did. Many students would just pick up the films from the slot box and leave, but radiologists, she found, always seemed willing to teach a medical student. Their days did not bristle with human interaction like the teams on the floor, so she figured they enjoyed it when she asked them questions. Plus, she should learn everything she could and not discount the field as a future specialty.

The door was open to the doctor's dimly lit reading room. "Can you give me any pointers about our obstetric patient's chest film?" she asked the man.

He squinted his eyes. "Sure, come on in."

Annabel handed him the envelope and, after reading the note from the referring doctors, he slipped it in the viewing box. "Aha. Says here the presumptive diagnosis is preeclampsia. So the status of her lungs is very important. Did you do a physical on her?"

"Yes, sir. Her lungs sounded clear to me."

"Isn't today the change-over for medical school rotations on your service?"

Annabel nodded. "I'm as green as a frog."

The doctor laughed. "Have a seat, young lady." He read the name tag on her jacket. "Dr. Tilson, that is."

The man took off his glasses and rolled his chair back a few inches. "Do you know the three features that make a case of preeclampsia 'severe?'"

"For sure, a high blood pressure. Over 160/110 mm Hg fits the category."

"A patient can have chronic hypertension with a superimposed high blood pressure from preeclampsia. Does she have a preexisting chronic condition?"

No one had mentioned that possibility, but then she remembered reading the pressures from the clinic notes. "No, her early visits in the prenatal clinic gave no history of chronic hypertension and her vital signs were all registered as normal except for the last pressure, which crept up."

"Excellent."

"There are many other abnormalities for severe preeclampsia, but I'm not sure exactly which ones qualify as the worst."

"And that's a hell of a blood pressure for a pregnant lady who is usually acceptable and low. At 160/110 … can you imagine? A woman could suffer a stroke!"

A no-brainer, she thought, but he was enthusiastic about teaching and so willing to talk to her.

"The second most important severe feature," he said, "is pulmonary edema. So your patient's chest X-ray is clear."

The certainty of no fluid in Mary Chandler's lungs made Annabel feel more comfortable. "Makes her situation a bit safer."

"Regular preeclampsia is still an alarming case. The third severe feature is elevated liver function tests."

"I believe those results are still pending."

He scooted his chair back in. "Of course, your residents must be focusing on stabilizing the mother's status over and above the fetal status. Seizures are a complication."

Annabel now remembered that; she was glad he reinforced that bit of knowledge.

He scooted back up to his table and scrutinized her. "Have your residents started her on seizure prophylaxis yet?"

"I don't know. I am behind with her case; haven't written up her H&P yet or reread the residents' notes since the patient arrived in her room. What is the drug of choice?"

"Magnesium. Magnesium sulfate. A blessing for seizure prophylaxis and delivery." He flipped the film down and handed it to her.

"Thank you so much for the discussion." She rose and slipped the result in the envelope.

"Any time."

In the main doctor's lounge on the first floor, Annabel slid up to a computer and plugged in her patient's name. She added the newer lab results to her index card; there were now a host of laboratory values: CBC with a platelet count, renal function tests, and the liver function tests or LFTs. Sure enough, the LFTs were higher than normal values. That now categorized Mary Chandler with one of the three severe criteria of preeclampsia. Although ... she was close enough to having all three. Annabel glanced at the wall clock. The day was zooming by and her appetite to learn more about obstetrics was ramping up.

Gone astray or hidden from action, Annabel didn't see the residents when she made it back to the nurses' station, so she stole Mary Chandler's chart from the rack and settled into the lounge to write her H&P. With all the lab results and the senior doctors' notes already written, her chore would be a lot easier, so she began:

Mary Chandler is an 18-year-old G1P0 woman at 29 weeks' gestation who presented to the ER because of a several hour history of dyspnea. She denied any previous medical problems and also stated her prenatal course has been unremarkable. Prenatal blood pressures in the clinic were normal except for a slight increase last week of 130/88.

Her presenting blood pressure was, however, 154/106, and respiratory rate was 30 breaths per minute. Oxygen saturation was 96%. Fetal heart tones stayed in the normal range of 110 to 160 bpm.

Annabel continued on, finishing with the "Diagnosis" and "Plan." Pleased with herself, she looked up to find Emmett over at the nearby table reading a newspaper headline.

"You sure are quiet," Annabel remarked. "That newspaper in here reminds me of a chief resident I had on internal medicine. He read us interesting tidbits from the paper every day."

He glanced over at the door. "Doubt if you'll experience that on this rotation."

"I suppose not. I'll go back to being clueless about what's going on in the world besides my rotation." She closed the chart while he put down the paper. "I bet you moved the stretcher out of Mary Chandler's room pretty darn quick after what happened."

"For sure ... after I moved her belongings."

"Hmm. Stretchers are substantial pieces of medical equipment to miss seeing. At least that's what I've always thought."

"Really? Like you've thought about that?" His thick eyebrows raised. A smile crossed his lips.

"Yeah. Just this morning, I woke up and figured there was no way I was going to stumble over a large object left a few minutes near a patient's doorway. And even if I did, it would be my own stupid damn fault."

"You thought all that, huh?"

Annabel shrugged. Emmett winked.

"Dr. Tilson, I'm so glad you're on board for the next two weeks."

CHAPTER 6

The vertical blinds were closed, blocking any remaining sunshine of the day from entering Bonnie Barker's room. A plush recliner was by the side of her bed. Tony sat there, the end of his sneakers bobbing forward and backward on the extended footrest. Annabel glanced at the clipboard hanging at the bottom of the bed. Her patient's vital signs were fine after her huge obstetric fiasco. "She's doing quite well," she whispered to Tony, "after all she's been through."

"They let the baby visit us before. I held her and Bonnie breast fed her. Or at least tried."

"I'm glad to hear it; no wonder she's so tired."

"Bonnie asked me if I was okay with the name she has picked out." He shrugged his shoulders. "At least she asked me."

"That's a start."

"Her name is Samantha, but she wants to call her by her nickname of Sam."

"Either name will fit her like a glove, I'm sure."

"I guess newborn babies are fragile, but the nurse told us to be really careful with her. She said the doctors seemed concerned and they'd know more later."

Annabel wondered, especially because of the previous mention of genetic testing. "I haven't done my medical school rotation of pediatrics yet, but I also think babies are delicate. My aunt and uncle had twins and they were so little, it made me nervous to hold them."

"Like trying to hold a butterfly and accidentally damaging its delicate wings."

"That may be more in line with holding a premature infant, one that barely weighs a few pounds."

"No thank you. No way."

Bonnie opened her eyes, and in another second, they fluttered shut again. "Another medical student will be here for the night," Annabel said to Tony, "and I'm leaving soon. Make sure Dad sleeps tonight too."

Tony stopped wiggling in his shoes. "I'll go take a dinner break, but I plan on spending at least tonight with Bonnie and Samantha … and sleep in this chair."

Annabel quietly padded out and went straight to the lounge, where Dr. Watson was reading a chart. Dr. Gash stood next to her. For a moment, she thought Caleb's hand was rubbing Ling's left shoulder, but it was by his side when she walked over.

"Annabel," Dr. Watson said, "you can go whenever you're ready. We're not having distinct rounds this late because Dr. Gash and I still have resident's work to do before giving a report to the night docs. However, try and give the medical student who's coming on soon a few pointers on your way out."

"That will be Stuart Schneider. He was with me on internal medicine." Ling looked up with an empty expression.

"He's really smart," Annabel said. "In the top of our class."

"Test-taking scores the first two years don't necessarily correlate with hands-on, clinical skills or smarts from there on in."

Annabel wanted to say that Stuart retained his rank during their third-year rotations, but she thought better of it.

"Anything you need to tell me about our patients that I may not know?"

"I don't think so. I do have a question, if you don't mind. The radiologist who pointed out Mary Chandler's clear chest X-ray mentioned magnesium sulfate in the treatment of severe preeclampsia. Since our patient almost qualifies as severe, are you going to use it as a treatment?"

"Absolutely."

"We must prepare for a worsening situation," Caleb added. "Because of the preterm gestation, we're also promoting antenatal lung maturity with corticosteroids just in case we have to deliver Mary Chandler's baby. What goes on with her condition overnight will tell us a lot as to how we'll proceed tomorrow."

"That's where the head honcho comes in," Ling said. "His name is Dr. Roosevelt Harvey, our attending. Most of the time, he's in clinic."

"She talks to him on the phone," Caleb said. He snapped a pen off his top pocket and handed it to Ling. She rolled away the one she'd been using, empty of ink.

Annabel went to the couch and opened up her OB book. Dr. Watson stood, took off her lab jacket, and started to leave with Caleb. "By the way," she said, "your H&P on Ms. Chandler was fine. We'll see you in the morning. Don't forget … your reading tonight is the physiologic changes of a baby's first breath."

That and a dozen other topics neither of you talked about today, Annabel thought. She could open a book while waiting for Stuart, but her stomach growled and she went out to the nurses' station to scrounge around for food. Not a shred was to be had in the lounge. Outside, a bowl of miniature candy bars was sitting below the counter, nestled in the corner. She picked up a chocolate-coated mint patty. The supply room was directly across the way. The RN in Mary Chandler's room before was inside, and Emmett stood nearby. He smiled over when he saw her. Annabel gave him a little wave, put the mint in her mouth, and was relieved to spot a man walking down the hallway in a medical student's jacket.

Although Stuart and Annabel were not tight friends, they were compatible on the same team, always helpful towards each other, and non-competitive. In a way, he inspired her. She did well, both academically and clinically, but Stuart usually topped off higher in the nineties on exams. She outsmarted him, however, with what could be considered more "street" smarts when it came to their team dynamics and patients.

Stuart was thin as a dime and he could care less about the stashes of donuts medical students would discover behind nurses' stations or in doctors' lounges. He was quiet and generally added his two cents worth only when called on. Most of the time, his head hung low, and he spared most people direct eye contact. He approached Annabel and gave her a quick smile as they turned into the lounge.

Annabel took a big sigh. "I hope you're ready for OB/GYN because I found out today that I wasn't." She pointed to the couch. "You can throw your stuff in here until you find the call rooms."

Stuart put a backpack down and pulled out a chair. He noticed the board on the wall and Annabel followed his gaze. "I'll tell you what I know about those patients, but I can't tell you what residents will be on tonight. I think Dr. Watson and Dr. Gash will be leaving soon." She shook her head. "Like me, I don't think you'll be comfortable with the way this rotation is structured."

"Did you do any pelvic exams or see any babies being born?"

"Ha! I saw enough to personally put off having a baby as long as I can and we'll probably only get to do a pelvic exam on the GYN service after OB."

A small muscle on his face twitched. "That's fine by me. I'm narrowing down what I'm interested in for residency and this won't be one of them."

"You made up your mind before starting?"

"Absolutely. Same thing with urology. There are pleasanter places on a human being to work with than inserting scopes into men's penises or doing manual exams on women's vaginas."

"I'm still open minded."

"I'm banking on subjects like psychiatry or neurology."

"I can picture you setting your sights on one of those. In the meantime, let me tell you about Bonnie Barker, who almost exsanguinated from her delivery. When you go into her room, her boyfriend is sleeping next to her in a chair. And I'll fill you in on Mary Chandler, an eighteen-year old with preeclampsia."

After ten minutes, Annabel called Uber for a ride home, gathered her things, and nodded good-night to Emmett and the RN who was in her patient's room before when her chief resident had blown a fuse. They still chattered across the hallway in the supply room as she left with a tempo to her step.

At 5 p.m., Emmett started off in the supply room all by himself. He was pulling a twelve-hour day, which he didn't mind in the least. His whole life, he had been a hard worker and could count on one hand how many times he had taken a day off from his present job, and those rare times he had been sick enough to qualify as a patient in the hospital where he worked.

With his orderly job, he had enough human interaction during the day that he felt no need for additional social interaction. His life was simple: a small house with a patch of land he tended to himself, a small chunk of time in the gym, and a bit of binge-watching when it came to streaming movies or series content on his tablet. Part of his simplicity and care-free lifestyle also came from the fact that he had never burdened himself with a wife and kids. He helped out the hospital obstetric patients and families, but the beauty of that rested with the fact that he could walk away from them at the end of the day.

There was simply enough joy, he believed, in watching other couples have kids. Like a grandparent, he could admire and get a kick out of babies, but he carried no direct responsibility for them. This was even more important when he witnessed the miniature premature infants coming out of the labor rooms, or the ones that came out with genetic malformations or maladies, or the ones that started out with a tumultuous, life-threatening birth. There was no way he would take on the remote possibility of being a father involved in any one of those scenarios.

Emmett reached up in front of the suspended shelving and stacked clear plastic bags with bedpans on an upper shelf. He then pushed the empty box to the corner and ripped open a large cardboard box with liter IV bags of Lactated Ringer's solution. There were four such containers, so he readjusted other LR solutions on a middle shelf to make room for his load.

One of his favorite nurses, Sherry, strolled in. The upper middle-aged, practical woman always wore tight, matronly-looking blouses that were tight across her chest, and he sometimes wondered if he'd be around when one of the buttons would finally pop. She also always wore the same clip in her hair every day with glassy beads. He came to understand her reason why when she told him that her only granddaughter had given it to her. ... on a Mother's Day, no less.

Sherry planted her thick, rubber-soled shoes in a dead stop and shook her head.

"Emmett, at least you didn't leave a stretcher at the door like in Mary Chandler's room where I could have landed on it." She gave him a serious scowl and then broke into a smile.

The big man chuckled. "The new medical student made an innuendo about that too."

"Dr. Tilson better keep her thoughts to herself. Dr. Watson is not all that nice, but she's worse when it comes to other females, especially if they appear to jeopardize her sovereignty."

"Women are other women's most successful enemies."

She leaned against the shelves and considered his statement. "Spoken like a master. I'd go a step further. I never want to witness a woman president in my lifetime because I wouldn't trust one with the nuclear button on her desk."

Emmett leaned down into the box, grabbed a few more bags, and stuffed them in above. "You're a traitor to your own kind."

"It's true and you know it."

He glanced outside where Annabel was nodding good-night over at them. "At least they let her leave on time," he commented and waved.

Sherry also acknowledged Annabel's departure with a slight flick of her hand. "Now give me two of those bags you're unpacking. This is the last doctor's order I'm following and then my old lady shoes will be close behind the homeward-bound path of that young, dynamic student."

Emmett handed her two bags. She ripped open the outer, tougher packaging bag of both, put the two LRs on the waist-high shelf next to her, and dropped the trash in the garbage. In the corner, she opened a medicine cart and pulled out a bottle of magnesium sulfate and a needle and a syringe. She aspirated 40 grams and then injected it into the medication port of the nearest bag.

Emmett stacked the next empty cardboard box into the last one and stood straight. "I'm out of here too. I'll take this stuff to dispose of on my way. Any more garbage from you?"

"No," she said, shaking her head and dumping the used needle in the sharps container on the wall. She stood in the corner as Emmett carried his bulky load out the door.

"See you tomorrow," he said, "when I'll be pulling another twelve hours."

Sherry plucked the bags off the shelf and placed them on the medicine cart. "Have a good one," she said. She dug into her pocket for the already-made-up admixture label regarding the magnesium sulfate and slapped it on the bag nearest the door.

Even though her shift was almost finished, Sherry's stamina was devoid of significant adrenaline, so she took her time. She took the Lactated Ringer bags and necessary tubing packets and arrived at Mary Chandler's room. They chitchatted while Sherry set up the infusion pumps. One was for delivering the patient's maintenance fluid and the other for the infusion of magnesium sulfate. She started a 6-gram bolus dose of the mag sulfate and, after that, started its infusion at 3 grams per hour.

Mary groggily watched as her nurse hooked things all together like voodoo and taped tubing, which now attached into her IV, down to her skin. She uncrossed her legs and asked, "What did those doctors say about my last blood pressure?"

"It dropped a few points in the right direction, so I think everyone is hopeful that your baby will not have to come early. Also, this medicine I'm giving you will help prevent you from having seizures, which can happen with preeclampsia."

Mary bit her lip. "Then I hope it gets in fast."

"In due time." She spiked the other bag with tubing and set it to run at 300 mL/hour. "This is just maintenance fluids," Sherry commented. Her patient's brown eyes were alert with alarm, so she continued. "It's called Lactated Ringer's solution. Consider it like the glass of water or cola that you would be drinking this evening if they would allow it. In case they have to deliver the baby quickly, they don't want you eating or drinking, especially because of the need for possible anesthesia. The IV fluids will keep you hydrated and they are running at a hefty rate."

"And my baby's heart rate is okay?"

"Nothing to be alarmed about, so try and steal some sleep. I'll be back tomorrow. Now comes shift change."

CHAPTER 7

Annabel lived southeast of the Cincinnati medical campus and University Hospital in a third-story apartment of a rental house where young working and academic types lived in the area. She felt at home as possible with her living situation, even though she missed her family and home in Nashville.

Since finding parking spaces on the narrow streets where she lived was near impossible after her long clinical days, she had taken up grabbing taxi services to go back and forth, and used her car less than before.

A dark SUV pulled up at the hospital entrance. "Annabel?" asked a woman wearing a stylish cap.

Annabel signaled a thumbs-up and scooted in. "You're the first woman Uber driver to give me a lift; not that it makes any difference."

"Yeah. Doesn't matter which gender has their hand on the wheel." She pulled away from the curb as her GPS app highlighted directions.

Annabel buckled up. "Ever feel unsafe, however, with who you've got in your car?"

"Not really. I don't take any bookings to remote locations. I transport only in the city area." She made a turn, and after they made an entrance onto I-75, Annabel pulled out her iPhone, ready to give Dustin an update of her day.

The police officer was someone she had known for a while, but he was new as her boyfriend. Being the cop that he was, he appreciated knowing a bit about her whereabouts, especially when she hopped rides in strange cars. She didn't mind. He didn't meddle with her activities; they had distinct separate lives in separate fields. However, the similarity was that they both helped people for a living. The characteristics of wanting to serve others, to see to the public's safety or health, made them similar humanitarians.

Holding her iPhone tight, she scrolled across the keypad:

"First day is behind me and I'm headed home. My reading is already stacked up!"

She waited for a response as the young woman cracked a wad of gum.

It'll always be piled high. You will never get out from under. BTW...did you deliver any babies?

"No, not as the low man on the totem pole."

"You figured that. I enjoyed last night. Can't see you tonight, can I?"

She smiled. "I wish, but no way. My unpleasant chief resident has given me an assignment."

Coasting along, the SUV stayed in the middle lane as she waited for Dustin's response.

"Okay. Pencil me into your calendar when you can."

"Will do. Give Solar a treat for me."

"For sure. Good night."

"You too," she replied.

The SUV took the exit ramp and headed into her neighborhood. She stopped thinking about the present and jumped ahead a year ... and to what that would mean. A year from now would be the end of April, the latter part of her fourth year, a milestone in her training. Applications for residency spots would have been previously sent out and evaluated. Medical students would officially be paired with programs they wished for ... or not.

What did she want to go into? The question in the back of her mind nagged at her. Whatever she chose would affect her the rest of her life. It was imperative that she considered all the options and make the very best decision for her talents and desires. During her surgery rotation, she had been interested in anesthesia, but now she just wasn't sure.

The driver slowed, stopped, and gazed back at her. "My roommate and I just split up. You're welcome to come over to my place."

Annabel grabbed her backpack. "No thanks." She scooted out, walked between the parked cars, and headed to the side entrance of her place where a young man was sitting on a step.

"Bob Palmer! What are you doing here?"

Bob was a close medical school friend. They had journeyed together so far on every third-year rotation – surgery, psychiatry, and internal medicine – until today. He was recuperating one more week from an illness he had picked up at the end of the medicine rotation and was now out of synch with her schedule. Even though he had passed the medicine final exam beforehand, next week he had one more clinical week to make up.

With his normal cheery expression, he looked hard at her. "I came to find out what OB/GYN is like."

"Today was only my first day!"

"You grasp everything in one day. Admit it. Besides, we must discuss our commitment to get a dog together."

She glanced down at his blonde hair and stylish haircut. "I haven't forgotten, but I have to tackle a ton of reading."

Bob frowned and hung his head. "Actually, sooner or later, I need to follow what you're studying anyway. Can we pore over the material together?"

"Bob, you should be resting."

"I rested and napped most of the day and was to the point that I yearned for fresh air. I'm only good for an hour or two anyway, and then I'll go home to bed."

"Which will be the most for me as well."

"So there you have it."

She squinted her eyes at him. "All right, then. What an unpredictable day." She turned to check if the SUV had left. "I think the female driver just made a pass at me."

"Why not? You're a hot chick."

She tapped her fingers on his head. "A chick without anything in her pantry. Why don't we go up to the intersection? My OB books are with me; we can grab a bite as we study."

The bell above the door tinkled when Annabel and Bob walked into Pete's Café up the block. Annabel settled her things at a table against the wood-accented wall and they went to the counter.

"Hey, Pete," she said.

The owner had a slight build and a warm smile. "Welcome back. You two students look like you could use some brain food. My special is a classic Colby Jack grilled cheese sandwich with a salad."

Annabel nodded. "If we can study over there for an hour."

"No problem. I love when you clutter up my place."

"You can skip the sandwich for me," Bob added. "I'll take your beer cheese soup instead."

"Coming right up."

"Throw in some water too," Annabel said.

At the table, they sat side-by-side on the bench. She opened a book and went to the index. "I've been given an assignment by the chief resident of what to read tonight. Like I can't pick out what I should be reading myself. For instance, the pharmacology of the certain drugs that kept coming up today, or postpartum hemorrhage, or preeclampsia …"

"Ouch. So what's the assignment?"

"The physiologic changes of a baby's first breath."

"We covered that a little bit last year in class."

"A tad, but that information is dusty, and look at this." She grabbed at least one hundred pages between her thumb and index finger, looked at him, and rolled her eyes. "This barely covers the topic."

"I suppose we must start at the beginning. Like with what is the most essential adaptation in preparation for birth."

"The adequate development of the fetal lung to support gas exchange."

"Exactly. I'm impressed with your chief resident's homework assignment. The transition from a fetus to a newborn has to be the most complex adaptation of a human being's experience. She must be a sharp cookie and a fine teacher to spring you with this."

Annabel wondered. Bob had a point. "To tell you the truth, she's starting out rough, but now that you mention it, I'll give her the benefit of the doubt."

She scrolled her finger down to the beginning paragraph. "At least there are charts that break up the physiology into parts."

Bob honed in closer and scanned the first box, an overview of the neonate's transition:

"Clearance of fetal lung fluid

Surfactant secretion, and breathing

Transition of fetal to neonatal circulation

Decrease in pulmonary vascular resistance and increased pulmonary blood flow

Endocrine support of the transition"

"Before I went to medical school," Annabel said, "I assumed the growing fetus' lungs were filled with amniotic fluid. Fetal lung fluid is different. It is secreted by the airway epithelium; production and maintenance is essential for normal lung growth. And in the last, third trimester of gestation, the lung tissue separates into septa … about four million distal saccules."

"And if the baby grows up and decides to, he or she starts smoking and destroys some or much of the hard work that Mother Nature did to build the respiratory system for breathing."

"So true." Annabel raised her head while Pete balanced both their salads in his hands. The waitress placed down the remaining items.

Bob pushed the textbook further away. "Thanks."

"You two reading how to use a stethoscope to listen to someone's lungs?" Pete asked.

"We're ingesting material a lot more complicated than that," Annabel said.

"You two can handle it, I'm sure. Need anything else?"

"We're fine," Annabel replied, not needing to tell him that they were now separated from their rotation. The Café thinned out as she started with her sandwich. Between bites, she read:

"The cardiovascular response requires striking changes in blood flow, pressures, and pulmonary vasodilation with the removal of the low-pressure placenta. The newborn must also quickly control its energy metabolism and thermoregulation. The primary mediators that prepare the fetus for birth and also support the multi-organ transition are cortisol and catecholamine."

"Modern medical deliveries have this down to a science," Bob said. "Helping the neonate transition by suctioning out its mouth, maintaining the temperature of the delivery room, and putting it in a warmer. Of course, all the rest of it, too, like cutting the cord ..."

"Where'd you learn all this? I'm the one taking OB, not you."

"You forget what I tell you. My mother is a nurse. Also, while I was resting today, I watched one of those clips on our list of useful video content."

"I remember your mom's career. You just don't talk about your parents that much. However, it sounds like you learned more than me today."

"Maybe today, but over the coming days, you'll learn more from real patients that you'll never forget."

"So true. That's a given. So speaking of real patients, don't forget that we're naming the dog we're getting after one of my prior patients, May Oliver. May if it's a girl and Oliver if it's a boy. She was a unique lady and I admired her. I wish she had not battled with and died from lung cancer." Annabel pictured her sweet expression and close-cropped haircut and thought about their conversations.

"I liked her too. We all did our best to stop her illness. She would have been tickled to know that you are going to use her name for our dog … a pet who will end up being a part of our lives and, I hope, a piece of our hearts."

"You are making me hungry for one already."

"How should we do it? Pick a dog out from a breeder's litter or go to the animal shelter and adopt? What's your favorite breed and when should we do it?"

She finished chewing a bite while Bob spooned more soup into his mouth. She shook her head.

"We're in this fifty-fifty. What are your thoughts?"

"I asked you first."

"You are cognizant that I have a love affair with Chesapeake Bay Retrievers and that my family lost Dakota. Finding a breeder in the region for them may not be easy and then it may take months before puppies are available. Also, our landlords may not appreciate that large of a breed."

"So let's consider the diversity available at the animal shelter. They must house a smorgasbord of breeds and mixes, sizes, personalities, and both genders. And more importantly, we would be saving a dog's life if we adopted from there."

Annabel picked at her salad. "What if … "

Bob put down his spoon and tilted his head.

"If you are feeling up to it, this week may be our best opportunity to pick up a dog. You could be at home with it and I'm also not on night call. Next week, you go back for only one week of internal medicine; maybe pull one night call, and I'll be on night call only. Like we thought before, between the two of us, one of us would be available to be with May or Oliver quite often."

A sly smile creeped over Bob's face. "And we'll split costs?"

"You're more strapped financially than me," she said fiddling with her shoulder-length hair. "But yes, we'll split the dog's bills or work something out."

"How about tomorrow?"

Annabel's eyes grew big. "Really?"

"Why not? If they close early before you're off, I'll ask them to stay open a little later. I'll pick up the essentials tomorrow. Don't worry, I'll make it a short run to the pet store."

"Why don't you call them tomorrow about the dogs residing there, so that we have an idea beforehand?"

"I will. I'll text you what I find out."

They both chuckled and then Annabel said, "After all, life shouldn't stop just because we're in medical school. We should not deprive ourselves of man's best friend."

"Precisely."

After moving plates around, Annabel slid the textbook back over. "We need to cover a lot more ground."

After the waitress removed their plates, and after an hour, Annabel and Bob adequately covered the subject matter highlighted in the first box they had read. She turned another page. "Cortisol is a big contributing factor," she said. "Here's another chart with all of the hormone's effects. I better understand and remember all of this tonight as well." She glanced at her wristwatch and Bob yawned.

"I will leave you to it, then," he said. "I'll walk you back to your place."

Bob held her backpack, they said good night to Pete, and nodded at the last remaining table of customers. The street lights lit up the uneven narrow sidewalks as they ambled down to her apartment. The leaves had not burst out of the tree buds yet and the air smacked of soon-to-be warmth and fragrance from new flowers.

"I hope you didn't overdo being out tonight," she said before they arrived. She glanced back; she was tall at five-foot-eight, but Bob squared off at six foot. "Are you still taking your antibiotic?"

"I am. A doxycycline twice a day, and the doctor's office scheduled me for a follow-up appointment in a few days."

"If you can't do those dog chores tomorrow, we can always postpone our plan."

"No way. Don't stay up too late either."

"I'll try not to. By 7 a.m. tomorrow, I'll be checking on my assigned patients, ready to give my Nurse Ratched reports on them in case she asks. To tell you the truth, I don't think she cares about what I have to say." They stopped on the path to the three-story common door. "Sorry. I'm trying not to be critical of her after what you said."

"Nurse Ratched?"

"Ling Watson, my chief resident."

Bob maintained a questioning stare.

"You know. The fictional character in *One Flew Over the Cuckoo's Nest*."

"No. I don't know."

"Bob Palmer, like *Gone with the Wind*, which I'm in the process of watching with Dustin. I guess you and I need to watch the movie version of that book. Both movies now seem pertinent to an OB/GYN rotation, particularly this one."

Bob's heart skipped a beat and his eyes sparkled. "There's a first time for everything. We haven't watched a movie together before. Why don't we stream the *Cuckoo* movie after we get our dog?"

"We have a deal. After all, the rate of medical student and physician burnout is at an all-time high. The new mantra and pertinent advice is to separate out time for ourselves. If we are not healthy and happy, how can we pass on effective care to our patients?"

Bob widened his grin and nodded. "I'll text you tomorrow."

He twirled around and took off to his car and Annabel entered the ground floor of her house. Besides needing to know the material she'd been assigned to read, she wanted to leave a decent impression tomorrow on Ling Watson and Caleb Gash. As she scrambled up the staircase two steps at a time, she figured her evening would go on later than she would like.

CHAPTER 8

Mary Chandler startled when the door swung open and the night shift nurse entered. She rubbed her eyes. The room had darkened and the RN flicked on the overhead light.

"Hello there," the nurse said as she bustled over to the white board on the wall. She crossed off the previous nurse's name, Sherry.

"This is me," she said as she wrote "Night nurse … Dorothy Clark." She was a lot younger than Sherry and wore makeup fit for acting in a romance movie. After moving the tray table to the side, she scrutinized Mary's belly. "Hope that baby doesn't come soon. You're not as big as most for your twenty-nine-week gestation. I bet you ate like a bird all along."

"What's your excuse for eating that way?"

"Pardon me?"

Mary pulled the crumpled sheet further up on her chest. All she wanted to do was close her eyes again and not talk to some nurse who didn't look old enough to have experience.

Dorothy went straight to the IV pumps. One liter bag was labelled as Magnesium Sulfate and the other was straight Lactated Ringer's. The infusion rates were perfect, as ordered, so she traced the tubing to Mary's hand and made sure the cannula site had not infiltrated and that it was taped down appropriately. She read the last vital signs from the chart and those were adequate as well. Her patient's oxygen saturation was in the high nineties and an adequate waveform pranced across the pulse oximeter monitor.

"Those residents have a handle on your preeclampsia," she said. "How are you feeling?"

"Sleepy."

"I'll leave you alone and check on you later."

Happy to see the RN leave, Mary tilted herself more to her side and rubbed her abdomen. "Don't believe her," she whispered down to her belly. "You will be big enough and strong enough, and, no matter what, you'll be my little angel. By the way, your name is Emma or Emmett. That is settled. Certainly if you are a boy, I won't be naming you after your father."

She rested her hand and thought back to less than a year ago when she was a senior in high school. Her best friend set her up for a date with her boyfriend Tom's best friend, Freddie. They double dated, went to a movie, and went to dance afterwards.

Mary had practically swooned over Freddie's charm and rugged looks. In addition, he was three years older than her, and out in the real world working with subcontractors building a home. Although he still lived with his parents, he made real money, paid for everything on their date, and even owned his own car.

That first night, he rushed to her side of the vehicle, opened the door, and walked her to the front door of her parents' house. He kissed her, kissed her again, and whispered in her ear, "Can't wait for next time."

Of course she'd been kissed and had dabbled in heavy petting before that night, but she was still a virgin.

On the second date, the two couples again double dated. They ate at a restaurant where the guys drank regional beer and the girls splurged on pina colada's with alcohol-soaked cherries. Over another drink instead of dessert, they all decided to go over to Tom's apartment. In retrospect, maybe the guys had decided that already.

When the four young adults landed at Tom's place, Mary browsed around and salivated to one day have her own place. Before that, however, she hoped that her dates with Freddie continued and he would soon be out of his parents' house as well.

"How about another drink?" Tom asked the group. He opened the refrigerator and pulled out a six-pack of beer.

"No more for me," Mary said. "The rum is still swirling around in my head."

"See you two later, then," Tom said. "Or not. Just lock the door behind you, Freddie, when you both leave." He slipped his hand into his girlfriend's palm and led her through the kitchen door and into his bedroom.

Freddie leaned against the counter and opened a beer. "Let's turn on his television. We don't have to watch anything if we don't want." He tapped her forearm to follow him.

In the living room, Mary noted the bedroom door closed while Freddie turned on the television. There was no couch. Only two slim leather recliners. He grabbed the two throw pillows from each chair and positioned them on the floor. Holding his beer, he lowered himself down and patted the carpet. "What should we put on?"

Mary shrugged her shoulders, but Freddie already switched to a sports channel. A male tennis player smashed his serve and his opponent didn't stand a chance at a return. "I already know the outcome of this match." He moved the beer bottle to the coffee table and scooted closer to her. "This was taped earlier in a different time zone."

Their beginning gentle kisses put Mary in the mood for more. Soon the moistness in her mouth tasted like a combination of pina colada and beer. Freddie began unbuttoning his shirt and soon had it behind him. His hands went under her sweater and he hoisted it over her head. He kissed her neck and rubbed away at her breasts like he was kneading dough. She considered that perhaps she would be better off with her top back on.

Now her thoughts wandered all over the place. He was already undoing the button on his blue jeans and unzipping his fly. She wanted to kiss some more, but he was moving way too fast. After wrestling his pants off, he crumbled them on top of his shoes. He tore off his underwear and tossed them by the flat-screen TV.

Freddie eased Mary flat on the floor and nestled one of the pillows under her head. She glanced at his penis, swollen and hard, but before she could touch it, he began wiggling her out of her casual pants.

"Freddie, I'm a virgin. I'm not on birth control. I don't think…"

"I know. Don't worry. I'll pull out."

She kept her thighs together. She didn't know about this. This wasn't good.

Freddie's weight was on top of her, his organ harder than it looked. He wiggled his way between her legs. She felt like a detached participant as he pushed his way forward. There was no pleasure when she felt a thrust in her vagina like a door had been forced open.

"There it goes," he mumbled next to her ear.

Another three shoves of discomfort, he pulled away. His hand wrapped around his penis, he trotted off to the bathroom. She slowly sat up in a daze. Between her legs, the light from the television revealed to her a light bloody discharge. She went to the kitchen to scout around for a tissue. By the time Freddie was back in the room, she was buttoning her blouse over her bra. He dressed while eyeing the tennis match.

Mary didn't have to worry any more about bloody vaginal discharges of any kind because her period never came later in the month, causing her to panic. Against her best judgment, she confided in her best friend, but that only made her feel worse. After all, the four young adults had not double dated again. Freddie had not so much as called her.

In partial denial of her situation, she missed her period again the next month. That was when despair and depression followed her like an evil shadow. Instead of being mortified by going to a doctor's office, she bought a "one-step pregnancy test." Sitting hunched over on the edge of the bathtub, her heart froze when she read the positive result.

That night, she confronted her mother with the news, and her mother broke the news to her father. Her dad yelled at her the most. "What were you doing having sex at your age? Who's the father? We taught you better," etc., etc.

Her parents were "right to lifers" and, following in her parents footsteps, she pretty much was one herself. She didn't know which option would be worse - aborting a baby or keeping it at her age and circumstances.

Telling Freddie was another story. Since she never heard from him, she went to his parents' house, where she found his mother to be hospitable. "I went out with your son," she said at the door, "and he hasn't returned my calls. I need to tell him something."

The woman rubbed her hands together. "Come in, young lady. I was just making a sandwich."

Mary stepped into the hallway, the smell of oven-baked cookies filling her nostrils. She nervously put her weight on one foot and then the other. What would Freddie say and do about her pregnancy, if anything at all?

"Well," the woman said, "I surmise you only want to talk to my son. Good luck. You seem like a nice girl, so my advice to you is to date someone else. He has growing up to do and I would hate for you to get hurt."

Mary took a deep breath. What an honest mother. Too bad it was too late to follow her advice. "Is he here?" she stammered.

"I hate to tell you, no. I made him go rent a place himself. He's too old to be a squatter in his parents' house while earning the fat check he makes. Besides, the fact is that we don't see eye to eye on anything and he leaves his stuff around like he has a maidservant picking up after him."

Mary bit her lip while her sandals were now rooted to the door mat. All of a sudden, the aroma of the cookies in the back of the house wasn't tempting.

"Damn if I know where he went," Freddie's mother continued. "He'll call one of these days, our relationship will settle into a more adult tolerance of each other, and life will go on."

Mary made a decision right then and there. Right now, she would keep Freddie out of the picture. She had enough to worry about besides hunting down the no-good guy who thrusted her into this position to start with.

After replaying the last year in her mind, Mary fell asleep. After several hours, she awoke and had a sensation of claustrophobia from the hospital room. She jostled around in the bed and fumbled with the sheet. After pushing the white linen off her breasts, she checked the clock on the nightstand. It was almost midnight and she grappled with telling Dorothy Clark that her GI tract felt like mud churning around in a pig's pen and she also felt warm. She pushed the call button.

The nurse came in along with the tech taking vital signs. "We're killing two birds with one stone," Dorothy said.

The tech took her temperature and then Mary extended her arm for the blood pressure cuff. The woman cycled the machine while Dorothy stood with her hands on her hips.

"It's really hot in here," Mary said, "and I feel sick to my stomach."

"So you're flushed and nauseated," Dorothy paraphrased. "You don't have a temperature and it's not hot in here. I can bring you something for nausea."

Mary and the tech made small talk and Dorothy came back with a round pill and a paper cup. Mary gulped down the medicine. "Thanks."

"You're welcome. And by the way … don't consider yourself singled out or on death's door because of these symptoms. They are to be expected."

Mary swallowed that advice as the two women left. There was nothing to be concerned about and, in the morning, maybe her doctors would give her excellent news and she could go home to her place. She wanted to go back to work in another day or two, where she worked at the front desk of the local library. Her boss had been understanding of her situation earlier in the day and had let her leave early.

Optimistic thoughts began circulating in her head. Her baby would go to full term, she had the infant's names picked out, and she would see her mother tomorrow. In her heart, she knew she would love her baby as much, or more, than she loved her mother. She let her eyelids close and she drifted off ...

A few hours later at the nurses' station, Dorothy Clark wadded up an empty bag of potato chips and tossed it over the desk to the garbage basket. "I'll never make a women's basketball team," she barked to the anesthesia resident on call.

"You hold down the court," the resident said. "I just topped off an epidural and I'm going back to bed."

Dorothy rose, stretched, and put the chip wrapper directly into the can. She decided to walk the hallway and check on patients. Those with laboring epidurals slept comfortably. Remembering Mary Chandler's prior complaints, she poked her head into her room and observed the woman sleeping. So much for her patient's prior flushing and nausea, she thought.

She then pushed a rolling medicine cart down the hallway and gave certain patients their medications. Lastly, she positioned herself back at the main desk. The rest of the shift flew by and, before long, Nurse Sherry was back for the day shift and the female medical student Annabel strolled in to begin her own rounds.

CHAPTER 9

Ready to start her second day, Annabel rode up the elevators to the OB/GYN floor. The man next to her coughed loudly and sent a spray into the air. One sign on the door read "Clean your Hands" and the other one said "Cover your Cough." She grimaced as the door opened and she hurried out.

As she turned right, she anticipated the questions that Ling Watson would throw her way this morning. She studied another two hours after Bob had left her last night and covered the subject of the neonate's physiologic changes at birth as much as possible in the short time frame.

The wing was vastly different from the day before when poor Bonnie Barker suffered her postpartum hemorrhage. Peace and quiet ran down the hallways like a gentle stream on a calm day. She went straight to the lounge and tucked away her backpack. The night nurse was giving Sherry a report, so she left them alone. She bumped into Emmet when she left.

"Hey, doc," he said.

"Hey yourself. Were any babies born overnight?"

"Not that I'm aware of. Deliveries come in waves."

"Really?"

"For sure. I can tell those fancy researchers working on their projects about the effect of the moon and the tides on women giving birth. I've been working here for years and I swear on the Holy Bible that deliveries occur in waves. Just wait…"

"Wait for what?"

"A full moon."

Annabel's eyes widened. "I'm aware of old wives' tales predicting a baby's gender, but I have never heard about full moons being associated with a surge in births."

"You have now. I'm telling ya."

"Then I will take your word for it."

Annabel pulled out her index cards on her patients and decided to round on Mary Chandler first. She hoped the young girl's preeclampsia would be so under control that the residents would send her home today after her mother showed up. But what did she know? Maybe it would take a week.

After all, she still had a lot to learn about the dreaded obstetric complication, particularly since she didn't get to read about her patient last night.

Down the hallway, she glanced into Room Six. It was as peaceful inside as the hallway, so she assumed that her patient had slept well. She must be fast asleep, Annabel thought, because she lay slightly aligned on her side, facing the window, and didn't stir.

"Miss? Doctor?"

Annabel turned towards the lobby. A slender woman wearing a matching blouse and pants waved at her as she approached. Large glasses framed her wide face. "I'm Kathleen Chandler. Do you know which room my daughter is in?"

Annabel was surprised at her early arrival. "Yes. Right in here. She'll be happy to see you before breakfast."

The woman slipped her cell phone into her shoulder bag. "I couldn't sleep; with coffee at a gas stop, it only took me two hours down the interstate. How is she doing?"

Annabel glanced inside without answering. Strange, she thought, that Mary didn't stir. She should be awake by now and overwrought with joy that her mother stood at the door. But no high-pitched voice called out for them and no big brown eyes looked their way.

Kathleen brushed past her. She slid her bag down her arm, dropped it on the chair, and thought to make less noise in case her daughter startled to see her. She tiptoed around the bed. A concerned expression crossed her face. "Mary?"

Her voice rose. "Mary?"

Mrs. Chandler shook her daughter's shoulder.

"She's not breathing!"

Annabel ran over. Mary Chandler was not breathing. She also had no pulse.

The simultaneousness of what happened next was sheer chaos with order. Annabel bellowed out for help and Room Six was invaded. Dr. Watson confirmed the absence of a palpable pulse in Mary's carotid artery. And in the thick of it, somehow Emmett took charge of Kathleen Chandler and escorted her away from her daughter's bedside.

As Ling Watson barked orders, the anesthesia resident, Kristin Fleming, took over at the head of the bed. As a respiratory therapist helped Kristin deliver oxygen and suction out Mary Chandler's mouth, Ling threw a head pillow at Annabel.

Caleb Gash pulled up his sleeves. Annabel froze, clueless about the pillow.

"Displace the uterus, damn it," Dr. Watson said.

Annabel startled. She put the information together that she knew about CPR and advanced cardiac life support. One difference, she figured, was that the heart compressions Caleb were about to deliver would not be effective unless the heavy uterus was displaced to the left. The gravid uterus, she thought, normally compresses the inferior vena cava ... which impairs venous return to the heart and reduces cardiac output. Resuscitating Mary would be futile unless they relieved the compression.

She jumped straight to the bed and used the pillow as a wedge to keep their patient slightly to the left. Caleb shot her a glance, put his hands on the patient, and felt for the best hand position on the sternum.

On Dr. Watson's orders, Sherry shut off the pumps and disconnected them so that a new bag of LR hung from a separate pole and Dr. Watson pushed drugs from the crash cart that had been shoved into the room. Sherry scribbled on a clipboard, documenting the drugs Ling injected.

Annabel's heart pounded as hard as Dr. Gash seemed to project his palms into the young woman's chest. What had happened here? Had Mary Chandler's blood pressure skyrocketed over night with no one being aware ... which caused her to stroke, seize, or have a heart attack? How often does preeclampsia cause a pregnant lady to die? This girl was way too young to die.

The scenario then struck her agonizingly hard. There was more than one patient here. What about baby Emma or Emmett?

Before they called off further attempts at resuscitation, another M.D. showed up. The two OB/GYN residents relented to his questions and suggestions. Dialogue was sparse, however, as the minutes ticked by. The end result of their efforts was so horrid that it became difficult to speak.

Dr. Watson used the fetal monitoring equipment. Like mother ... like baby. No spontaneous heartbeats occurred again for Mary Chandler and no fetal heart rates registered from the fetus.

"Call it," the senior physician said. "Time of death ... seven thirty-six."

The respiratory therapist stepped back away from the bed. Kristin Fleming snapped off her blue vinyl gloves. Ling dodged her glance between the dusky dead patient and the new physician, and Dr. Gash somehow sneaked out the door.

Annabel backed up to the sink and pretended to wash her hands thoroughly. Clearly unnerved, Ling updated their attending. "Dr. Harvey, again ... this was the preeclamptic patient, Mary Chandler, who I told you about yesterday."

Annabel dried her hands while Ling reiterated a thorough synopsis of the patient's admission, diagnosis, and care. Both their moods were grim and serious; she felt grateful that she was only the medical student.

Dr. Harvey pulled the sheet up on Mary. "Obviously, she'll go for an autopsy." He carefully scanned the whole room and then pointed to the IV pumps with fluid bags above. "And send them to the lab for analysis."

"They are just ..." Ling started.

"Did I ask you what they are?" he asked. "I can read the labels."

Annabel held back as Dr. Harvey, Dr. Watson, and Sherry exited Room Six. The stark white sheet outlined Mary's pregnancy, now no more than a stillborn who never had a chance. A wave of sadness came over her like her chest was being squeezed. At least, she thought, this young woman would be buried or cremated with her fetus. They would be together forever.

In the hallway, Annabel saw Dr. Harvey and Ling duck into an empty room with a whimpering Kathleen Chandler. Their hands supported her under her armpits, leading the way, as if she would lose consciousness.

Someone pulled at her sleeve. It was Stuart Schneider.

"Didn't you go home yet?" Annabel asked.

"I slept longer than I wanted. Sorry I didn't give you a report when you arrived. However, not much went on and I slept much of the night."

"Lucky you."

He glanced up from the floor and practically whispered. "What happened?"

"The young girl with preeclampsia died," Annabel began. The two students made themselves less conspicuous and huddled outside the room where the senior doctors had taken Mrs. Chandler. Over the next ten minutes she shared the events with him, telling him what transpired.

"Jeez," Stuart said, shaking his head. The door finally opened and Dr. Harvey and Dr. Watson passed them. Kathleen Chandler stayed put. Her sobbing ramped up from inside the room while she placed a call.

"Mike," Kathleen Chandler said into her cell phone. "I have the worst possible news."

A pause ensued and Annabel and Stuart heard what came next. "I got here and ... Mary ... she died."

On the other end, Kathleen's husband responded to her with a long, silent pause, after which he said, "What did you say?"

Kathleen put her other hand on her lips as if to stop an onslaught of tears that were somehow going to flow from her mouth. "I said our daughter is dead. Downright dead."

"That's what I thought you said. It can't be. Women don't die because they're pregnant, especially not our daughter."

"Mike," she cried, "you better get here."

He controlled his disbelief and his anger. There was no doubt as to what she told him. His wife needed him. "I'm on my way."

When Mike Chandler ended the call, his fury built up like a volcano ready to erupt. How could their only daughter be dead? How could she have died in a hospital where she went for help? Better yet, how did his sweet, immature daughter get pregnant to begin with? He still had a difficult time facing that fact in the first place.

Stuart wrinkled his face at Annabel after listening to the one-sided conversation they just heard from the room. He shook his head, leaned into her, and spoke softly. "I'd better go."

She nodded and he took off. Mrs. Chandler still hung back in the room; Annabel wondered if she'd ever come out.

Annabel hurried to the nurses' station and, behind the desk, the door to the lounge was closed. Trusting her instincts, she figured it was shut tight for the senior doctors inside to be left undisturbed. Too bad her books were in there, she thought; she could use the time to read. However, she probably couldn't concentrate on studying after what happened even if she tried.

"Best that you don't go in."

Emmett stood next to her, his eyebrows arching up while he leaned his elbows on the desk. "Dr. Harvey must be taking control in there. He gives them residents latitude until they mess up. Then he sets them straight again and everything goes back to normal. But this time, who the hell knows what happened."

"You must see things," Annabel said, "and notice which doctors are good ... and which ones need improvement."

"Oh yeah. Like the patients really love Dr. Harvey. Bedside manner and all."

"I saw what you did ... escorting the patient's mother, Kathleen Chandler, out of the chaos. That was a thoughtful gesture on your part."

"Yeah. I come in handy once in a while."

"She told me, you know. Mary Chandler. She had made up her mind for sure; she planned on naming her baby Emma or Emmett."

He turned to her with a gleam of moisture in his eyes. "A kid named after me. Like being handed a gift. I would have had something to brag about after all these years."

It dawned on Annabel that she shouldn't just be standing there. She had never gotten any farther than Mary Chandler's room. There were other patients to see on the floor.

The door to the lounge jerked open and Ling tapped the secretary on her shoulder. "I need to start filling out the death certificate and other paperwork."

The seated woman anticipated her question and handed her a stack of papers bound together with a pink paperclip.

"Thanks," Ling said and noticed Annabel. "You might as well come in."

Annabel trotted in after Ling, and her senior resident closed the door again. Dr. Watson sat at the round table and spread the papers beside Mary Chandler's chart. Caleb left the couch and joined her.

"You must be the new student," the attending doctor said. "I'm Doctor

Harvey."

"I'm Annabel Tilson."

"I heard a good word about you from your internal medicine attending. I also got wind that your father is an esteemed neurosurgeon in Nashville."

His introductory remarks were unexpected; she was at a loss for words. He poured a cup of coffee from a pot shoved on the far end of the counter. "Would you like some?"

"No thank you," she said, finding her tongue again.

Dr. Harvey stirred in a packet of sugar and motioned her to the couch. He appeared to be a solid sixty years old and wore a toupee that looked like it would blow off with a sneeze. His shoulders sagged off his light build and he wasn't wearing a white coat. She figured he had rushed there after being summoned to the emergency and wasn't quite prepared to be on the delivery ward.

"The residents will fill out the paperwork, the young Mary Chandler will be picked up for the morgue, and I suppose her mother is going to be glued to the waiting room until her husband arrives. Maybe as we sort things out, we'll have some answers for them.

"You oversaw your first patient with preeclampsia. In our field, it is a pregnancy complication that we treat with utmost respect and diligence. Hence, did we do something to fail in the care of our patient?"

CHAPTER 10

Ling and Caleb continued with their official paperwork while Dr. Harvey gave Annabel more of his attention. He dreamed up questions for her slowly and methodically like the way he sipped on his coffee.

"The diagnostic criteria for preeclampsia is hypertension, edema, and protein in urine or proteinuria, but do you know what they used to call it?"

"No, sir."

"Toxemia of pregnancy. Don't use that term, however, because toxemia is a misnomer. There is no toxin circulating around these women's blood and causing preeclampsia.

"Overall, what is the incidence of hypertensive disorders in pregnancy in the US?"

As she blinked, Annabel drew a blank. "I'm not sure."

"Estimates are between three and ten percent. What causes most patients to die from eclampsia?"

Annabel wanted to make a stab at guessing, but she figured it would be worse to come up with a ludicrous answer. She shrugged her shoulders.

"Pulmonary edema. With no evidence of that on Ms. Chandler's chest X-ray or by auscultation, this is a unique case and off the bell-shaped curve of normalcy.

"Okay, here's an easy one. What is the last of the three major signs of preeclampsia to appear?"

"Edema?"

A muscle twitched near Dr. Harvey's eye. "No. It was the third criteria we talked about. Proteinuria, primarily albumin.

"Since you don't seem to know much about your previous patient's illness, maybe you are aware of what to look for, say, in clinic visits, before a patient develops the hypertension?"

Annabel crunched up her face and wanted to crawl under the table. Ling glanced at her, her lips twisted in a wry smile.

"I'm not sure what you're looking for," she answered.

"Dr. Tilson, when your patients are seated before you, it will have nothing to do with what I am looking for. It is all about reading about your patients while you are managing them; watching and learning every single day of your medical school journey."

He crunched the empty cup in his hands. "Before hypertension sets in with these patients, there is a first sign that is quite dependable. A weight gain of more than two point two pounds in a week or six point six pounds in a month is often regarded as significant. An astute clinician following patients along prenatal clinic appointments will pick up on this sudden excessive weight gain."

Jammed into a spot that she couldn't dig out of, Annabel swallowed hard. He was supposed to be asking her about the physiologic changes of a neonate, but how was he supposed to know that? Ling offered no mention of tying her up with a different reading assignment the night before and Annabel felt cornered to not mention it to her attending.

"Since you exhibit a hole in your knowledge starting out on this rotation, please be aware that during pregnancy, a gradual increase in weight is normal ... a half a pound to a pound per week."

Dr. Harvey rose and went over to make more fresh coffee. He shook his head, wondering how Annabel was given such complimentary accolades from other medical professionals.

The residents peeled away from Mary Chandler's medical and legal documentation of death and Dr. Harvey signed a few of their sheets. "Let's make quick rounds together," he said, stretching his arms out to the side, "and then I'm leaving for the office."

They visited three patients and, each time, Dr. Gash properly summarized the patient as they cluttered up the hallway. Annabel hung on every word, now feeling more ready than the previous day on how to present obstetric patients. These patients were different than recapitulating surgery, psychiatry, or internal medicine patients.

They went outside Bonnie Barker's room. "Perhaps Dr. Tilson can tell you about Ms. Barker," Ling said, "although I don't think she's seen her patient yet today."

Dr. Harvey held the patient's chart and peeked at Annabel's note from yesterday. He eyed Ling suspiciously. "Under this morning's circumstances, did you stop in on your patients yet?"

Ling shook her head.

"Makes you all even," he said. "Let's hear it, Annabel. I realize the patient came in before you started the rotation, but you had the opportunity to familiarize yourself with her case and write a progress note on her."

Annabel's confidence finally inched up with the new attending and she plunged into her presentation. "Ms. Barker is an eighteen-year-old white female who was gravida one para zero on admission, at full term, with a negative prenatal course and history. Yesterday, she delivered vaginally, and after the placenta was delivered, she experienced significant vaginal bleeding, estimated to be at least one thousand ccs.

"The residents did a bedside uterine massage, but with continued bleeding, they took her to the OR. She was resuscitated with IV fluids and doses of oxytocin. Her diagnosis was uterine atony."

She thought ahead but was unsure as to how much detail Dr. Harvey wanted. After all, she was not presenting a whole initial history and physical. Then she thought about the woman's newborn, so she decided to include the baby too.

"The pediatrician was called; the baby's initial evaluation or Apgar scores were something like seven and eight. I believe the pediatricians are monitoring her and doing some testing."

Dr. Harvey attempted to shove some of his shirt's loose fabric, which hung around his belly, into his pants, but it didn't work.

"Much better," Dr. Harvey said.

Better than what? Annabel wondered. Better than the wrong impression he formulated about her?

"So what are the risk factors for uterine atony?"

Annabel didn't have a clue.

"Working with me, it's better to be straight, such as 'I don't know.'"

Annabel cringed. However, she liked a straight-forward doctor. "I don't know."

"Uterine atony is always on obstetric exams. There are two opposite risk factors: a rapid labor and/or delivery ... or a prolonged labor. The rest of them are overdistention of the uterus, an intraamniotic infection, high parity, which we don't see often anymore, oxytocin use during labor, and magnesium sulfate."

Annabel wished she could rattle off information like that. At the least, she better understand it all by the time she took her second official board exam or USMLE - United States Medical Licensing Examination. That test, Step 2, would be a two-day exam in the fourth year of medical school. The three Step exams were weed eaters … they pulled the lower tier of student or resident test takers and gobbled them up with cordless weed trimmers.

Roosevelt Harvey nervously glanced at his watch and practically galloped into Bonnie Barker's room. "Congratulations on the birth of your baby," he said, shoving the bedside clipboard into Annabel's hands. He looked between Bonnie walking out of the bathroom and Tony, who sat on the windowsill. "I'm Dr. Harvey, the senior doctor in charge."

Bonnie bounced her head up and down and lowered herself into the recliner like she had hemorrhoids. "It hurts to have a baby," she squealed. "Since you're in charge, remind me not to do it again any time soon."

"You are a sturdy young woman; it took a lot to get through such a complicated delivery." He shook her hand, which surprised her, and she began to smile.

"Dr. Tilson, what are Ms. Barker's vital signs since yesterday?"

Annabel grabbed the bedside clipboard. "Her blood pressures have been less than 130 or 120 and diastolics are all normal. No problems with her respiratory rate or pulse, and she's afebrile."

"I can go home today, can't I?" Bonnie asked.

Roosevelt peeked in the chart. He sat on the edge of the bed and read the latest notes in each section. "Hemoglobin and hematocrit have stabilized. Other labs are fine. No signs of infection. Let's plan on releasing you tomorrow if you continue on this path."

Tony sprang up from the ledge, more excited than Bonnie.

"I can't wait," she said. "But I hate to go without my baby, Sam. Maybe they'll tell me more today."

Dr. Harvey looked straight at Tony. "Are you a visitor or a significant other?"

Tony winced. "Half and half."

Roosevelt didn't want to touch that one. "Be sure and holler if you think of any questions today. Dr. Watson and her team will be here if you need them."

"Yes, but can I have something more for pain?" Bonnie asked. "I still hurt down there."

He glanced at the pain order she already had in place. An extra pill on top of what she was receiving was reasonable.

Ling Watson sighed and shifted her weight from one foot to the other. It was time to move on.

"Yes, that's not a problem," he said. He leaned into Ling's left ear and softly told her, "Another 200 mg Motrin."

Ling stepped close to Tony and perched herself on the windowsill. She opened up the chart to an order page, took a pen, and scribbled. She ended by rolling her eyes.

"One more thing," Dr. Harvey said, looking at Annabel. "Mrs. Barker is breastfeeding, so we must take that into account. Motrin is the preferred pain medication for nursing women. Unlike narcotic pain pills, ibuprofen-like meds will not make her or her baby sleepy."

Annabel nodded, grateful that despite his hurried schedule, he was taking time to teach.

Outside the door, Dr. Harvey absentmindedly patted the top of his head, making sure his toupee was still in place. "When Kathleen Chandler's husband arrives, and if he would like to speak to the senior doctor, then give me a call."

He disappeared off the labor and delivery ward to his own office where the waiting room was full of waddling pregnant women and women anxious to put their pap smears, exams, and requests for birth control behind them for the day.

Ling dropped the brown binders on the round table in the lounge. "There are no orders in these charts that can't wait," she said to the unit secretary, who poked her head in and then went back to the desk.

"I sense a break in the action," Caleb said. "Who's joining me for a late breakfast or early lunch or whatever you want to call it?"

"Isn't the earlier drive-through breakfast biscuit holding you for a while?" Ling asked.

"Up until this minute."

Dr. Watson threw him a glare and fumbled in her locker.

"You coming, Annabel?" He started for the door.

Wondering, Annabel followed his springy and energetic gait to the cafeteria. When he arrived earlier, she didn't notice him with a take-out breakfast and he didn't sit down to eat. How did Ling know he stopped at

McDonalds? Were they together before they arrived on the wards?

Annabel picked her lunch out a lot quicker than Caleb, so she already was seated at a table by the time he arrived.

"It's nice to get away," he said, placing his tray across from hers. "We had a hell of a morning. I don't want to see any more OB deaths during residency. And after residency, I don't want to think about it. CPR and resuscitation skills for obstetricians out of training end up being rusty; between you and me, I think they depend on anesthesiologists being around and backing them up."

"You all pulled your weight this morning as residents, though," Annabel said, complimenting him.

Nearby, there were four people sitting at a table and a female wearing a college sweatshirt diverted her gaze to Dr. Gash. He kept a beard, short on the sides and fuller on his chin, which took advantage of his square jawline. Annabel wasn't surprised when he stole a sideways glance at her in return.

Annabel lowered her voice. "You've seen other OB fatalities?"

"Oh yeah, and they aren't pretty. In this specialty, you'll overhear docs talk about cleaning up after midwives. Don't get me wrong … they are not one-hundred-percent bad, but there are those that don't meet the minimum state licensing requirements and standards as well as those that are flat-out negligent. Midwives are more common and more needed in areas where there's a shortage of OB/GYNs. Unfortunately, those are regions where hospitals are often a hell of a ways away in an emergency."

He shook salt and pepper on a bowl of chili as Annabel hung on every word. So far, she had never heard anything good or bad about midwives.

"There are pregnant women," Caleb continued, "that view hospitals, modern technology, medications, and having their babies in sterile-like environments as anti-natural. Like a mother not vaccinating their children against diseases. I mean, vaccines work and they are the biggest success story of modern medicine. Anyway, these pregnant women think that childbirth should be totally natural. If you ask me … subconsciously they want to give birth like women did in the Stone Ages."

Annabel grimaced and speared a cherry tomato from her salad.

"Well, not that bad," Caleb admitted. "Anyway, for the last ten years or so, home births are on the rise. Women *choose* to give birth in their own home. But in the event of an emergency, do these midwives have a backup plan?" Caleb paused. "No," he said with emphasis.

"Then how did you happen to stumble upon a fatality where a midwife was involved?"

"EMS rushed in a dead baby after a botched at-home breech delivery by a midwife. The ER and OB docs then tried their damnedest to save the mother, who was also ambulanced in. That case was doubly negligent because, apparently, the midwife never talked to the parental couple about the dangers of vaginal birth after cesarean section or VBAC, which the mother had a history of."

"Jeez," Annabel said.

"That father or husband? In a couple of years, he won't need to work another day in his life ... if that's what he wants. A jury will find it inhumane to not award him a multi-million-dollar lawsuit against the midwife."

Annabel shook her head. "I bet he'd trade back that windfall if he could have his wife and newborn back."

"No doubt. I later stumbled upon him downtown after one of his attorney appointments. He told me something I'll never forget. He said that if he ever bought a Lamborghini later on, he was going to put an infant car seat in the passenger side ... to remind him how he came to acquire the vehicle and to always remember his wife and child."

"I'll peek in the next, or only, parked Lamborghini I spot to see if there is an infant seat."

Caleb gave her a quick nod. "Since there aren't too many of them cruising around, one of us will discover it."

CHAPTER 11

As the elevator door began snapping shut, Caleb thrust his hand in and paused it. He sprang in and held the door for Annabel.

"Thanks for suggesting lunch," Annabel said. "I don't rank as high as you with Dr. Watson. I wouldn't have suggested it in front of her."

They stood on one side of the elevator. A neatly dressed man stood against the other back wall, his hand gripping a shiny aluminum cane. He tapped its rubber gripper on the floor several times. When they didn't ride up immediately, he pushed the button for the OB/GYN floor several times.

"It worked out," Caleb said softly. "Grabbing meals while monitoring and taking care of obstetric patients can be a luxury. Like today. You never know what's going to happen. And with Ling, sometimes you have to ignore her shortcomings. Between me and you, I think she's getting worse lately. She needs a vacation or something."

The man between them took one step when they resumed moving, ready to spring out as soon as the door opened. When they arrived, he pulled ahead with a tilted gait.

"He's three-legged and burning rubber," Caleb said as they walked past the waiting room.

"He's anxious, here to see a family member in labor, or he's mad-as-hell about something."

"Hey, you." A woman's voice they recognized approached from behind. "Doctor?"

Annabel and Caleb whirled around. It was Kathleen Chandler and the man from the elevator behind her.

"You two were in the room," Kathleen said. "This is my husband, Mike Chandler. Mary's father."

"You were afforded a lunch hour?" he said sarcastically with a British accent. "My wife and I surely won't be eating anytime soon. Our daughter passed away," he continued. "We aren't doctors, and my wife isn't a midwife, so we don't even know what questions to ask. But if there is no absolute understandable reason why Mary died, a lawyer is going to be asking our questions for us."

Annabel gulped for air and her heart pounded while they all suffered an uncomfortable silence.

"I'm Annabel Tilson, a medical student. Our attending doctor can help you. We can call him."

"And where is our daughter?" Mark barked.

Annabel glanced at Caleb, who peeked down at his shoes. Surely Dr. Harvey and Dr. Watson had told her that a legal autopsy would be performed.

"You can inquire downstairs in the basement where they've taken her." Hopefully, Annabel thought, no one had started the autopsy yet and Mike Chandler would still be able to see his daughter.

"We'll be back," he said.

Annabel and Caleb made sure they were out of range. "I'm sorry," he said. "I have more to lose than you if they end up being pissed off at me. I'm in an OB residency and you're not."

"Thanks a lot, Caleb."

"You handled them perfectly." He rubbed his fingers in his beard and then used his iPhone to alert Dr. Harvey that the Chandlers wanted to talk to him.

Caleb pulled ahead as Annabel walked past each labor room. A few of the doors were closed and she wondered if any new patients had been admitted. Then she realized she hadn't given Bob and their potentially nonsensical plan a thought all day. She pulled her iPhone from her pocket and found no email or text messages from him. Maybe he aborted their dog plan but she doubted it.

Bob might be at a Petco or PetSmart right now shopping for a sturdy dog collar and a nylon leash. Or he was in the process of making other decisions: what type of food would he start their puppy or dog on and which bowl should he buy? Those were fun items to shop for and they might belong to the dog and the two of them for the entire life of their pet. Yet, although she was missing the shopping trip with him, it was handy that he was available to do it. More important was their decision of which dog to adopt. She was part of that no matter what and, now that the time drew near, she couldn't wait. Maybe tomorrow at this time, she'd be a dog mom.

One of the day shift RNs rolled the red medicine cart ahead of her. The woman pulled the twelve-hour shift on the days when Sherry had off. She stopped, parked herself outside Bonnie Barker's room, and stared down at an open chart.

"Dr. Tilson," she said as Annabel began passing. She gestured at an order page, her bracelets clanking together at the bottom of her lanky arm. "This looks like chicken scratch. What did Dr. Watson write? It's for Bonnie Barker."

Annabel stopped. The nurse's name tag said "Melba Fox, RN." She peered down. "Looks like morphine 200 mgs, but that can't be right because that's too high."

"Not necessarily. Ms. Barker is already on a nonsteroidal, which isn't holding her pain in check, so she needs something in addition to that. And you're a medical student. You haven't been around long enough to understand that some of these patients are previous or presently drug addicts. That means that they have an accumulated tolerance to opioids and need and take far more than anyone else. I see it all the time." She flicked her hand in the air. "After all, look at her. Eighteen years old with a baby already. And a newborn with some kind of a problem, which is what I heard. In all fairness, she's a druggie and her baby is suffering the consequences."

Annabel narrowed her eyes and studied the woman with thick-penciled eyebrows.

"Really," Melba said. "I don't mean to sound cynical like your chief resident. I'm not that bad. I am just reporting what I see around here."

"I hope the opioid addiction problem isn't that bad." Talking about Bonnie Barker's baby made Annabel turn around and walk over to the nursery. Maybe baby Samantha could use a visitor.

Bob Palmer's common occurrence these days was to sleep late for two reasons. Ehrlichiosis was the medical reason; besides other significant signs and symptoms, the tick-borne disease made him especially tired. His energy level returned only somewhat faster than a snail slinking across the street and he hoped that by next Monday, his return to the last week of internal medicine would be almost normal.

The second reason for sleeping in late was simply because he could. Since starting medical school, he couldn't remember a few days in a row like this when he woke with the sunrise peeking through his window treatments and then he would fall back asleep several times until it was midmorning. It was glorious. However, deep down he knew it only qualified as a treat, like a present that would befall a kid on a major holiday, so he better not get used to it.

Today, however, he not only didn't sleep in, he was more vibrant and snappy. The thought of finally getting a dog with Annabel made him spunkier, both because of a new pet, but also because he'd be working with her in a separate collaborative manner. Different from the way they had been working together on medical rotations. Now they would have an outside interest all to themselves, a healthy way to step aside from the wards, sickness, and studying, as well as to take a break from following orders and the attentiveness and empathy they needed when dealing with patients.

Annabel Tilson had caught his attention the first two years of medical school when everyone was getting their feet wet and becoming accustomed to the crazy education and training they had signed up for. But he never had the opportunity to get to know her better. That changed when he landed on the same rotation as her in surgery. However, a friendship grew rather than a love interest because Annabel became enamored at that time with their chief resident.

Because they intensified their friendship, that hurt him rather than helped him. She went on to meet and later date the policeman, Dustin Lowe. Putting the situation into perspective, he realized that the only way she "saw" him was as a true friend, even when he had accompanied her to Nashville when her family dog died. Meeting her family in Tennessee also brought him closer to her and he enjoyed the whole household, but it made him more certain. Romantic notions about him did not fill her head like the way he thought of her.

Bob weighed his options quite often and always came up with the same result. If he stated his feelings to her or if he made a romantic gesture, he stood the chance that would make her uncomfortable; he could even lose her as his very best friend. He innately sensed this and his feelings usually didn't lie.

It had been a tough situation to deal with on a regular basis on their shared rotations. But now their schedules were unhitched ... which was why he had to drum up a more permanent method of seeing her. Dustin Lowe might be sharing his bed with her, but Bob could share a dog with her and continue their strong-bonded friendship.

For now, it was the best plan he could come up with and it better work. He not only loved her, he practically adored her. She was a knockout, but she was so much more than that; personable, agreeable, and thoughtful to just about everyone. And she always dove to the bottom of a situation with more streetwise smarts than he ever possessed, which always struck him as ironic since she came from a more well-to-do family than he did.

So, he thought, as they were about to embark on a new journey together, he'd be sure to keep a tight rein on his emotions and not display his feelings and jeopardize what they had.

Bob dragged himself out of bed, showered, and dressed in cotton sweatpants and a t-shirt. He savored a flavored coffee at a coffee shop and then drove to the back of the shopping strip to the pet store. He realized most customers probably shopped online because there were only a handful of customers in the spacious store. This was a new experience for him, however, and he preferred picking out the items in person.

One whole side of an aisle displayed leashes and collars for dogs of every size, which posed to be a problem. How could he buy anything if he didn't know how big the dog would be? Yet how would they bring home a dog if they didn't have the proper gear?

He spotted one collar of its kind ... a red collar with five solid bells attached. Labelled for a "large" dog, he figured he could tighten it for a medium dog as well because of so many punched holes. Not only Christmassy, but it was also unique, fun, and frivolous. Their dog would clatter with tinkling bells every time he or she would make a move or run. He clutched it in his hand and then moved on to leashes, where he found a perfect matching off-white nylon leash with two red stripes.

With help from a young woman with a bouncing ponytail, Bob decided on dog food and a bowl for water and food. He paid and left and found himself debating over his next move while sitting in the driver's seat of his Honda Fit. He was doing fine as far as his energy level, so why not poke into the animal shelter instead of calling them? At least get a head start before Annabel was sprung from the hospital.

He drove a few miles north and down a less-travelled road to a cul-de-sac, where he heard the cacophony of dogs barking. The county had built a new shelter with outside dog runs with funds acquired over several years from a fundraising organization. He went inside where a woman stood at a long desk and a couple peered into the cat window of a spacious room. Another woman mopped the floor to the side.

"Do you have dogs to adopt?" Bob asked at the desk.

"Always," the woman said. "Behind that door." She finished tying a scarf around her forehead and pointed.

Bob nodded and went inside. On both sides of the aisles, there were concrete kennels with in-and-out wall openings leading to dog runs. Every stall seemed to house one dog or more. Although some of the dogs seemed not to care that he was there, the barking picked up from the ones who showed interest as he walked along. The ones that glued their eyes on him all said the same thing. He interpreted each one of them: "Take me home with you. I'm a good dog and I'll love you forever. None of us should live like this."

Bob's heart broke. There were too many of them: a coonhound with a shiny coat, a poodle mix with dirty curls, a Labrador retriever mix panting like she was ready to play ball. He slowed his pace and sauntered up the other side of the middle counter. After passing two short pit bulls, he came to the happiest face of all. The dog in front of him wore a smile despite the four walls surrounding him.

Bob bent his knees and lowered himself while the dog's tail swooshed back and forth like a motorized feather duster. "Holy cow," he said, "you are the handsomest dog I've ever laid eyes on. Happy too."

The dog was a mixture of white and tans and light reds all streaked along his long hair like an artist had whipped up paint and streaked it on a canvas. He stepped closer to the bars of the door and sniffed Bob's hand.

Bob read the index card posted on the door.

"Retriever mix? Approximately nine month old male. Neutered."

Bob put his hand in to pat the dog's head. "I think Annabel needs to meet you. I hope she falls for you like I am."

Back outside, the couple looking at cats had a cardboard box with a handle. "Our daughter is going to love her," the woman said as they opened the door to leave, their new cat scratching the box from inside.

Bob smiled at the woman at the desk wearing the attractive scarf. "That nine-month-old on the left with the unusual coloring … what can you tell me about him?"

"The lanky Retriever mix?"

"That one."

"We think that's what he is, but we can't be sure. We've only had him going on three days. If you want him, I suggest you grab him. As handsome as he is, he's not going to last. Plus, we think he's housebroken and friendly and he's not an annoying barker like some of them.

"And as you know, we do euthanize here, so if he doesn't go, he's destined for ashes." She frowned with displeasure. "I'm citing the eventual sad reality of many stray dogs and cats running wild that breed like rabbits because they aren't fixed and don't have homes."

Bob sighed and propped his elbow on the desk. "How did he end up here? Do you have any history at all?"

"A man brought him in. Said he can't keep a dog because he's hardly ever home. He thought someone dropped him off either at his house or close to it. It was like the dog knew he got dumped off and needed safety, so he hung out in the man's garage after the man left the door open. Like I said, I bet he's a good dog."

Bob's eyes narrowed. The seconds ticked away. He could barely stand leaving the dog at the shelter. But Annabel was in this thing too.

"What time do you close?" he asked.

"Five o'clock."

"Would it be possible for you or someone to hang around later? Otherwise, my friend and I may never make it in here together and we most certainly are going to adopt."

The woman bit her lip. "I suppose I can stay over and get some extra work done."

Bob didn't want her to change her mind.

"See you around six, then."

CHAPTER 12

Annabel tapped on the window of the newborn nursery where baby Samantha Barker slept in a clear plastic bassinet. At least the infant had been transferred and upgraded from the neonatal intensive care unit. She must be making progress from whatever ailed her on delivery, she thought, and more importantly, baby Sam may not be an infant born to a narcotic-addicted mother like Melba Fox, RN had told her.

A male nurse peered through the glass at the onlookers with wide grins. It was amazing the faces people made at the infants who had no concept yet of who, what, and where they were. Visitors waved, bobbed their heads, or stood transfixed like the little beings were all flown in on wings and dropped into the bassinets by angels. Siblings wiggled their fingers from their ears with their tongues out. Childless women tended to watch the infants with relief about their own status or with longing to have their own in the near future.

The RN pointed at Annabel, and although no visitors were allowed for another hour, he waved her to the door.

"Can I visit baby Barker?" she asked softly.

"Since you're a student, I'll give you slack. If you want to give her a little comfort and pick her up, however, check with Dr. Thomas in the back. He just received the baby's genetic test results."

Annabel strode over where the middle-aged man stood hunched over a chart. When he glanced up, the poor outcome of his surgical cleft lip and palate repair, from the days when that surgery as well as other plastic surgery had not been perfected, became obvious.

Annabel introduced herself. "Mrs. Barker is one of my patients," she said. "I came to check on her baby."

"Did you rotate on pediatrics yet?" He set down the chart and crossed his arms.

"Not yet."

"It doesn't always work out that way ... for students to take OB/GYN first followed later by pediatrics. You're lucky because that is the natural order of the two specialties."

"I see your point. I never thought about it that way."

"Since that is the case, you will almost certainly not have heard of the problem that Samantha Barker was born with. And even when you take pediatrics, chances are you won't see a patient with it. The incidence is only one in ten thousand."

Annabel's chest tightened for a moment. Infants are so fragile and innocent; they do not deserve for anything to be wrong.

"The first obvious symptoms made us suspicious. The babygrams or skeletal survey showed up as being osteopenic or osteoporotic, so we sent samples off for specialized genetic testing. Unfortunately, the results confirmed that there is an issue. Samantha has brittle bones."

Without blinking, Annabel waited for more. Was "brittle bones" a loose term for a real medical problem?

Sensing her naivety, he said, "Osteogenesis imperfecta or OI. Poor baby Sam has, and will, continue to suffer imperfect bone formation. It is a disorder that goes way back to ancient times. She didn't sign up for the unlucky cards she was dealt, but was dealt a problem because of genetics. If you did well with your genetic courses, she inherited OI in an autosomal dominant manner."

Annabel clasped her hands and rubbed her fingers back and forth. "Although I don't understand yet what that entails, this is very sad news to break to a young single mother who experienced a postpartum hemorrhage." She glanced over at the baby and frowned. "Let alone this newborn who had no say in the matter."

"I agree. I know about being born with something wrong right off the bat." He paused and tapped above his upper lip.

"In my specialty, I see it too often for my liking ... inherited diseases from little differences in the DNA of a chromosome. A transposed or messed up A, T, C, or G from what's normal in the nucleotide pairing of a human being."

Annabel envisioned the DNA base pairs of A and T, and C and G - which stood for adenine and thymine, and cytosine and guanine - and their helical structure when all linked together. Mother Nature was cruel when she mutated them negatively, and yet on the opposite side of the spectrum, mutations along the course of human history accomplished remarkable things as well ... like bigger brains and opposable thumbs.

"Will you be telling Bonnie Barker today? The OB team plans on discharging her tomorrow."

"Then she'll be going home without her baby because we must keep an eye on Samantha for a longer period of time. So far, it is remarkable that we transferred her out of the neonatal intensive care unit. These newborns are at higher risk for pulmonary infections and, with their smaller stomachs, they are more susceptible for GERD. You know, gastroesophageal reflux disease. Plus, she will not have feeding requirements like other newborns or children because they often end up at the very bottom percentile of the Growth Curve. Not because of failure to thrive, but sometimes due to dwarfism."

He glanced toward Sam's bassinette and said with emphasis, "It is our responsibility to not over-feed Samantha."

"I'll be sure not to mention the diagnosis to the mother until you do. Would it be all right if I visit and pick up baby Barker?"

"Be gentler than you would be with any other newborn," he said and motioned her over. "And, if you are a remarkable student wanting to learn as much as you can, add OI to your list."

Annabel smiled. One more topic to read, she thought, or at least an abbreviated summary because her OB/GYN one and only exam needed her primary focus. However, she would get her hands on an abbreviated summary of OI.

She leaned over the bassinette, took the swaddled neonate in her arms, and darted her eyes back to Dr. Thomas with alarm. Samantha had bluish gray sclerae.

"Yes, the whites of her eyes have color. A feature of OI."

Annabel nodded.

"Don't fret too much," Dr. Thomas said. "Out of a person's differences come great successes and the birth of extra creativity. Look at me. Part of my face was unsightly when I was a child and I was bullied like hell and made fun of. Instead of rolling up in a ball and letting life pass me by, I became stronger and excelled. I became the first person in my family to go on and earn an advanced degree. I also chose pediatrics because I can empathize with the plight of children, especially those who are different than the norm."

Annabel held the baby ever so gently. "Thank you for sharing," she said. She hoped she would see him again during her pediatrics rotation. She picked up more information from him that she could bank away and always remember, than from her present teammates.

Dr. Thomas gave her a good-bye tap on the shoulder and went out the back door. She knew of no other way to hold a baby except gently, but with this one she followed his advice and cuddled with extra care. What if, because of her frailty, she suffered a shortage of hugs and physical closeness as a baby, as a child, or her whole life? Annabel held her closer and the baby opened her eyes. She slipped her index finger into Sam's light grasp and their eyes locked.

"Welcome to the world, Samantha. You'll be fine, just fine."

Dr. Harvey and the residents were gathered in the lounge when Annabel returned. The attending doctor had stripped off his white jacket and was preparing yet another cup of coffee. She hoped it was decaf because he twitched and paced like he was waiting for the delivery of his own infant. They ignored her as she slinked to the couch and decided to heed her gut inclination not to interrupt the brooding group about baby Sam's diagnosis.

"Mike Chandler and his wife are still downstairs in the basement with their daughter," Caleb said to Roosevelt. "Sorry if we called you too early."

"That's okay. They'll be more ballistic if they come up and wait on me. In the meantime, we still have no answers about the woman's death." He wrapped his fingers around the handle, and with his other hand, he tapped the mug with his fingers.

"Since you all did H&Ps on her, was there any inkling that she could have had a diagnosis we didn't know about? Say, for instance, a Wolfe-Parkinson-White syndrome heart condition? Or a weird subset of sleep-apnea? Or maybe there was a heart problem at birth that she never followed up on but was supposed to? Patients often don't go back to their doctors. They start feeling better and believe that the diagnosis went away."

At this point, Caleb and Ling leaned against the counter. He was pouring her a coffee while the attending trailed off mumbling to himself. He finally snapped out of it. "Does anyone know if Mary Chandler was her parents' only child?"

Caleb poured creamer in Ling's coffee. "I believe so," he said. "At least

72

Mary told me it was going to be the parents' first grandkid."

The door to the lounge opened wider and Kristin Fleming poked her head in. "Emmett wheeled a patient up straight from admissions. She's an induction on the OB schedule for today. She already told the nurses she'll want an epidural so holler after someone's seen her and gets her labor going."

"We'll holler," Ling said. "And Annabel, pick her up as a patient. Do your H&P soon with or without us, which will be more experience for you that you are lacking. You'll have to think on your feet without copying our notes."

Annabel held her tongue. More and more, Ling was treating her like it was her first day of medical school.

The phone mounted on the wall rang; Ling answered and raised her eyebrows at Roosevelt. "It's the director of the lab downstairs," she said and put the call on the speaker.

"It's Dr. Harvey," Roosevelt said. "Is there anything you determined from the items we sent down from Mary Chandler's room?"

The man cleared his throat. "We finished analyzing the IV bag contents that were hanging on the infusion pumps upon your patient's death. I bring bad news. Very bad news."

Roosevelt Harvey placed his coffee squarely on the table and stood tall. He signaled to Ling to close the door.

"I'm listening," Roosevelt said.

"There were two one-liter Lactated Ringer's bags, one of them drained more than the other. The one clearly labelled as 'Magnesium Sulfate 40 mgs' only contained Lactated Ringer's solution with no Magnesium in it at all.

"The other bag? Testing that bag which had no label, in other words, the straight Lactated Ringer's solution, revealed that it contained 40 grams of magnesium sulfate. The infusion rate on the pump was at your probable rate of her maintenance fluids."

Roosevelt Harvey gasped and looked at Ling.

"300 mL/hour," she stuttered.

"300 mL/hour is correct," the director said. "I'm sorry to break this to you, but more sorry for the patient."

Roosevelt's head nodded up and down and up and down like a marionette on a string. Refusing to let the information sink in as fact and not fiction, he stayed speechless for a few moments.

"I'm not a praying man," Dr. Harvey managed to say, "but I'm going to say all the Hail Marys that go on a rosary bead that you mixed up the bags yourself when they were deposited there."

"Doctor, I'm sorry. The bags, the labels, and the pump in front of me spoke for themselves."

Roosevelt dropped his head and closed his eyes. "Thank you. You are doing your job. I know what you'll be doing next. Filling out all the incriminating paperwork."

"Every drop of it."

Dr. Harvey hung up. Ling sat at the table, knowing not to open the door again. She nervously patted her shoe on the floor. Caleb rubbed his bearded chin. The two of them searched each other's eyes, wondering if either or both of them had anything to do with the mistake.

Annabel tried to keep her pulse in check. The discovery was abominable and the fallout to her superiors might impact them the rest of their careers.

"We have our cause of death," Dr. Harvey said painfully. "Mary Chandler received a lethal fast dose of magnesium sulfate."

The group piled out of the lounge like it was on fire. Her team had other blazes to put out because of this news and were probably, in more ways than one, in deep trouble because of the medical error. At some point later, she needed to tell them about Samantha Barker's diagnosis.

While she thought about it, Annabel plopped herself straight into the end of the couch and went to a major pharmaceutical textbook to reference magnesium sulfate more thoroughly. It was a Godsend in obstetrics, but it was obviously lethal if overdosed or used in the wrong way. She scanned the primary description: … *a small colorless crystal used as an anticonvulsant, a cathartic, and an electrolyte replenisher in the treatment of pre-eclampsia and eclampsia; it causes direct inhibition of action potentials in myometrial muscle cells.* For its main mode of action, the summary stated … *excitation and contraction are uncoupled, which decreases the frequency and force of contractions.*

Annabel squirmed before even coming to the overdosage part. The drug posed as an acute toxin by most routes: inhalational toxicity, skin or dermal toxicity, and toxic if swallowed. But an outright overdose brings bigger problems like a slowing heartbeat, severe confusion and muscle weakness, drowsiness and dizziness, all succumbing the patient to a loss of consciousness.

She closed her eyes tight. Mary Chandler had ended up pregnant at a young age and there was no mention of the father of the baby. Apparently, he was out of the picture. She bet Mary would have thought twice about having a few minutes of sex with him if she had had a crystal ball to look into the future.

She opened her eyes and considered the end result. The eighteen-year-old had died a shocking, terrible, unforeseen death. Magnesium sulfate had been the premier drug of choice for her preeclampsia, which in and of itself, was a dangerous situation and diagnosis, but it went without saying that safety in the use of of all drugs was paramount ... especially in a hospital!

CHAPTER 13

Roosevelt Harvey mustered up his courage as he took off down the hallway. Sometimes the responsibilities of being the attending doctor in a teaching hospital were enormous. It was better to be straightforward with the Chandlers about what had been discovered than procrastinate to buy time. The chances of them not suing the hospital and the doctors involved were slim. Honesty and timeliness were paramount and he would maintain the ethical and moral standards he believed in and always practiced.

After being given instructions by Dr. Harvey, Ling and Caleb had their own tasks to perform. They huddled inside the supply room to make a game plan and split up their chores. Ling spotted a stepping stool and sat down on the top step. She swept her hand back to grasp her ponytail, her ring gemstone lacking its luster as she changed her expression into a deep frown.

"I'm as tired as a bear in a den," she said.

Caleb leaned in. "You should be perky. They say women often look rosy with an 'afterglow' after good sex and last night was felicitous, if I must say so myself."

A moment of silence ensued. "Maybe for you," she quipped.

Caleb felt a twang of ridicule besides being surprised. "Do you really mean that? I had no idea."

"I'm just tired, that's all."

"You're tired after getting adequate rest? We managed at least seven hours, which is a windfall for residents."

"Yeah, well, for once, I'd like to be a normal person who sleeps that much every night."

"There are a ton of people working other jobs and doing other things who get less than seven or eight hours a night. It's not just us, you know."

"Don't you think you've pontificated enough?"

"I'll shut up."

She tilted her head and stopped fiddling with her hair. "I'm half sorry. Half the time, I feel defeated."

"Defeated about what?"

"This case, for instance. A dead patient. No. A dead patient and baby.

We're not in it for that. Being a doctor in and of itself means to 'do no harm.'"

Caleb maintained eye contact with her, trying to relay some empathy. "In actuality, you did not harm her. A mistake was made, which is what you are going to go talk to the head nurse about. Health care is run by humans, and although our record of safety is almost clean as a whistle, humans *will* make mistakes."

Caleb extended his hand, hoping to help her down. She clasped it and stood in front of him. "You go see the new patient Kristin told us about, especially before the stupid bleached dark-blonde medical student goes in there."

Dr. Gash let go of her hand. "Ling, you were a medical student once. I hope no one belittled you like that. Rumor is ... Annabel Tilson is far from stupid."

"You can stick up for her. What? Have you become enamored with her?"

Caleb frowned. "I'd better go take care of our new patient." He turned and glanced back over his shoulder. "And I don't think she colors her hair. She's as natural as the sunrise."

Ling fumed as Caleb disappeared down the hallway. But forget about him, she thought. She marched past the elevator area and waiting room to the gynecology section and knocked on the first door.

The tall woman who swung the door open was the hospital's head nurse and administrator of OB/GYN. "I just housecleaned that chair and alleviated it of a backlog of files. Have a seat. You're Dr. Watson and, of course, I'm Elaine Rice."

Ling wondered if the woman's nasal voice had anything to do with her crooked nose. "I'll sit, if you don't mind." She looked at the chair like it was a piece of chocolate cake. "A plushy, upholstered seat cushion is a rarity for a resident. I guess the hospital reserves that for their own main employees rather than the doctors and residents who keep hospitals afloat."

Mrs. Rice threw her a dirty glance. "Feel free to speak your mind, Dr. Watson."

"The reason I'm here is to discuss Mary Chandler. You must have been informed of her death yesterday."

"Yes. My hand is on the pulse. It was an awful occurrence and I was informed immediately."

"Have you been told yet what killed her?"

Mrs. Rice squinted. "Apparently not."

"We only just found out. I'm sure diligent hospital employees will be calling you any minute."

"Please lay the groundwork, Dr. Watson."

"Your staff screwed up the labels and contents of two IV fluid bags yesterday on Ms. Chandler's treatment of preeclampsia. Magnesium sulfate was bolused and dripped into our patient at an obscene rate ... which was the rate of the hydration we had ordered for normal Lactated Ringer's solution."

Elaine Rice gripped her hand into a fist and placed it on the desk.

"Sherry was the nurse working yesterday who was taking care of her and her unborn child. She's not here today, but I believe it was her actions that led to the demise of our patient. Poor Dr. Harvey is dealing with the patient's parents as we speak. He spoke to the mother before, but now the father is here. Mike Chandler is spending an inordinate amount of time in the basement with his dead daughter before the medical examiner begins his autopsy."

Elaine Rice squirmed and her hyponasal speech became worse. "I'll talk to our laboratory immediately as well as do a thorough nursing investigation."

"I'm new to such matters, but I'm sure that's what your hospital attorneys are going to advise. Keep us abreast of what you find out."

"I agree. It would be unwise if the medical team and the hospital staff do not directly communicate. Misinformation could jeopardize getting to the bottom of this."

"Or put you in a worse situation."

Ling rose and was at the door. "Nice meeting you, but the nurses you hire leave a lot to be desired."

Mrs. Rice stared past the open door. What ever happened to tactful, non-accusatory, professional speech from a resident, she thought. Not only did she have a possible overtly negligent nurse on her staff to deal with, but a bitchy resident was running loose too, who basically thought she was mightier than the attending physician.

With Melba Fox, RN finished with her last round of dispensed drugs, Elaine Rice found the medicine cart stashed in the supply room. She hovered over the book that would incriminate and hold accountable a formerly trustworthy and dependable nurse. She licked her index finger and skimmed to Mary Chandler's page. The doctors had clearly written the mag sulfate order as well as her maintenance fluids. Ms. Fox had also checked off and logged in a time when she had carried out the orders.

Someone can check off doing something as much as they want, Elaine thought, but if they aren't doing it correctly, then what good is it? Except that it set a more accurate timeline of administration and death to the patient.

Sometimes she hated her job; this was one of those times. Next stop was administration and, no doubt, their decision would be to put the middle-aged nurse on a leave of absence when she showed up for work the next day.

Glad to get away from the drama on the ward, Annabel strode into Room 4, where her new patient and husband were settling in. The man wore a T-shirt and blue jeans, which defined his muscular build. He unpacked a navy nylon bag with his wife's things in them and neatly stashed clothes and toiletries on tables and in drawers like they were away on vacation.

Already dressed in a hospital gown, the woman sat with a pleasant smile in the room's comfortable chair as she watched and directed her husband. Annabel nodded at them as she perched herself on the end of the vacant bed.

"I'm Dr. Tilson, one of the medical students. One of the residents will be in shortly. May I ask you some questions?"

"Sure," the woman said. "This is a teaching hospital, so we expect students. They were loitering around for my first baby too. I'm Amy Wagner and this is my husband, Harry."

Annabel had read the woman's limited paperwork which functioned as her ticket for admission. The thirty-one-year-old had last been seen in the clinic a few days ago. Despite her large girth from her pregnancy, she appeared to be in excellent condition like her husband: her legs and arms slender, firm, and shapely. Her skin glowed like all she did was eat fruits and vegetables and take fast-paced walks on nature trails.

She was just the patient she needed to work-up, Annabel thought, to fend off the cloud that had fallen on the rotation.

"So this is not your first baby?"

"Second one. We have a little girl at home. This one's a boy."

"Any other pregnancies at all?"

"No."

Annabel grabbed an index card from her pocket and wrote G2P1. "I read you had a previous C-section. What was the reason?"

"Ha! My outlet was too small for a big girl!"

Harry placed a framed picture of his wife, his daughter, and himself on the nightstand. The family huddled close to each other in front of a Christmas tree.

"I tell it differently," he interjected. "There was no way Amy was going to spill out our daughter, who was as plump as a honeydew melon."

"You must have welcomed the C-section."

"We did," Amy said.

Annabel thought about follow-up questions about this pregnancy while Harry crouched down, slid off his wife's hospital slipper socks, and put on the ones they'd taken from home.

"What did the obstetricians in the clinic tell you about this baby's size?"

"He's not as huge as our Susan was. They've monitored me by ultrasound. You know, years ago, they used to automatically do follow up C-sections on women who had their first baby by surgery. Nowadays, they decide on each case separately."

"Yes, they have you down for a trial of labor after cesarean section or TOLAC," Annabel said. "And why did they admit you now?"

"I'm overdue, so no sense in letting little Wagner grow any more!"

"What about the last nine months? Any problems we need to know about or any medical history?"

"Not at all. I'm pretty healthy too."

"She's a skier," Harry said.

"What kind?"

"Both," Amy said. "Snow and water."

"She's being modest," Harry said. "Snow includes downhill and cross country and water depends on how many feet she wants to put in skis ... or not ... and get pulled by a boat at a hundred miles an hour."

"I bet you have that short blonde haircut to fit it snugly under a winter ski cap," Annabel said. "Much of what you're talking about sounds exciting. Has little Susan stood on skis yet?"

"Amy is going to see to it," Harry said, beaming.

Caleb made an appearance at the door and came straight in wheeling an ultrasound and a fetal monitoring machine on a cart.

"Mrs. Wagner, I presume," he said. "I'm Dr. Gash. I saw you in clinic once or twice."

Harry shook his hand and introduced himself.

"Dr. Tilson," Caleb said, "are you almost finished with your H&P?"

"We're making progress, but I still need to examine Mrs. Wagner."

"You can close the door and watch while I do an ultrasound. Since Mrs. Wagner underwent a previous C-section, we'll assess her lower uterine segment one more time to determine whether sufficient thickness is present to support labor."

Amy took the clue and wiggled up on the bed. Caleb prepared the patient's lower belly and was soon rolling the ultrasound around. He nodded and pointed out the black and white picture to Annabel as he went along.

"That's my son in there," Harry beamed. "He'll be on this side of that incubator by tomorrow."

"Since when is my uterus an incubator?" Amy commented.

"It counts as a controlled environment; it most certainly is an incubator." He took her hand and kissed it.

Caleb stopped and wiped off the gel on Amy's abdomen with a hand towel. "You're set to go with our original plan."

"Easy for you to say. I guess the next item on the agenda is an IV."

"Precisely."

"May I start it?" Annabel asked.

"Caleb raised his eyebrows. "If Mrs. Wagner allows it ..."

"I'll give you one chance," she said. "Two tops."

"With the few that I have inserted, I'm not too bad. I'll ask the expert anesthesiologist to help me out if I fail, so as to avoid the tech as the middleman. I do need to wrap up my H&P, however, and listen to your heart and lungs."

Annabel still needed to write up the H&P on Mrs. Wagner, but the IV was the first priority to start her patient on oxytocin to begin inducing labor. She grinned; she was finally learning some obstetrics.

She familiarized herself with the supply room and grabbed what she needed. A large-bore IV was not needed, but she didn't want something too small either. She chose an 18-gauge IV catheter knowing that a 20-gauge was a backup plan for a smaller vein. After shoving more supplies in her pocket, she headed back to Amy's room.

Harry ambled from one side of the bed to the other, forcing his wife to smile as he clicked cell phone pictures of her.

"You are the proudest father I've come across so far," Annabel said, "and your baby isn't here yet."

She realized her first and second patients were not so lucky; one with an uninvolved father who only donated his sperm, and the second with a father who wanted to be involved, but the woman was not letting him.

"I'm sure Amy will have this one on skis early too. I am active in sports, too, and I'm a health fanatic. Little Bobby is going to be a chip off the old block."

"You hope so," Annabel said. "Sometimes kids don't follow their patents' agenda. I bet you two are stellar examples, however."

Annabel set her supplies on the tray table and tightened a tourniquet around Amy's arm. A straight, plump vein popped up on her hand. She leaned in, wiped it with alcohol, and opened the IV packaging.

"We also have a dog at home," Amy said. "His name is Blue. He's a German Sheperd and is baby number one. He plays with Susan and he also is the protector of all of us like he's the house sentry."

"He sounds marvelous. It turns out that I may be getting my own dog later today. Your enthusiasm over Blue makes me all the more excited."

Over the dog discussion, Annabel had pricked the area with local anesthetic and had slipped in the IV to make its mark with a quick blood return. She heplocked it and secured it with tape to Amy's hand. It wasn't going anywhere when she finished.

Harry's big tall frame peered over her shoulder. "Way to go for a medical student."

"Thumbs up," Amy said. "And you're really getting a dog today?"

"Yes, with a friend. We're going to take care of the dog together, even though we don't live together. As students, our schedules fluctuate."

"Good luck with that. Dogs shouldn't be experimented with, but you'll probably do fine. As long as you and your friend are cooperative with each other."

Annabel trudged to the door, where she dumped the needles into the sharps container. "He may be my best friend ever. We'll never know unless we try."

"Dr. Tilson," Harry said, "you must tell us tomorrow what happened."

"Sure thing."

Annabel took one step into the hallway. Emmett came zooming out of the next room and grabbed Annabel by the arm.

CHAPTER 14

Emmett's bushy eyebrows stood out over his wide-open eyes. He grasped Annabel's white coat by the sleeve and yanked her from the hallway straight into Bonnie Barker's room.

For just two days of being on the rotation, Annabel trusted Emmett even more than some of the other medical people working in obstetrics. He seemed trustworthy, did his job without fanfare, and treated the patients and staff with respect. With curiosity and concern, she let him pull her next door.

"You're the closest one," he said as they turned at the doorway. "I walked into her room and ... look."

As Annabel approached the bed, she thought Bonnie was dead. Her own heart jumped like a car's ignition had just been turned on. Her heartbeat raced as she simultaneously docked her fingers on Bonnie's carotid to feel for a pulse. Please, not again, she thought.

"Emmett, get help."

The orderly took off and she zeroed her attention on her patient. She felt it. A faint pulse under her fingertips. She exhaled, allowing herself the small relief of that discovery. But there was still a crisis as she watched the woman's chest and tried to discern her respiratory rate. There wasn't much of a rise to her chest, so she grabbed the nasal cannula off the wall oxygen device and stuck the prongs in her nostrils. It was a band-aid only because her patient had little in the way of respiratory effort. She needed help; otherwise, surely in a minute or two, she would need to do chest compressions.

She heard them barrel in before she saw them. Kristin Fleming appeared to her side and then Dr. Gash. Emmett followed with the crash cart.

Dr. Fleming's actions were quick as thought as she unlocked the bed and moved it away from the wall. "Emmett, see if any nurses are around or get me respiratory stat."

Kristin waved at the cart. Annabel pushed it closer and, reading the anesthesiologist's thought process, she opened the drawers for airway equipment. She handed her a laryngoscope blade, one she knew was of an appropriate size for an adult, and then laid three sizes of endotracheal tubes at the top of the bed. Caleb listened with his stethoscope to Bonnie's heart.

A stout young man from respiratory therapy sidled next to Dr. Fleming and hooked up a suction catheter. Kristin yanked on nylon gloves, opened Bonnie's mouth, and in two moves with the blade and the tube, had Ms. Barker's trachea intubated. The therapist hooked it up to an Ambu bag and squeezed oxygen into Bonnie while Kristin verified breath sounds.

Dr. Fleming nodded. The tube was in the right place, not the esophagus, and both lungs rose with bilateral breath sounds. Another therapist wheeled in a ventilator and the team finalized everything they had done.

"Her heart likes that much better," Caleb commented. "But I'm not crazy about it. She's slow ... in the fifties. Now she needs to be in the unit."

"Yes, get her transferred to the ICU right away," Kristin said. "What on earth happened?"

"I intend to find out."

Annabel thought back through the afternoon's events. "Bonnie Barker complained about pain when we rounded on her early today. I think Dr. Harvey and Dr. Watson came to a treatment decision and the nurse dispensed her medication this afternoon. The RN wondered what was written."

"That's a start," Caleb said as the therapists and Emmett unhooked connections and began wheeling Bonnie Barker to the ICU.

Caleb ran to find her chart. He needed to document the occurrence as well as write orders for the transfer. He also needed to alert Ling, wherever the hell she was, and put in for a medical consult with internal medicine for management in the ICU. The electronic medical record was another thing, but he also needed to investigate what Annabel had spoken about.

Annabel tailed after him. She could almost see the wheels in his brain churning. They both heard the running of shoes on the shiny corridor until Ling stopped short next to them. She tried to catch her breath. "Our patient passed me on her way to the ICU with a breathing tube jutting out of her mouth. What the hell?"

Caleb and Annabel glanced at each other first.

"Annabel showed up first."

"She was nonresponsive and barely breathing."

"And I have my hands full at the moment," Caleb said. "We honestly don't know what happened yet. Maybe you can follow Ms. Barker over to the unit, give them ventilator settings, and request help from internal medicine or a hospitalist."

Ling's ponytail swayed as she turned on her heels and left.

Annabel and Caleb looked at each other again.

"That was a surprise," Annabel blurted out.

"Easier than I thought," he said. "Perhaps she figures she'll follow the path of least resistance."

Annabel nodded. "We better take a look at Bonnie Barker's previous orders and then the medicine cart to check what was or was not given."

"I hope Emmett didn't grab her chart when they went over."

"If he didn't, they'll be calling for it any minute."

They hustled to the stack of charts at the nurses' station and Caleb found it under the lip of the counter.

Dr. Gash flipped to the end of the "Orders" tab to look for recent activity. There were a set of orders from earlier in the day. They both angled so close to each other their sleeves touched. He pointed.

"I'm having difficulty reading this order," he said.

"Dr. Watson's handwriting is ..." Annabel started.

"Illegible. The 200 mgs looks fine. What's in front of it, with normal scrutiny, looks like morphine because the "m" and the "o" are clear." He averted his gaze to Annabel and his eyes popped wider.

"Shit," Annabel whispered. "Bonnie Barker received 200 mgs of morphine. Dr. Watson should've written the real pain medicine of Motrin really clear. The nurse, her last name is Fox, said something to me about it in the hallway and I sort of questioned her thought process."

"Let's check the medicine cart."

They ripped across the aisle and into the supply room. Annabel opened the record lying on top. "Sure enough, it's what we thought."

Their eyes met.

"We should reverse the actions of the opioid," Annabel said.

At the same time, they both quipped, "Narcan."

"Come on." Caleb waved past the doorway.

Before they made it to the staircase to run up to the unit, Dr. Harvey stepped out of the family consultation room near the waiting room. They almost banged into him. He wore a forlorn expression. His toupee lacked buoyancy and sat atop his head like someone had sat on it.

"Are you two going to a fire?" he asked. His attention focused on Annabel; sometimes students divulged more than their higher-ups.

Annabel held her tongue for an extra moment, hating to saddle her attending with another team medical emergency. "Ms. Barker is in the ICU on a ventilator. She mistakenly received morphine instead of Motrin."

Roosevelt Harvey gasped while Annabel peered into the room he had exited from. The Chandlers had fortunately not been close enough to hear their conversation about another patient. Mike tried to control his sobbing wife while he wiped tears away from his own eyes.

Dr. Harvey, Caleb, and Annabel swiftly left the corridor and caught the attention of visitors in the waiting room as they walked shoulder-to-shoulder with their heads down.

"Are you sure about this?" Roosevelt asked.

"The entry is in the record," Caleb said, shaking his head. "I can understand why the mistake was made."

Roosevelt stopped short. "There is no excuse for errors!"

Caleb and Annabel flinched.

"What? Tell me your interpretation of the mistake."

"The nurse may have misinterpreted Dr. Watson's handwriting," Caleb said.

Dr. Harvey sagged his shoulders more than usual. "God forbid," he mumbled as he opened the door to take the stairs instead of the elevator. He took one step at a time like it was a chore and he was out of steam. "We all have patients to take care of, there are women in labor, and I'm due back over in my office. You all are making a mess and all I'm doing is putting out fires!"

Caleb reached for the doorknob and they exited next to the ICU. The automatic doors opened and the first person they saw was Ling.

"Dr. Watson ... Dr. Gash and Dr. Tilson just informed me that Ms. Barker received high-dose morphine."

"Based on her pinpoint pupils, I guessed that. What stupid idiot did that?"

"Your handwriting may have been misconstrued based on what your teammates are telling me."

Ling took a second to process that and then gave Caleb a heavy glare. "What you are implying is preposterous. There must be more to it than that."

"Let's put this to rest right now and check with the RN." He tilted his head towards Annabel.

"Melba Fox," she said.

"We'll talk to her," Ling said, "but we need to give Bonnie Barker an opioid antagonist."

The group went into her ICU room and Dr. Harvey examined her. Bonnie was covered with a sheet to her shoulders and the tubing to her endotracheal tube pulsed with the respirations from the machine.

"Here's what you're going to do, Dr. Gash. While Dr. Watson and I go talk to the nurse, you're going to methodically treat her overdose. You can start off by titrating slowly and staying right here for a few doses. Since she is on the ventilator, we don't have to worry about her oxygenation. Start with an initial dose of 0.4 mg of naloxone IV and you can use repeated doses if necessary.

"Dr. Tilson, you will stay with Dr. Gash to learn an important point. Even though you both may think she begins to come around and breathe adequately, the duration of action of the morphine will probably exceed that of the Narcan, so she needs to be kept under continued surveillance. No extubating her prematurely. No taking her off the ventilator just because she may open her eyes.

"Meanwhile, Dr. Watson and I will go talk to the RN who was responsible."

"This will be a slow, easy process," Caleb said after he gave Bonnie her second dose of naloxone. "As a matter of fact, it's best if we reverse at least half of the overdose and let her rest tonight on the ventilator."

"That makes sense."

"I'll give her a third dose in a little while. In the meantime, grab a chair."

Annabel perched herself at the end of the nurses' station and took out her cell phone. The volume was turned down all day, so she checked immediately if Bob had contacted her, hoping that today was yet another improvement in his energy level. Especially since he was the appointed task master for setting up for their pet. The dog might end up memorable in more ways than one and more pleasant than the events that took place on the ward.

Her index finger plugged in her opening password and she went to text messages where his message popped up. Even if he had not made progress with their agenda, she was glad to see it.

Hey, workaholic medical student. Don't deliver too many babies today. Save some for your residents!

What a doofus, she thought with a smile.

'Shopping' for dog 'basics' is done. And you won't believe it. I scouted out dogs at the kennel ... where some dog, I think, stole my heart. I'll be curious to see what you think about the furry beast.

Annabel stroked her hair and hunched over the phone. A pathological euphoria swept over her and she contained a giggle. He might not be available to text back right away, but she responded.

You did take a picture, didn't you?

Nope. Sorry about that.

Caleb put two Styrofoam cups down with steaming black coffee and rolled out a chair. "It's late in the afternoon for this, but I'm offering some to you in case you want to ruin your sleep tonight and study like me."

"Is that your agenda?"

He frowned. "I may use the coffee to keep alert for a movie instead. God knows, after today, I deserve it." He nodded his head toward her phone. "You seem chipper."

"Another student and I may be getting a dog."

"One of those four-legged things that need to be walked, and fed, and brushed, and taken to the vet? And jump all over you with muddy paws, and jump into your bed at night just when you've gotten to sleep, and bring in ticks and fleas? Besides the fact that they go through worse terrible twos than a little human being because they pull stuffing out of pillows, yank toilet paper out of the dispenser, and eat your sump pump?"

He leaned back with assurance. "And unless you get yourself a trained security dog, he or she will lick the very palm of an intruder breaking into your apartment or house. He'll soil your car with dog hair that will become a permanent fixture to the upholstery and it'll bark like a spoiled child when you pull through a drive-through bank window because it somehow knows they keep biscuits behind the counter."

Annabel's eyes grew with disbelief. "It can be that bad? Is there anything else you want to add to that?"

"It's worse than that," he said forcing a scowl that he didn't mean.

"Hmm. Maybe my whole idea is a bit premature."

"Are you kidding? Don't deprive yourself. There's nothing like a dog."

CHAPTER 15

Dr. Harvey stopped in the obstetric hallway and tapped Emmett on the shoulder. "Have you seen Melba Fox?"

"Right in there. Since Bonnie Barker was temporarily transferred, she's putting a few of her things out of sight. The patient's boyfriend was just here too, and he frantically left for the ICU."

"I suppose he's another unhappy camper," Ling said.

"He should be." The attending poked his head in the door. "Ms. Fox, may I talk to you?"

Melba strolled over. She nervously rotated her bracelets on her wrist. "I hope Bonnie Barker returns to her same room."

"We do too. Obviously, discharging her tomorrow is out of the question. I understand you may have given her an overdose of narcotics this afternoon."

Melba guessed she would be facing this type of confrontation. Since she learned of Bonnie's respiratory depression, emergent treatment, and transfer, she'd been shaking in her shoes.

"I followed orders, Dr. Harvey. Reading certain doctors or resident's handwriting can be a big problem for nurses."

Ling put her hand on her hip and seethed.

"However," Melba continued, "I read Dr. Watson's order as most likely being Motrin. In retrospect, it was damn cryptic to make out. Fortunate for me at the time, Dr. Tilson was nearby and I asked her what it said. She said, 'Morphine 200 mgs.' Which is what I gave. I feel so terrible about this, I'm almost in tears. I should know better than to trust the input of a medical student."

Ling slid her hand off her hip and relaxed just a bit. At least the accusation against her had taken a little turn. Most of the heat for the situation had been turned to Annabel.

Roosevelt worked at tucking the bottom of his shirt into his trousers for the umpteenth time that day. He narrowed his eyes.

Emmett listened intently, fiddling with the supply boxes on purpose. In his opinion, Annabel Tilson came to Bonnie Barker's aid immediately when he reached out and grabbed her. She rendered aid efficiently at the time and he believed she was more professional in two days than what he saw of Ling Watson all the weeks and months she came and went from obstetrics at the University Hospital.

"I don't mean to interrupt," Emmet said, "but the medication log book is right here on the cart."

Dr. Harvey liked the large man with the tattoos on his forearm. He nodded his approval for Emmett to grab it.

Roosevelt's gaze froze upon reading the order. "Dr. Watson, this is atrocious, and indecipherable. What did you think? By only writing an 'm' and an 'o' legibly, then someone reading it was given the liberty to fill in the rest themselves?"

Ling bit her lip. She didn't sweat when she worked out, but now beads of perspiration formed under her armpits.

Dr. Harvey looked up. "And I suppose our medical student needs a scolding too."

Worried, Emmett backed up. Annabel didn't deserve what was coming to her.

Tony had left the hospital for a few hours to grab lunch and run errands. He'd taken another day off from his job as a coach, so he tried to fit in a few personal tasks while Bonnie began snoozing off to sleep. Otherwise, he stayed in her room like they were bounded by a history of forty years' worth of wedding anniversaries ... which wasn't the case at all.

When he came back, bad news hit him worse than a dismal season for the soccer team he coached. He wanted to kick himself for leaving.

He stopped first at the newborn nursery. Dr. Thomas noticed him at the window swinging his head back and forth like he was humming a tune to baby Samantha. The pediatrician stepped outside and asked, "Are you Samantha's father?"

Tony nodded. "How can you tell?" He put on a wide smile and laughed.

"She's a doll baby like most infants. I planned on going over to see you and your wife soon because I must tell you some important news."

"We're not married, but go ahead."

Dr. Thomas rubbed above his lip and chose his words carefully. "We discovered a problem with your baby, which may end up causing lax joints, poor muscle tone, and poorer motor skills than other children her age. It affects bones; they may easily fracture."

Tony looked down at his sneakers while trying to grasp the pediatrician's words. He knew a few things about kids who couldn't compete in sports, even about a bone disease he once heard about.

"It's called osteogenesis imperfecta."

Tony gripped his hand as hard as he could. No, no, no, he thought. "How come? How did she get it?"

"I'm sorry. It is a genetic disease."

"Does her mother know yet?"

"No. Would you like to break it to her and I come by later or tomorrow and answer both your questions?"

"That may be best. She suffered with a postpartum hemorrhage; I'd better dish out the news in drips and drabs the way I see fit, according to the way she responds and handles it."

"It sounds like you know best. Why don't you call me when you're both ready for the medical facts; when you're ready to hear more?"

"Thank you," Tony said. Disheartened, he headed to Bonnie's room, where he found it empty as a discarded soda can.

At the nurses' station, Tony learned of Bonnie's transfer to the ICU. "Because she's on a ventilator," he was told. Upstairs, he was lucky with the visiting hours and went straight into the intensive care unit where he found Annabel and Caleb sat at the end of the desk.

"Where is she? I came back to the hospital to find two catastrophic events with the two most important people in the world. Don't you people believe in phone calls or text messages?"

"Dr. Tilson and I are treating your girlfriend right now," Caleb said, "which is our number one priority. Dr. Watson will be calling you any minute."

Annabel realized the young man said "two catastrophic events," so she ventured saying, "Dr. Thomas must have told you about Samantha. He is an excellent pediatrician and she is in skilled hands. I went over and held her before. She's the sweetest thing."

"I hope so. I mean, I think so," Tony said, focusing on Annabel. He took a deep breath. "This is a lot to process."

"Both of them are going to be fine. Bonnie is in the room straight ahead. She was given too much pain medicine and Dr. Gash and I are slowly reversing those affects."

"Somebody made a mistake?"

"Basically, that is what happened," Annabel admitted.

"I'd better go see her." He slid away and, inside the room, pulled a chair as close to her as possible.

"He was more tolerant than I would have been," Caleb said when Tony stepped away.

"He's a dedicated father already," Annabel said. "I sure wish the two of them would get their act together."

Bonnie Barker was in some kind of a dream. Or was it? A euphoric feeling swam around inside her head and her body felt heavy as a load of concrete. She hated whatever was going on with her throat, as if it was jammed up with something.

Her eyelids were possibly slammed shut with industrial tape, she thought, because she couldn't budge them open. She was damn tired, but why? The last thing she remembered was being in her labor and delivery room, the bed semi-inclined, as she became overwhelmingly tired. Now, however, she lay flat and the mattress seemed different.

Since she came into this hospital, dreadful events had befallen her. In her prenatal clinic visits and in her overall understanding of childbirth, never did she learn about excessive post-delivery bleeding or what had happened to her. Certainly a woman could bleed a bit during delivery, but nothing like what had transpired after her delivery. And then the doctors-in-training inserted their whole hand inside her and on top of her and massaged like that was going to stop the flow. How barbaric!

On top of that, there was something they were keeping from her about her baby. They were "testing" Samantha, but they still didn't divulge a word. They must have information by now. They were hiding something, and why were they so jittery when she held her own baby and breast fed her? It was as if the nurse from the nursery was afraid she would break her own newborn!

Over the course of a few more minutes, Bonnie seemed a little more lucid. She heard a droning noise like a machine, cyclical in nature, and became more aware of her chest rising and falling. Then, for sure, fingers slipped into the palm of her hand. Human touch; warm and comforting. Then she heard a female voice. That medical student, Annabel Tilson.

"I popped in to check if she's stirred yet," Annabel said to Tony, who sat at Bonnie's bedside. "Feel free to talk to her. We'll let her sleep overnight, but I assure you, she's not deeply sleeping like she was before."

Tony nodded and Annabel left.

So Tony was next to her, Bonnie thought, as she felt his fingers rub hers. Why did he continue to be around so much? After she found out about her pregnancy, she saw him the least. Over time, however, as the girth of her abdomen grew, he came across as being more interested and spent more time with her.

She had dated Tony for half a year before her pregnancy. Nothing special, yet nothing too boring either. When she found herself accidentally pregnant, abortion was not even a consideration. She wanted kids eventually anyway. Why not just go ahead with it? She was independent, very bright, and ran a daycare center since her high school graduation. She handled the business aspect of it but, in essence, she would be able to mind her own child while she worked. It made for a decent plan.

Now that she thought about Tony, she wondered. When he stopped coming around so much in her first trimester, wasn't it her who had pushed him away? He coached kids for a living and he never once gave her grief because she had erred with her birth control. One day, he even said, "Hey, Bonnie, isn't it about time we got married?"

To which she had spoken hastily, but believed what she said. "That's what people used to do in the old days because they had to ... save face in public and get married because the woman was pregnant. Being pregnant and unmarried doesn't matter anymore. We don't need to become a married couple."

Tony appeared unhappy about her remark and yet he never brought it up again. That was his style, however, to accept another person's wants and desires. He never asked again or persisted about things that mattered to him.

Tony inhaled and noisily exhaled over many seconds. "I sure hate to see you this way," he said softly, leaning over their hands. "They goofed up your pain medicine and that is the reason they transferred you here and why the machine is helping you to breathe. You had your own troubles before, but now it's their fault. I won't leave you. When you are awake, you can always tell me to buzz off." He chuckled and said, "Which is what you pretty much did months ago."

He rested his left elbow on the sheet. Bonnie listened to every word and hoped he would continue to keep her company. Plus, she wanted to hear more.

"They told me bad news today, though. Our daughter has a genetic disease that makes her bones brittle. It comes with other problems too. If our relationship stays the same, it will be that much harder for us and Samantha. She deserves the both of us together. You may not love me, but I'm sure smitten with you. Ever since I met you the night you were wearing the powdered sugar from the beignet you were eating. That date was a setup, remember? The four of us met for dinner at that New Orleans style restaurant and we both realized we loved the same music and the same courses like geography and art and we both hated Mexican food and over-sized cars."

The words sank in as Bonnie listened. Hearing about her daughter's illness saddened her very core; she had been correct to worry. And yet this man in his twenties showed remarkable maturity. She had also read him wrong. Terribly wrong. In her whole lifetime, she might not ever meet a man as steadfast, sincere, dedicated, and responsible as him. And what had she done? Assumed he only went through the "motions" of a distraught unmarried father and that he had pretended to want more in a relationship with her and their baby.

Now her heart warmed. He cared. He really cared about her and baby Sam. Samantha ... an ill little girl that he could easily have little to do with if he wanted, especially since she had pushed him aside.

She couldn't wait to wake up, pull him close to her, and tell him they were overdue to get married. After all, she wanted to tell him that she needed a buddy to eat beignets with and that he would be the best dad in the world to Samantha.

Annabel and Caleb entered the lounge hoping the team would soon discuss their patients and that the night call team would soon take over. They both secretly wished to put the last ten hours on the obstetric ward behind them.

Dr. Harvey was still there wearing a scowl on his face. Annabel realized he missed all his afternoon office hours. That would leave him a group of unhappy patients and a rescheduling nightmare. Being an attending affiliated with a teaching hospital as well as managing private patients, she thought, must take courage and dedication. Playing double jeopardy may have occasional rewards but, on the whole, must be fraught with stress. That would be an enlightening research project, she thought; comparing the number of heart attacks of university attendings with private practice doctors. She bet some group would dump a lot of money into that one.

"Dr. Tilson!"

Annabel startled as Dr. Harvey thumped his fist on the table, prompting her to sit before him. Caleb circled wide, headed to the couch where Ling sat cross-legged.

Annabel sensed jitters in her stomach. Dr. Harvey was not his usual self that patients loved. Actually, all afternoon, he was going downhill. Why did he seem angry at her? She had been in the unit with Dr. Gash. Earlier, she had even been instrumental in getting Bonnie Barker the help which she needed. She also completed a work-up on her new patient, Amy Wagner, a flawless, healthy obstetric patient for an induction, who posed no problems since her admission. Roosevelt splayed his hand on the tabletop as if to keep from thumping it again.

She clutched her hands on her lap and waited.

"The main principle of a doctor's Hippocratic Oath is to 'do no harm.' Ms. Barker almost died of a morphine overdose when she should have received a simple 200 mg tablet of Motrin. I understand you read Dr. Watson's pain order as a long-lasting narcotic and instructed the nurse, Melba Fox, to give it."

The accusation struck her in the gut and her stomach rumbled from fear. "No, sir. I actually questioned her interpretation when she said Dr. Watson's handwriting looked like morphine. I told her that 200 mgs seemed too high for it to be morphine. But she said I didn't know any better. If I may paraphrase, she said something like many patients on the obstetric floor have a history of taking drugs and it was not an uncommon prescription for those who have developed a tolerance."

"Let me get this straight. We have here an RN's word against a medical student. One versus the other. What kind of a rotation am I staffing here? One where I must act like a detective and dole out polygraph tests?!"

He rose suddenly. "You take off for the day. It's that time anyway. We can see our patients without you before handing them over to the night team. Be back in the morning and reconsider the accusation you've made."

Annabel stood. In all her rotations, she'd never been so humiliated. Her word was never doubted like this before. She caught a sly upturn of Ling's mouth while she grabbed her things. She stepped out of the room. Her stomach churned, but worse than that, she wanted to call it quits.

CHAPTER 16

Annabel's heart pounded from a mixture of emotions: anger, unsureness, and sadness. Anger at wrongly implicating her in Bonnie Barker's overdose, uncertainty whether this incident would negatively impact her grade or further status on the rotation, and sadness for both her young patients who encountered obstetric complications and for herself because her luck ran out to be working with such a dysfunctional team.

And although she was a student, teaching was minimal. The four years of medical school was called "medical education." So where was the medical education except for what she was learning by reading and observing?

She pushed through the revolving doors at the hospital's front entrance and stood on the pavement half disoriented. She had to think about it ... had she driven in that morning in her own car or with an Uber driver? Since Bob wanted to scout out the dog shelter, she remembered her thought process. She had driven in her own red Nissan SUV because that would be less complicated. Knowing she could barely think straight, she was so upset, she shook her head back and forth.

At her car, she threw her things on the back floor, started the ignition, and held the steering wheel with an isotonic death grip. More than anything, she hated this rotation. She couldn't wait for it to be finished. However, it had only started.

She put the car in drive and took off. What a bad day to go scout out dogs, she thought. Maybe she should cancel with Bob. She toyed with the idea but, earlier, he had done their shopping and gone without her to look at them. What would she think of the one that "stole" his heart? If the previous hours were any indication, she would probably not see eye to eye with Bob either.

After heading east, she arrived at his apartment complex, realizing that she should have texted him that she was on the way. But she still seethed over the day and, if she had a choice, she would go straight home, curl under her covers, and sob into her pillow. She walked past the empty pool not filled for the springtime. She glanced at the horizon. Although the days were getting longer, the sunset was not complete. She went to his first-floor unit and knocked.

"Hey," Bob said, opening the door. He wore a smile, sweat pants, and a long-sleeve medical school sweat shirt. "I will owe the lady at the front desk my first born if we don't get over to the shelter. She is staying over for us."

Annabel frowned.

"Uh-oh, you don't appear too chipper."

"You're putting it mildly."

"You can tell me about it. Let's take my car." He stepped back inside and grabbed his keys and wallet and handed Annabel the leash and collar, and led the way to his Honda.

"You should be resting. Our timing is terrible."

"Then there will never be the right time. Sometimes you must cross the Rubicon and do what you made excuses to put off."

Annabel sighed. There was truth to that. She examined the items in her hand; not the standard fare for a dog collar or a leash. She liked them, but her enthusiasm was still dampened. As Bob commented about the weather and the shelter, she half listened. Finally, they drove in silence.

After repeating his drive down the long country-like lane, Bob pulled his Fit into the parking lot next to the only vehicle around, no doubt, belonging to the thoughtful employee waiting on them.

Annabel dangled the items as she followed him in. She still didn't know any more about the dog he was interested in other than from his text message. "Do you mind if I look at all of them before we commit?"

"Sure thing. Start from scratch like I did."

The female employee stepped out from behind the desk. "I wondered if you would show up again. Don't take too long, okay?"

Bob nodded. "This is Annabel. We hope to make a decision, but don't get mad at us if we happen to go home empty handed."

"I'll try. The bottom line around here is to find *good* homes for these dogs and cats. They are better off here than if they end up with owners who want them as a decoration and will not take care of them as they should."

Annabel went through the door first. Bob stepped in behind her but stayed put at the front of the room. He followed her with his eyes, watching her demeanor and body language as she began down the right aisle. A bustle of activity ensued from the pens. Dogs barked, toenails pranced on the floor, and some tails wagged.

Almost to the end, she paused before a black and white terrier mix. "You look as troubled as I feel," she said. The dog's roommate came over and the first dog jumped up and they frolicked. "At least there's a buddy with you that you can play with." She moved on to the other side.

Annabel locked eyes with a dog several kennels down before she passed the one beside her. His long, bushy tail swooshed back and forth as he stared at her. Fully alert, he drew her to him. She gave in and walked past the others.

"Oh my. You are a beauty." She tilted over to check the dog's sex. "A handsome fella." She frowned. "There's not much for you to be happy about between those four walls, yet you're smiling like I am passing you a steak. Where'd you inherit such a magnificent coat from?"

Annabel lowered her body, balancing herself on her toes. He came closer and sniffed her hand and his tail sped up. Their eyes continued to survey each other. "You're not a slobbery kisser and yet you are clearly pleased with me."

The dog sat. His tall, lanky frame had long hair and his chest was mostly white. The back of each leg was furry, enough to brush, and his colors were a remarkable mix of light reds, white, and tans. How could she turn him down and not adopt him?

She thought about Bob. She was so fixated on the dog before her, that she must take him ... even if he was not the one Bob wanted. She stood and looked in Bob's direction. He covered his face with his hand. When he took it down, he choked back emotion and nodded.

When Bob stepped over, the dog stayed in a sit, watching them intently as if not wanting to be rude and interrupt them.

"He's so polite, isn't he?" Annabel commented.

"Like The Dog Whisperer trained him himself."

"No. He has been waiting for us."

"We have the same taste in dogs."

"His name is Oliver, you know."

"It is now."

"It says here he's a retriever mix. Nine months old and neutered."

Bob nodded. "Well?"

Annabel sighed and allowed a smile.

"Is that your first smile of the day?"

She lowered her head. "Unfortunately."

"Come on." Bob opened the door to see the woman waiting expectantly. "We'll take him. The one I was looking at earlier."

"I've got the adoption papers right here," she said.

Bob and Annabel both signed and he took out the fee of fifty dollars.

"How sure are you that he's a retriever mix?" Annabel asked.

"We're guessing. What I suggest is that you send off his DNA for a breed analysis. The information is useful for training and taking care of him properly. For instance, does he like to retrieve, or swim, or herd, or be a couch potato?"

Annabel and Bob looked at each other.

"We can split his fee, his DNA analysis, and vet visit," Annabel said.

"No problem."

The three of them went into the back room and the woman opened the bars to their new dog's kennel. The woman spotted their collar and took the old one off. Annabel placed the red leather with attached bells on his neck and cinched it in place. The dog looked from one to the other and then Bob hooked him to the leash.

"Your new name is Oliver," Annabel said. "This is Bob and I am Annabel. Welcome to your new family."

"Bye, Oliver," the young lady said when they made it to the front entrance.

"Thank you for extending your day for us," Bob said.

"For this result, I'm glad I did."

"Let's see how he behaves on a leash," Bob said outside. He walked along the edge of the grass and Oliver never pulled; the new odors beneath him smelled a thousand times better than the stale concrete he was sprung from. After he lifted his leg and peed several times, Bob opened his hatchback and waved his hand. "Jump up."

Oliver jumped in and after they were underway, he stood in the very back with his front paws on the back seat and scanned the front of the car. Occasionally, he rested his head on the upholstery.

"I hope your night is uneventful with him," Annabel said.

"On the contrary. Our first night will be memorable no matter what. I assume he'll be with me since you're the one heading out at the crack of dawn."

"I'm worried sick about going back in tomorrow."

He glanced over. She twisted her hands in her lap and looked out the window like she didn't want to talk. Before leaving the less-traveled road, Oliver barked several times, perched towards the right back window. "It's just a squirrel," Annabel told him. "But at least now we know what you sound like."

By the time they arrived back at Bob's apartment, the outdoor lights had snapped on because of the fading light. He opened the back of the car. "I'd better teach him not to dart out when I put the hatchback up. For right now, I'm going to snap this leash on quickly."

Oliver didn't seem to mind and sat in agreement while Bob hooked him up and then tugged. The dog jumped down and pranced around on the pavement with exuberance.

"Come on in," Bob said when he took out his apartment keys. "And you, too, Oliver. Welcome to one of your homes." He dropped the leash and Oliver went straight in. The dog scoured the floor and Annabel filled one of the dog bowls on the counter with water and set it down. Oliver drank greedily. The two students watched as the dog examined his new surroundings. When he finished, he jumped up on Bob's couch.

"Oh, no, Oliver," Annabel said.

"No problem. Like I told you once, most of this furniture came from Craig's List. After what he's been lying on, he deserves it."

Annabel sat down next to the dog. "Wow, you have special privileges already." She nestled her hand into the fur around his neck. "I wish I could hang out with you tomorrow," she said softly. "Human beings can be the worst species in the whole world. Mostly everyone I'm working with right now is deplorable or morally corrupt."

Bob fell into an oversized leather chair and eased his legs onto the ottoman. He studied the two of them, knowing how troubled she was with the rotation. He grinned. For Oliver's first night with them, he was proving to be useful and therapeutic for Annabel. The worried expression she'd worn during their trip had faded; her eyes softened when she talked to the dog, and twice she leaned over and kissed his forehead.

"Before you go, do you want to tell us about it?" Bob asked.

She stroked her shiny hair in the front of her collarbone and considered his question. Bob waited.

"The most awful events unfolded today," she started with a choppy voice. "My attending practically kicked me off the ward, the chief resident is nothing short of malicious, and I've been accused of being the responsible party for overdosing a patient with morphine. And that's just the start of it."

"Get it all off your chest. Oliver and I can listen all night."

If Annabel needed to survive the next day on obstetrics, hanging out with Bob for too long was not a smart idea. She summarized the basics for him over the next half hour.

Bob was also tired but leaned forward in his chair several times, appalled at the details. He wished he was rotating with her at the same time. That way she would have company and he could back her up with her issues. Although, he thought, he also respected the fact that she could handle herself.

The dog's head was nestled on her lap, so she slid it off. "Oliver, I need to take off. You be a good dog for Bob."

Bob rolled the ottoman out of the way and rose from the chair. "Hold on a moment." He reached over for his iPhone. "Mind if I take a picture of you and Oliver? The first day here?"

Annabel smiled. "Sure."

He clicked, they switched positions, and Annabel took one of Oliver and Bob. Then she clicked a selfie with all three of them huddled together.

"I'm sorry you're going through this," he said. "Don't get sidetracked, however, and not study enough."

"So true. But if Dr. Harvey doesn't give me a decent clinical evaluation, I'm toast."

"Worrying won't help." He walked her to the door.

"Bye, Oliver." She inched down and patted his head.

"I'll bring him to the vet tomorrow for shots and whatever else he may need. I'll text you."

"Thanks, but don't you overdo it. We'll settle up the finances soon." She grabbed the door handle and glanced down again. "I sure hope he is indeed housebroken!"

At home, Annabel perched herself on a kitchen stool. She realized she deprived herself of dinner and opened a large yogurt. She had a strong desire to talk to her parents, but she also needed to touch base with Dustin. She checked her phone to find no messages from him.

Hey Dustin, she texted. *I think you're working a late shift, so I won't disturb you. But hello anyway!*

She took a few spoonfuls straight from the container and her phone dinged.

I'm at my desk at the moment. How was your day?

She laughed out loud. Not wanting to type out an obscenity, she decided on grawlix symbols.

*!#@%

That bad?! he responded.

Affirmative. But on the bright side, I got a dog tonight. My medical school friend, Bob, and I are going to 'share' him.

Hmm. You can tell me about that later. Solar has also learned a new trick. You won't believe it.

Seeing is believing, you know.

Then what night are you coming over? After a nice dinner out, of course.

I'll let you know. Obstetrics is crazy.

Okay, love, later...

She scrunched her eyebrows. Hmm, he never used that term before with her. She kind of liked it, she thought, as she went back to her home page. But her phone dinged again. This time from Bob.

The three pictures popped up. Her heart warmed; they were priceless, especially the last one with two smiling medical students and a goofy, grinning, happy dog between them.

CHAPTER 17

Annabel stirred a half hour earlier than normal. Most likely, she thought, because her vivid last dream was about a laboring patient wrenching in pain while health care professionals passed by her room without going in. She tossed off her covers, went to the kitchen, and selected a flavored K-cup. The Keurig machine was a new acquisition from the end of her internal medicine rotation, given to her by Bob. It made her think of him as she put on the single serving. She wondered how Bob's night was with Oliver.

She puttered, getting ready with the mug of French Vanilla in tow. After dressing a bit more stylishly for the day, including sterling silver earrings under her long hair, she called for an Uber ride and went downstairs.

For 6 a.m., it was apparent it was going to be a beautiful day as she stood on the curb. She forced herself into an optimistic mood as much as she could as a black sedan double parked and the driver rolled down his window. "Annabel?"

She threw her backpack in first and scooted in. "How are you today?" she asked.

"Not too shabby for this time of day."

"That makes two of us."

He drove off and turned his music volume up, which suited her just fine. She pressed "home" in her phone contacts. Since her father, Danny, was a neurosurgeon with a busy practice and her mother, Sara, was a teacher, the early hour was no problem at all.

"Hey, honey," Danny said. "Is everything all right?"

"I thought women have a sixth sense about things and not men."

"I've lived a hard, eventful life. I learned a thing or two along the way. Like when my kids are going through a rough time."

Annabel had to agree with him. The poor man had gone through terrible times because of a noose around his neck for years - a certain female health care worker. However, he was super smart and talented in his specialty. Always, in the back of her mind, he was her greatest inspiration.

The driver pulled onto the entrance to I-75 and the Cincinnati traffic picked up.

"You started OB/GYN," he said. "It should be too early to form a concrete opinion, but how do you like or dislike it so far?"

Annabel made sure not to speak louder than the music. "Too many things are going wrong, including patient care. Like a patient being bolused and dying due to an overdose of magnesium sulfate for preeclampsia. And then, specifically for me, being blamed for a different patient's medical narcotic error. The patient is on a ventilator overnight, Dad."

Danny was upstairs in the main kitchen where his wife and best friend/brother-in-law, Casey, sat with steaming coffee and wearing pajamas. He met their eyes. "It's Annabel," he said.

He went back to the call. "I'm sorry about this. You must straighten this situation out right away. First of all, the current opioid crises makes healthcare professionals and laypeople sensitive about the whole issue and sometimes stories get blown up out of proportion. Secondly, if a patient was harmed in any way because of the error, that misunderstood mistake could jeopardize your grade, your reputation, and be a blemish on a clinical evaluation. Go to your attending right away."

"Dad," she almost sobbed, "he's the highest-ranked person to accuse me based on what a nurse told him."

Danny shook his head at Sara and Casey. "Ask to speak to him alone. Somewhere with no distractions. Attendings are multi-tasking all the time, so that will be difficult. Try your best. You would never do something like this. Also, in general, the medical field is not without human error. We are aware of this; there are procedures in place to avoid it. Take, for instance, the sequence of 'time outs' before a surgeon actually makes an incision on a patient."

She inhaled deeply. "You're right, but somehow on this rotation, there is less respect towards students. I felt like more of a team member on other rotations and not like some side show."

"You let me know how it goes. Would you like to talk to your mother? She's here with Casey. I'm leaving for a morning surgery schedule, your mom needs to get ready for work, and Casey's paramedic shift is this afternoon. If he's even going to put in a decent day's work, that is."

"Hey," his friend yelled.

Annabel snickered, knowing the two men had a humorous running commentary on Casey's paramedic job. "Okay, Dad, thanks. Hate to dump you with the bad news. I'll tell Mom my fun news."

"Bye, honey. Your mom and I will fill each other in tonight."

Danny handed Sara the phone, rinsed his empty mug, and headed to his car.

"Annabel," Sara said, "what's going on?"

"Bob and I got a dog last night. You all are going to love him."

Sara furrowed her eyebrows.

"Put her on the speaker," Casey said.

"You're on the speaker now," Sara said. "How and why did you get a dog? How will that work out?"

"For the time being, Bob and I are separated from the same schedule. Between the two of us, we think this can work out. We picked him out from a shelter. Another dog can't replace Dakota, Mom, but I think this one may be good for me."

"All right. I'll give you and the dog and Bob my blessing. Take care of him and yourself."

"What did you name him?" Casey asked.

"After one of my former patients, whose last name was Oliver. Casey, he's the most gorgeous thing!"

"You sound happy about him. Give him a biscuit from Uncle Casey."

"Thanks."

Sara cut back in. "I haven't asked you in a while. Are you and your sister talking to each other yet?"

Annabel hated to tell her mother what she didn't want to hear. "Not yet."

"You two are wasting precious time. She's the only sister you have left."

Annabel gulped. Her oldest sister had died, ironically enough from a medical problem which theoretically should not have happened. And she and Nancy, her younger sister, had had an argument and fallout.

"Mom, I'm not the one being immature."

"Since you are older and the mature one, why don't you take the bull by the horns and call her?"

"Mom, please, I tried already. Right now, I'm dealing with more blazing fires than her."

"Okay, sweetheart."

"Bye, you two. Hope to see you soon."

"Bye yourself," Casey said.

"Love you," Sara said and hung up.

Annabel focused on the song the driver bobbed his head to. Blake Shelton crooned "I'll Name the Dogs."

Ha! she thought. She had named Oliver and hummed along just thinking about him.

The driver dropped Annabel off. She was early and hoped to bump into Stuart before he left after being on call overnight. Better than hunting for him upstairs, she could spot him anywhere. In the hospital's lobby, Stuart sipped a frothy cappuccino outside the coffee shop.

"You're studying before 7 a.m.?" She rested her backpack on the table and added, "You're amazing."

"But not as dramatic as you."

"What did you hear?"

"Probably rumors. You didn't tell some nurse to give a patient 200 mgs of morphine."

"You're correct, but convince my attending." Annabel pulled out a chair.

"I'm not assertive enough to speak up about certain issues, but if you need me to, I will."

"Thanks, Stuart. Are you faring any better than me by doing the night hours?"

"My problem is I don't like the subject matter."

"Really? I assumed most guys looked forward to it. After all, I assumed since it has to do with female genitalia and your gender gets a hard on about that, they'd mostly love it … if I may be blunt."

"Hey, all barriers about anatomy and sensitivity about discussing body parts and what they do go out the window in medical school. This is different. Seeing bulging vaginas with heads popping out and afterbirth is opposite than a turn on. And a resident told me last night what's worse is doing smelly exams in the clinic on women with discharges and foul odors from bacterial vaginosis."

"Oh, Stuart. That's more information than I need. A resident said that?"

"Yeah."

"Come to think about it, that's a different perspective I didn't think about. However, there are other areas in medicine that aren't fun either. Take being a gastroenterologist, working in a GI suite a good deal of your time, and doing colonoscopies. Or being a urologist and sticking scopes up penises, especially the ones with venereal diseases or whatever."

"See. There you go."

"In any case, we've come across some bad attitudes. Why does it seem like the residents now are moaning more than usual?"

"Maybe they wouldn't be happy no matter what they do. You know, burn out and all. Perhaps more of that is going on." He licked his lips to clear off the steamed milk foam from his cappuccino while Annabel eyed his paper cup. Maybe she would supplement her earlier Keurig with what he was drinking.

Annabel leaned forward. "I miss you, me, and Bob rotating together. There is safety in medical student numbers. Who woulda thought?!"

"Speaking of Bob ... do you know how he's doing?"

"He's following the predicted path of recovery from his tick disease. Next Monday, he goes back to internal medicine and finishes up and we embarked on getting a dog together yesterday."

"How's that going to work out for you?"

"I don't have a clue, but we're off to a decent start." They both got up and Annabel slung her backpack over her shoulder. "I have the unpleasant task upstairs of trying to talk to Dr. Harvey in private about this accusation against me. Otherwise, it will never get cleared up."

"I'm headed out. By the way, Amy Wagner's induction is going along well and Bonnie Barker slept through the night on the ventilator. The medicine service is extubating her soon."

"Thanks, Stuart. Catch you tomorrow, I hope."

Annabel skipped the added coffee indulgence and went upstairs. She dumped her bag in the lounge, threw on her white jacket, and was still early. Before Dr. Harvey made an appearance, she hustled to the ICU and witnessed a great relief. A doctor and a nurse exited Bonnie's room, where the young woman was devoid of her breathing tube.

As she walked in, Bonnie cleared her throat. Annabel remembered to scan the monitors; her patient's vital signs registered as normal as if she was walking around a shopping mall. She wondered, however, what Bonnie was told about what had happened to her and how she would react to such information. She stepped to the bedside cautiously.

"Dr. Tilson, I made it, didn't I?"

"You did. Believe me, I am as relieved as you are to find you awake and without breathing assistance from a machine."

She leaned her upper body towards Annabel and her eyes widened. "If this traumatic experience had not occurred, I would not have seen the light."

"What light?"

"Don't say anything, but Tony talked to me. I realize what a super guy he is and how much he genuinely cares about me and Samantha. But I also heard that our baby is not one-hundred-percent well."

"Yes, Sam has what's called OI."

"We must talk to the pediatrician. I bet Tony and I will become experts and do what's necessary for our child."

"What a positive attitude. Samantha is a newborn with two mature parents." Annabel thought about the answer to the next question. "How do you feel about the wrong medicine you received yesterday?"

"Like I said, I learned something. It could have been a lot worse if you hadn't come in my room to help me out."

"A school of thought says that I may have caused it."

Bonnie tilted her head and pursed her lips. "Is there any truth to that?"

"No, Bonnie. In a miniscule manner, it could be construed that I enabled the sequence of errors, but that's a stretch. If I had done anything to overtly put you here, my conscience would be killing me and I would be questioning my presence here as a medical student."

For a moment, Bonnie put her hand on Annabel's sleeve. "I believe you."

"Thank you." Annabel unwrapped her stethoscope from her neck. "Won't Tony be relieved to see you this morning?"

"He may be here any moment. Crazy Tony didn't even go home. I was told he's over in my obstetric room sleeping in the chair."

"He is dedicated."

"Like a faithful dog."

Annabel smiled. She thought of Oliver. Hopefully, he would be a dog that followed that description. "May I listen to your heart and lungs?"

"Absolutely. Do your thing."

The two women laughed and Annabel placed her stethoscope over

Bonnie's right lung and told her to take a big breath.

Annabel scrutinized Bonnie's chart and gathered every update she could. Only one more lab was pending, an arterial blood gas ordered by the internal medicine doctor after he took out her endotracheal tube. She waited on writing a progress note until after formal rounds, if that was even going to occur.

After using the staircase back to the OB/GYN floor, she stumbled on Dr. Harvey getting out of the elevator. Her heart pitter-pattered in her chest and she ramped up the nerve to ask to talk to him.

"Dr. Harvey," she said, "I am terribly uncomfortable with what transpired yesterday. May I talk to you about it further?" She grimaced with her selection of words. He could shut her down with her weak appeal.

"We covered the situation already, Annabel." He kept walking and she stayed next to him.

"Dr. Harvey, this is extremely important to me. I am a rock-solid student who deserves to be heard. If you don't mind, sir."

Roosevelt glanced back over to the lounge where no visitors were in sight. He turned on his heels and wandered over beside a potted plant. "I'm listening."

"Dr. Harvey, the morphine order did not originate with me. Clearly, the order to give it came from what was handwritten in Bonnie Barker's chart by the resident. The absolute fact is that every person who looked at the chart had difficulty with interpreting it. Melba Fox interpreted the order her own way and I had little to do with her decision. I questioned her thinking, but she did her job of dispensing medication the way she saw fit. Honestly, Dr. Harvey, if I may be so bold. I've been implicated as the fall guy."

Roosevelt listened more attentively than yesterday. The day was early and burdens had not yet sagged his shoulders or dampened down his toupee. "Hmm. I suppose medical students make good scapegoats. I remember being told to start an IV on an old man. He ended up slapping my hand. He told me he didn't want no God damn medical school student touching him. I told him that even he had learned to crawl before he walked. I was accused of being disrespectful to him." He squinted his eyes and repeated his "Hmm."

Annabel took in a long breath, hoping his comment was because she'd made the situation better and not worse.

"I worry about our patient, how she is doing this morning, and how she is going to react to all of this."

"I just rounded on her. She is off the ventilator and extubated. Her pulse oximeter registers an oxygen saturation of ninety-nine percent. Her lungs are clear, her heart a normal rhythm. Her CBC and electrolytes are normal and an ABG is pending. After discussing with her the events that happened, she is grateful that nothing worse occurred. She also knows about her baby's diagnosis from her boyfriend, and wants to focus on her family."

Dr. Harvey made no attempt to move. "What is her baby's diagnosis?"

"She has osteogenesis imperfecta. The baby is being handled with special care and attention. Dr. Thomas seems to be an expert about the genetic disease."

"The baby does have a rare problem. Did you know those babies sweat a lot?"

"I did not know that."

"Somehow that fact stuck in my mind from doctor lounge talk with pediatricians." He smiled, surprised he remembered, and added, "It appears you are multi-versed and up-to-date about your patient. And, it also sounds to me like she trusts you."

Dr. Harvey nodded not once, but twice.

"Bravo, Annabel."

CHAPTER 18

Ling Watson arrived in the lounge and scoffed at the board on the wall. Two new patients were written there, the black magic marker ink seemingly mocking her in big letters. "At least I don't need to work them up," she mumbled while she grabbed her white jacket off the coat hanger.

The ward secretary held a chart and peered into the doorway. "Good morning, Dr. Watson. Here's this patient's paper chart to refresh your memory. She was discharged a few days ago, but I'm supposed to tell you that electronic medical records has no discharge summary on her."

Ling glared at her and pulled the chart out of her hands. "The day hasn't even started."

"Make it worthwhile then," the woman said in a neutral tone.

"Smart-ass," Ling muttered. She needed to dictate the discharge dictation as soon as possible, she thought, before the records department gave her a demerit like she was in grade school.

The phone rang several times. "Where the hell is everybody?" She yanked the receiver off the wall. "OB." An ER physician advised her of an admission. "Why didn't you page me?" she asked.

"I did," the man said.

"Not that I'm aware of. I'll be there when I can." She hung up, snapped her pager off her pants, looked down, and frowned. She had not turned it on.

A nurse stepped in. "Is it okay if Dr. Fleming does an epidural in Room 4?"

"Wouldn't I shout from the rooftop or write it all over the board if I *didn't* want the patient to get one?"

The nurse didn't flinch. "Is that a yes?"

"Yes, with a capital 'Y.'"

"Moron," Ling said after the RN stepped out. She turned around and glanced at the coffee pot. Empty as a sinkhole waiting for a car. "Damn it. Must I do everything around here?" She opened the cabinet above the counter and saw a bag of house blend sitting on a plate. After wrapping her hand around it and yanking it out, she realized too late why the plate was there. The bag was already cut open and coffee grinds flew everywhere … the counter, the floor, and her blouse and white coat.

She stood staring, the expletive curled on her tongue, ready to explode out of her mouth like she'd spit out putrid milk.

Caleb walked in and approached her from behind. He spoke softly. "I brought you a present since we didn't wake up together at your or my place." He held up a Dunkin Donut bag off to her side.

She spun around. "Do I look like some obese pregnant lady who stuffs herself with donuts? Spare me the gift. Decrease my eighty-hour work week instead." Her voice rose and Caleb was taken aback.

"Unburden me of the exams," she continued with more potency, "and the research, and the presentations. Get rid of my educational debts, the medicolegal pressures, and the relentless paperwork. Blow up the ineffective electronic medical systems and make the administrative intrusions disappear!"

Annabel and Dr. Harvey walked toward the lounge. Annabel was ecstatic; she had taken her father's advice and talked to her attending right away. Now … if the dynamics with the most important person on the team had improved, she hoped she had less to worry about him writing an unflattering clinical review of her at the end of the rotation.

Caleb Gash was ahead of them, strutting along with his canvas bag with books, papers, and whatever snacks he lugged in for the day. In his left hand, he dangled a brown paper bag. Annabel and Roosevelt caught up and he turned into the lounge.

Dr. Harvey stopped at the doorway to smile at the secretary and the RN at the desk. He jolted his head, his ears questioning the loud voice he heard just inside, behind Caleb, whose back faced the door. Annabel realized her attending was listening.

After Ling finished with the part about the obese pregnant ladies eating donuts, the eighty-hour weeks, the exams, and on to blowing up medical records and making intrusions disappear, Dr. Harvey had had enough. He walked in.

"Not to mention," Dr. Harvey said, startling both Ling and Caleb, "obstetrics is a branch of medicine affected disproportionately by medical malpractice. Insurance premiums of one hundred thousand dollars a year are becoming commonplace nationally. You have that to look forward to. Bad outcomes in obstetrics can lead to multimillion-dollar awards."

Caleb stood there with a silly grin. Ling moved her head to the side at first with a questioning expression. But then she surmised that her attending really realized how crappy she had it.

"That too," Ling said.

Roosevelt stared at the coffee grinds splattered on her clothes. Annabel glanced at the spillage sprinkled all over the floor. Caleb slid the donut bag on the round table beside him.

"Dr. Watson," Roosevelt said. "I want you to do these things in order. Write up a medical error incident report on the Motrin order you wrote yesterday for Bonnie Barker. Don't write down any 'hearsay,' only the facts pertaining to your part in it. Then, straight away, go over to the OB/GYN department office. Wait for me there. It may be some time because I need to round on the patients here first. You can leave now."

Ling's mouth opened with surprise. Why was he instructing her to leave the ward when there were patients to take care of? Plus, she wanted to make her coffee and then clean up the mess. She hesitated, but Dr. Harvey held his ground. She had a bad feeling about this.

She stepped past them and found the courage to walk out to the desk. She asked the secretary for the necessary papers to fill out her report.

Roosevelt proceeded to address Caleb and Annabel. "You two meet me upstairs in the ICU. Based on Dr. Tilson's progress report on Ms. Barker this morning, I believe we can transfer her back down here. We'll start there. I won't be far behind you." He grinned, glanced at the brown bag, and back at Caleb. "Mind if I help myself to that donut?"

Caleb shook his head. Annabel nodded to the door and they both left, closing the door behind them. Roosevelt opened the bag and pulled out a blueberry donut. "My favorite flavor." He placed it on a napkin, called the department's main office, and asked for the chairman.

Roosevelt cleared his throat as Dr. Roger Winstead picked up the phone. "Roger," Dr. Harvey said, "it's Roosevelt. We have a situation with resident Ling Watson. We *must* pull her from her clinical duties and seek out immediate help for what appears to be physician burnout."

"Although I trust your judgment, let's sit down about this," came the response.

"Exactly. I've sent her over. It'll take me a few hours here to fill in.

Any way we can jockey around schedules for an upper level resident to fill in?"

"I absolutely don't think that's possible."

Roosevelt knew what he had gotten himself into. This was the rare circumstance where an attending must sacrifice outside duties to be fully available for the university teaching team. Work like a resident. His other partners in his private office would need to step up and split up his private patients.

Dr. Harvey grimaced. "Holler if that situation changes."

"You'll be the first to know. I'll see you when you get here. Don't worry about Dr. Watson. She can crack open a novel to read while waiting. I bet she hasn't done that in a long time."

Dr. Winstead hung up. He huffed out a big breath. He needed to follow the recommended department protocol to deal with her. However, it always killed him that not too long ago, residents and students got through their training years with longer work hours and stress than the current trainees ... who moaned about and broke down about everything. He understood both sides of the spectrum, but he felt like an army sergeant witnessing his men wanting clean sheets and pillows while taking cover in a bunker.

Roosevelt stayed put and enjoyed every morsel of the blueberry donut. Since he'd be working like a resident today and in the near future, he might as well eat like one too.

Annabel and Caleb waited in the ICU for Dr. Harvey.

"I'm way too worried about Ling," Caleb said. He sat on the edge of the counter while Annabel pulled up Bonnie Barker's ABG result on the computer.

"I'm more worried about what's going to happen to us. It's about time we started functioning like a real rotation. I'm not here to stick my head in an obstetric textbook. I'm here to learn from patients and upper level doctors." She jotted down Bonnie's arterial blood gases on her index card, but Caleb wasn't listening. "Are you worried about your relationship with Ling?"

Caleb sighed. "I can't figure her out these days. She sure was nasty to me this morning. Recently, I thought about throwing in the towel. This morning may have been the last straw."

"Relationships are complex. You'll know when to end it, and I agree. From what I've seen and heard, there is often some event that breaks the camel's back and one party throws in the towel. You must do what you have to do. Was it serious between the two of you?"

Caleb slid a little closer. He considered the question before answering. "No. Not serious. 'Light' would be more like it. And I think it started because I was kind of struck by her status as a chief resident."

"Oh my God, that sounds familiar. I was crazy, insanely hooked on my chief resident in surgery."

"Really?"

"Yeah, but don't repeat what I said. However, not only was I infatuated by his chief-residentness, but he was my type. Handsome, smart, slim athletic build, charismatic, a damn talented surgeon and teacher, and the list goes on. To my heart's delight, after some time, he asked me out, but the dates were a set of misfortunes."

"Wow." Caleb laughed. "Chief-resident-ness?"

"Yeah. I just made that up."

"I like that, but sorry, the dates didn't work out. At least you had a resolution to your crush on him. But, hey, where is our attending?"

"You shouldn't have left him the donut!"

"Actually, I should have bought more."

"Speak of the devil," Annabel said as the doors snapped open. Dr. Harvey walked slowly towards them, too busy tucking in his shirt, and stopped across from them at the desk.

"Ms. Barker's ABG is back," Annabel mentioned. She rattled of the numbers: the arterial blood pH, oxygen saturation, and partial pressure of carbon dioxide.

"Perfect, and you gave me a thorough update of her before. Hand me her chart."

Annabel gave it to him and he went through it standing up. She was impressed; he took his time and was not distracted by nurses, the sound of monitors, or X-ray equipment rolling past him. He finally grasped it in his hand. "Let's go in."

Bonnie was bolt upright in her bed, a tray table and a breakfast tray in front of her. She decided not to put a spoon of oatmeal into her mouth as they sidled up to her bedside.

Bonnie shrugged her shoulders. "I was hungry. My nurse called the kitchen for an early breakfast."

"Perfect," Dr. Harvey said. "If anyone deserves extra attention, it's you. We are so sorry about the last twenty-four hours. Everything is being done so what happened to you never happens again." With a slight tilt of his head, his eyes reassured her.

"All your labs and vital signs look real good. Having a postpartum hemorrhage and then a setback with a pain medication was no fun, I'm sure. I'm going to transfer you back to your obstetric room and we'll shoot for tomorrow as far as discharging you. That will also give you more time with your baby in the hospital and a chance for Dr. Thomas to answer any more questions you may have. How does that sound?"

"Maybe Samantha can go home with me."

"Maybe so. Dr. Thomas must make that decision. Do you mind if I listen to your heart and lungs?"

"Dr. Tilson did that already, but help yourself."

Roosevelt finished and Bonnie went back to eyeing her oatmeal.

"We'll see you later on our ward," he said. The three of them marched out and Dr. Harvey wrote for and informed the staff of her transfer. "After she eats that porridge she's delighted with," he added.

Roosevelt left with Caleb and Annabel on either side of him.

"Amazing," Annabel said, "that she's taking her situation so well."

"You and I both gained her trust and we are sincere about her and her baby. She's no dummy and she picked up on that. I will add her and her baby to my prayers as well."

Annabel was surprised about his "prayer" remark. But there was no rule against that, she thought. On the contrary, some people were afraid to mention prayer or their religious affiliation whereas others seemed entitled to do so.

"By the way," Roosevelt said, "the RNs involved with giving Mary Chandler an overdose of magnesium sulfate as well as Melba Fox who made the morphine mistake were both put on leave by the Head of Nursing. And, as you both may have surmised, Ling Watson is going to be placed in a time-out as well. You need only deal with me for the time being."

Annabel and Caleb managed to lock eyes past Dr. Harvey. Annabel's lips curled in a slight smile. Their own private attending just for the two of them, she thought. She put vigor in her step as they approached the elevators. She held open the staircase door instead of letting the men push the elevator button.

The three of them were a single file of white coats from one side of the corridor to the other as they strutted down the obstetric wing. "I nabbed you two from the lounge before. Did either of you have a chance to pop in on our patient from late yesterday, Mrs. Wagner, scheduled for an induction?"

"Not me," Annabel said.

"Nor me," Caleb said.

"Then what are we waiting for? Let's check up on her TOLAC!" He looked straight at Annabel.

"Trial of labor after C section," she said.

"Did one of your residents check if that was a feasible plan?"

Annabel thought fast. "I believe so ... with an ultrasound. Which helped to determine if the previous scar and lower uterine segment seemed adequate enough to support labor."

Roosevelt popped his index finger in front and wiggled it affirmatively.

They made a right turn at Amy's doorway and Annabel led the way inside.

CHAPTER 19

Amy Wagner forced a smile when the three doctors walked in. Her husband, Harry, sat on the bed with one leg dangling to the floor and one bent on her sheet.

Dr. Harvey introduced himself as the attending doctor. "How's Mom and Dad doing this morning? Making progress?"

Amy nodded. "I'm in labor because that oxytocin you gave me is working like rocket fuel."

Roosevelt scanned the monitor. "Your baby's heart rate looks good."

"Baby Bobby is going to be a skier like his mom," Harry said, "so his heart better be healthy."

Amy grabbed the bedsheet in her hand and squeezed while a tinge of pain passed over her lower abdomen. Her husband wrapped his hand on her forearm and then let go.

Roosevelt let the contraction pass. "Do you mind if I examine you while my team is here?"

"Most certainly, I don't mind."

"Even though we teach here, I still like to ask. Occasionally, there is a patient very sensitive to groups and, unless it's an emergency, we can render a bit more privacy."

Caleb closed the door and Dr. Harvey pulled on gloves. Amy scooted further down on the bed and spread her legs. Roosevelt quietly examined her and rolled back on his stool. She resumed a more comfortable position and Harry helped cover her up.

The attending snapped off his gloves. "Do you mind if I talk shop to the resident and student?" His tone was soft and reassuring. "Otherwise, I can do it outside."

Amy and Harry glanced at each other. "Please, I'd love to listen in," she said.

"Then you're included." Roosevelt took a spot facing them all. "Generally, if the cervix is dilated beyond two to three centimeters, the patient has a favorable cervix. Mrs. Wagner is at or passing six centimeters. Dr. Tilson, that means she is making continued progress and has reached the active phase. What labor parameter is next?"

"Second stage of labor?"

"Precisely. Explain, please."

"Second stage is the complete dilation of the cervix to expulsion of the infant."

"And normally, in a multiparous woman, how long should that take?"

"I don't know."

"Caleb, tell Annabel."

"Up to two hours; an hour longer if an epidural is in place."

Roosevelt scanned all their faces.

Harry touched his wife. "Maybe our baby will be here by lunchtime."

Dr. Harvey laughed. "That may be cutting it a bit close. Hopefully, by dinner time, baby Wagner will be suckling at Mom's breasts and you two will be blowing out his first-day candles."

Roosevelt herded Annabel and Caleb out, leaving wide smiles on the faces of Amy and Harry. In the hallway, he closed their door again.

"So," Roosevelt said, "I want to start with some basics for Annabel about the pelvic exam. The formal teaching of the exam in medical school is fraught with anxiety, especially for the guys. Students are always taught to consider the concerns and fears of the patients, yet I also think about the concerns and fears of the student. Yes, the student!

"The exam of the patient in labor is always a bit easier on both parties because both sets of people know that the woman is going to deliver and all focus is on that part of her body. However, during other physical exams, there is a huge interaction going on between the two individual human beings, each one bringing his or her own knowledge, beliefs, status, attitudes, and experience to the process. The interaction needs to be mastered by the clinician to make the patient relax and feel comfortable and they themselves must do the same. There is a layer of complexity to the clinician's examination of genitalia and breasts."

A visitor passed by and Roosevelt quieted.

"Anyway, just know that an obstetric exam and a gynecologic exam is a rare breed. When you perform one, it is an art. At no other time is a woman's body touched by a stranger or a semi-stranger in that manner. Try to master it with sensitivity for the patients and also be cognizant of your own feelings. Your attitude may also give you clues as to whether the field is something you'd be interested in as a specialty. I also recommend any of the books that address the feelings students may encounter while examining a patient."

A nurse stopped, waiting to interrupt. Roosevelt seemed to read her mind. "I just examined her. Active phase. Oxytocin working like a charm."

"Thank you, Dr. Harvey," she said. "By the way, there is an admission in the ER. Dr. Watson was informed, but no one went to see her yet."

"I am going to break away," Roosevelt said. "Caleb, you go see the patient with Annabel. I am a beep, a phone call, or a text away. I'll be back after going over to the chairman's office."

With his usual tranquil manner and confidence, police officer Dustin Lowe entered his favorite diner. He walked in solo, but was meeting another officer he worked most closely with. It was late morning and the place bustled with patrons.

Dustin grinned at Sean as he walked to where he was sitting at a window booth. The older officer had twenty more years on the job than him and as Dustin slid into the booth, he recognized that more space was allotted to Sean's side. His paunch needed the room.

"You order yet?" Dustin asked.

Sean nursed a cup of coffee. "No sense in waiting. I take longer than you."

A familiar waitress came over. "What'll ya have, Dustin?"

He scanned other tables. It was fifty-fifty. Half the plates were piled with remnants of waffles, eggs, hash browns, and sausage, and the other half were in front of the afternoon eaters, with cheeseburgers and French fries.

"Do you all ever serve anything that is green?"

"I can put food coloring in a glass of milk for ya."

"I'm yanking your chain, but that was very funny."

"Yeah, you must like it here. You bring that girl of yours in here once in a while."

"Annabel. Annabel Tilson. I think of her when I come in during work. I also think of my former partner."

"When are you bringing her back in here? You must be taking her out more to fancy restaurants."

"Sometimes. I see her less than I'd like. Her being in medical school and all."

"Okay, since she's not here, order what you want and not what she'll tell you to eat because she's concerned about your health."

"What a fine idea. How about a couple of eggs over easy, bacon, and toast? Don't forget the coffee."

"You got it." Like a salute, she tapped her pink diner cap.

"So what's the update on her and you?" Sean asked.

Dustin rubbed his chin. He could hear the staff washing dishes. Off to his right, the parking lot was like a pit stop off an interstate. Cars pulling in and out and doors opening and closing. He looked back at Sean.

"Sometimes I don't know whether to be ecstatic or cautious. She's getting under my skin."

"Then what are you cautious about?"

"Her past dating history was a bit indiscriminate. I believe she's over that. So more than that, I'm afraid our relationship is too good to be true, and the more I see her, the more I like her. She's barging in on my thoughts all the time. I guess I'm guarded because I don't know if she feels the same way; I don't want to press the relationship to another level if she's not up to it."

The waitress passed and set down Dustin's steaming black coffee and Sean's order.

"What does an old married guy think about that?" Dustin continued.

"Love is a flower. You have to let it grow."

"Love? I didn't say I was in love with her."

"Perhaps you're not, but from where I'm sitting, you seem pretty close to it."

Dustin's heart thumped. He stared out the window. A lanky older teen with straight, combed-back blonde hair got out of a sedan. He yanked the hoody of his jacket up on his head.

"Women," Dustin said. "How do you find out what they really think about you?"

Sean laughed out loud. "I asked the love of my life to marry me. She said yes, so that's how I found out." He chuckled again and reached for the salt and pepper.

"You have to be kidding."

"Nope. In your case, you better not try it. She might say no and you would not be pleasant to work with after that."

"You're preposterous. I've known her a little less than a year and we've only been dating a couple of months."

"What difference does that make?"

Dustin shook his head. "That potbelly of yours has gone to your head."

The waitress set down Dustin's food, topped off Sean's coffee, and left. He watched the old kid with the hoodie walk behind a woman coming towards the diner, his right hand jammed into his pocket. The guy looked both ways as if monitoring for traffic crossing an intersection.

Dustin twitched his mouth. In general, it was not cool enough outside for a man that age to really need a thick fleece hoodie, but a bit more suspicious to use it to cover his head while entering a public building.

The front door of the diner opened as Dustin swiveled in the booth to look towards the door. The young man shoved the woman aside and yanked a gun out of his jacket pocket. Without flinching, he aimed the weapon to the side of the cash register and pulled the trigger.

The man at the register grabbed his left bicep in pain as the young man aimed instead at the manager off to his side.

Dustin slid out and stood. The manager was about to be shot, so his hand gripped his firearm and, with no hesitation, he fired.

Dustin's bullet made contact with the young man before he pulled the trigger again. With a fast rush, Dustin tackled him to the floor and then pinned him down. Sean followed and attached handcuffs to the assailant.

After flipping him over, the man winced with pain. Sean called EMS and two ambulances arrived. Dustin stood watch while the paramedics secured the cash register employee on one stretcher and the assailant on another.

"Officer," the employee said to Dustin, "EMS says I'm going to live. Thanks to you."

The paramedic nodded his head. "A bullet to the biceps. After the docs fix that up, you'll be fine ... except they'll be restricting your gym workout to less than a hundred-pound weights for a while."

Two professionals picked up the stretcher and loaded him in the back of the vehicle.

The man, now without his hoodie and gun, was spread on another stretcher where a paramedic held pressure on his bleeding. His partner started an IV and they slipped him into the second ambulance.

"I can't thank you both enough," the manager said when Dustin walked back inside. "I remember that guy. He worked here months ago. Not only did he skim money out of the cash register, he was late for work half the time and would disappear out back to smoke. I fired him as nicely as I could, but I was uneasy about him. I guess my instincts were correct."

"Appears so. Another patrol car will be here soon, since Sean could use some help. I'm leaving to follow the ambulance."

"Again, thanks. Paramedics would be taking me and a lot more customers with them if you two hadn't been here."

A group of customers nodded and added their thanks.

Dustin left his partner and followed the medical sirens in his own vehicle. The diner, he thought, was a stomping ground for him and Annabel on occasion. The two of them could have been sitting there when he was off from work … the two of them instead of him and his partner. He may not have been carrying his weapon off duty. He shuddered. It was one thing if he were to get hurt, but he wouldn't be able to bear it if she was injured.

Life was too short, he thought. Things can happen in a second. How could he, or anyone, count on their future? He thought about Annabel; her warm smile, earnest yet fun personality, and her tall, slender build. Her eyes, he thought, depending on the light, appeared blue or brown, and her long hair was like a model's curls pampered by a beautician's magic. Yet Annabel's was as natural as sunshine. Plus, he never before dated someone as smart as her.

Dustin wondered about the man in the ambulance ahead of him lying flat and receiving medical care. Being fired was his own fault and revenge had been his sad response. More importantly, he turned back to thinking about his current relationship.

Annabel was special and his mischievous partner had actually mentioned the "M" word. That was a new idea he had not considered. With such uncertainty in the world these days, like what had just happened, maybe he should kick the idea around in his mind. Sean's idea was refreshing. Or considering a pun on words, his "proposal" was interesting!

Roosevelt tried to hurry to the chairman's office, but he wasn't getting any younger. After crossing into his fifties, his right knee bothered him. It felt like there were opposing forces at work around his knee cap pulling in opposite directions. Retiring early in his fifties, or having an early knee replacement was not on his agenda, so he listened to his knee each day and walked an appropriate pace to not aggravate it. He grimaced when he realized the foolish thing he had done before leaving the house ... he had neglected to take the single over-the-counter NSAID he took each morning.

He opened the OB/GYN department door and greeted the secretary. "Is Dr. Watson here yet?"

"She is. Would you like me to get her?"

"No, not yet. Dr. Winstead and I are going to talk first."

"He has visitors. He said for you to go in when you arrive."

Roosevelt absent-mindedly began tidying his shirt into his trousers. "Who's with him?"

She glanced at the note in front of her. "A Kathleen and Mike Chandler."

Dr. Harvey sighed. He had spent quite a bit of time with them already, as had the medical examiner. Maybe they were still looking for closure, although he doubted that would come any time soon. He couldn't imagine how anyone would move forward after the death of their only daughter and unborn grandchild, especially under the circumstances that took their lives. He patted his toupee and knocked on the chairman's door. Dr. Winstead was not behind his desk, but was across from the couple on the couch. The three of them made a small attempt to rise, but Dr. Harvey motioned for them to stay put. "May I?" he asked, pointing to the nearest leather chair.

Roger nodded and wore a serious expression. Kathleen wore a black skirt and crossed her legs and her husband finally looked like he'd gotten rest since yesterday.

Dr. Winstead leaned forward, appealing to both of them. "Would you mind if I encapsulate to Dr. Harvey what we talked about?"

"No." Kathleen sighed.

"The Chandlers have hired attorneys from a well-known law firm which specializes in medical cases. They are preparing a lawsuit against the hospital that will claim negligence for the deadly medical mistake responsible for their daughter's death. Against the wishes of their attorney, they are not going to name the OB/GYN doctors involved or our department."

Kathleen rubbed her dry eyes. "We read everything we could get our hands on in such a short time. Even the medical consultant for the law firm said that magnesium sulfate was the correct treatment for Mary's preeclampsia and in the correct dosage as you all ordered."

"In other words," Mike said, "we are not people who want to milk this occurrence and try to profit from it. We are just and fair people. The doctors in this case were doing every single thing to help our daughter. And, actually, we have no beef against nursing staffs, but an overt error was made." He tried, but failed to contain the spark of anger rising in his voice. "We would go after you too, if one of the doctors had written for phenobarbital or whatever it's called instead of magnesium sulfate."

"We understand," Roosevelt said, his concern for them genuine.

"Also," Dr. Winstead said, "Mary is being cremated this afternoon. There is a service at the funeral home tomorrow morning. I would love for one of the team members to attend. I know you can't, because your presence on the ward is now imperative. Mr. and Mrs. Chandler also understand that I have duties here tomorrow that I cannot leave."

"We will be represented," Dr. Harvey said, "I guarantee it. And for those of us who can't make it, our hearts and souls will not forget your daughter and what happened."

Dr. Winstead stood and shook Mike's hand. Dr. Harvey did likewise at the door.

"There's one more person I would sue if I could," Mike added. "The father of the baby. Our daughter clammed shut to tell us who it was and she didn't seem to care. But all along, I had a sneaky suspicion about the circumstances which led her to be pregnant in the first place." He fought back a tear. "And now, like my wife so flatly stated, she's downright dead."

CHAPTER 20

"My heart bleeds for that couple," Dr. Harvey said when the Chandlers left the chairman's office.

"Who do you have in mind to represent the department at their daughter's service tomorrow?" Dr. Winstead asked.

"Annabel Tilson. I need Caleb to help me with patient care. Plus, Mary Chandler was one of Annabel's first patients who she spent time with. There is also another problem. Ling Watson is scheduled to present grand rounds next week, but we're taking her out of the picture until she is straightened out to assume patient care again."

"Ask Caleb to do it."

"Then I'd be lumping him with way too much responsibility. I want him focused only on patient care. Patients and the department cannot afford another crisis." He frowned. "What if we asked the medical student? She would undertake the ultimate early experience at speaking before her colleagues and medical staff as well as what it takes to prepare something like this. I would be careful to cut her slack on the wards and also make sure she is getting enough study time."

"Talk to her about it. I'll approve it only if she agrees and if the responsibility doesn't totally rattle her composure. If she commits, please help her out if you can."

"I'll be sure to give her guidance."

"Let's talk to Ling Watson. She's not going to take this well and I hope she's not in denial about her behavior." He pressed the intercom and asked the secretary to send in their chief resident.

When Ling entered, she flicked back her ponytail and squared her shoulders.

"Have a seat," Dr. Winstead said, pointing to the chair across from his desk. "I think you know why Dr. Harvey took you off the ward this morning."

"I'm simply overtired and having a bad day," she stated, gripping the armrest. "Sometimes my best work comes when I'm a bit drained. The cases energize me. But not today."

"Dr. Watson, fatigue is not a badge of honor. It's a sign of danger. Do you really want Dr. Harvey to reiterate all the reasons why you should be taken out of your residency for, hopefully, only a short time?"

Ling held her breath. Damn it, she thought. She couldn't think straight; couldn't make up her mind to hear him out or not. It might be too painful to listen to him echo what she couldn't admit to herself.

"I didn't think so," he said. "Fortunately, an excellent chairman of Psychiatry is employed at the University. She runs a program for the health and well-being of medical staff and they address these very issues of what you're going through. You possess all the signs and symptoms of physician burnout."

The two attendings were in this together, she thought. She stood on trial and didn't stand a chance of changing their mind.

"That was easy," Caleb said in the ER. "An antibiotic for a urinary tract infection, and the pregnant lady we just saw can be sent home. She was a smart one to come in with the initial symptoms of burning and frequency instead of letting the infection fester unchecked."

"However, couldn't she have scheduled an appointment at the clinic?" Annabel asked.

"True. Trips to emergency rooms are becoming more commonplace for problems which can easily be taken care of in a doctor's office or clinic." He put the patient's chart in the rack. "And everyone wonders why the cost of healthcare keeps going up. That's a small additional reason.

"Come on; let's get a cup of coffee out in the lobby on our way upstairs."

The barista noticed Annabel coming across the lobby. "What'll it be?" she asked. "Cappuccino, an Americano, chocolate-covered blueberries, or espresso beans covered in chocolate?"

"Sounds like you earned a history here," Caleb said.

Annabel laughed. "Guilty as charged. I'll take a French vanilla cappuccino and grab a box of blueberries."

"I'll take an unflavored milk coffee," Caleb said. "A latte for short."

The barista whipped up their drinks. "One vanilla cap and one regular latte," she said and rang up their items.

"I can't wait to see Amy Wagner's third stage of labor," Annabel said as they left. "You better not let me miss it. I have yet to see a 'from beginning to end' normal delivery."

"But here's the thing. You never know what's going to happen. It's a crapshoot. The more I do OB, the more grateful I am that I'm a guy."

Upstairs, Dr. Gash steered them into the lounge to finish their hot beverages. They both studied the wall board from the table as Dr. Harvey walked in. He closed the door behind him, looked at them, and raised his eyebrows.

"Honestly, Dr. Harvey, we just walked in," Caleb said with a guilty expression on his face. "The ER patient was not an admission, just an early UTI."

"In that case, you should have bought one for me." He nodded at their paper cups.

Annabel and Caleb glanced at each other with a grin.

"I have two things to talk to Dr. Tilson about, but you stay too, Dr. Gash." He dragged out a chair. "Annabel, would you mind attending the gathering at the funeral home tomorrow morning for Mary Chandler? It would be respectful and a kind-hearted gesture if someone from our medical team attended. This is not under your job description, so feel free to say no. You would not need to show up here tomorrow morning. We'd expect you around noon."

Annabel didn't give it a second thought. "I'd be honored."

"I'll let the chairman know and his secretary can text you the location." He put both elbows on the table and rubbed his hands together. "I have another request, which is more complicated. How would you like to become a very rare student? Would you be willing to present grand rounds next week? We'll discuss the topics, we'll give you lots of slack with your other work, and I will give you guidance. We'll make sure you are still allotted study time."

The request came as a shock. She couldn't fathom standing up to lecture those with more experience than her. Which was practically everyone who would be in the lecture hall. However, she trusted Dr. Harvey. He would not throw her to the wolves; she was sure of it. But why was he asking *her*? Then she realized the department had taken Dr. Watson out of the picture and they were in a pinch for a speaker. They were willing to try her out and give her the opportunity. She gulped.

"I want to say yes, Dr. Harvey, but using me may be a mistake. I can't pull off personally and professionally what someone with more experience can."

"I have faith in you."

Annabel glanced at Caleb. He seemed as surprised as she was and kept quiet.

"Okay, Dr. Harvey. Please don't be disappointed in me, however."

"That's the least of my worries."

Annabel finished her drink, savoring every last bit of foam at the bottom of the cup. Roosevelt and Caleb had gone off for patient care and left her with a list of scut work to do. She went to the computer in the corner of the room, hunted down lab values on laboring patients, and wrote them on her index cards. She checked the board again, where a nurse had updated Amy Wagner's labor progress. Her husband and nurse were rallying her along. She was bravely or stupidly going "natural" and refusing any type of anesthesia. Annabel couldn't decide which behavior was more accurate ... brave or stupid.

Her phone dinged and she pulled it from her pocket.

Oliver had no accidents overnight, Bob wrote. *He is housetrained like a Westminster ribbon winner! You going to pop by tonight?*

She was glad for the timing of the text, since she had a few minutes.

They don't give ribbons out to those dogs just because they don't pee in the house! I would love to come over. but I'd better study. The attending also gave me a 'project.' I'll explain later. She hit the arrow to send and then had an idea and began writing again. *He gave me tomorrow morning off – to attend a patient's funeral home function. Why don't you come if you're up to it? Oliver too. (He can stay in the car and I can see him!)*

Would that be appropriate for me to be there? he wrote back.

Department wants representation. Another student would be wonderful.

Sure. I'll plan on it.

However, how are you feeling?

Amazingly enough, I slept ten hours. Repeat ... Ten hours. With a dog at the bottom of my bed ... a first. It was scrumptious.

Annabel laughed out loud. *You're crazy. And you're spoiling him already.*

So what's your point?

She tried to hold back from laughing again and smiled. *All right, then, see you both tomorrow. I'll give you the details later.*

Bob texted her a "thumbs up" emoji. She pocketed her phone as Emmett tilted his head around the door.

"Come on in," she said. "How are you today?"

Emmett opened his mouth wide with a smile, displaying a chipped tooth she had not seen before. "Better than I deserve. I notice Dr. Harvey is here today more than usual and Dr. Watson isn't."

"How perceptive of you, Emmett. Appears to be the way they want it for a while."

"I figured. That will make your rotation easier."

"Like I said," she whispered, "that's perceptive of you."

"Nicer for me too. The twelve-hour days I pull are long. They will be more tolerable if the personalities around here are more balanced."

"I agree."

"Dr. Gash said you're welcome to come into Mrs. Wagner's room any time. She's getting closer to pushing that baby out."

"I can't wait." She moved away from the computer. "Thanks, Emmett."

"If I can help you with anything, you just let me know." The man pointed at her for emphasis, his arm flashing his muscles like logs and the pigmented figures on his skin.

She walked beside him down to Amy's room. "Don't faint in there," he said with a wink when she turned in to observe her first full delivery.

Amy Wagner breathed deeply and rhythmically between a contraction and glanced over at Annabel and managed to chuckle. "I should start charging an admission fee."

"Especially for medical students," Annabel replied. "We're as useless as an un-baited fishing hook."

Caleb sat on the stool at the bottom of the bed and Dr. Harvey stood off to the side. The nurse was ready to help in any way possible. The fetal heart rate monitor raced along with its tracing. Harry, for the moment, stared with a mixture of fright and amazement at the action going on between her legs.

"More," Amy said, looking to her husband. He snapped out of his trance and popped open a tiny plastic container of Vaseline. He dabbed a bit on his index finger and applied it to Amy's lips.

"My lips and *me* are so dry," she said. "I could drink a pond."

Harry put the petroleum jelly on the nightstand and sat back down on his own stool. "Come on, hon, concentrate. You can do this."

"Easy for you to say." The next contraction clamped down and waves of movement rippled across her abdomen. Amy leaned forward and grimaced with all her might. The baby's head bulged, pushing against her vagina like it was desperate to get out.

Harry's face went a shade whiter. "Are you still sure you don't want any anesthesia?"

Her pain eased. "Too late for that!" she exclaimed. "You're the one who could use some. What I need is to get baby Bobby out of me and food and water into me. Damn! I haven't had anything to eat in a gazillion hours!"

Annabel glanced at the nurse. They both tried to suppress a smile.

The next wave of pain started. "A Big Mac and French fries," she blurted out, and then concentrated on her breathing. Now she absolutely didn't care what was going on down there and who was doing what. Certainly, all modesty and attempts at dignity were thrown out the window.

Dr. Harvey stepped right behind Caleb, who was gowned, gloved, and masked. "You're almost there," Dr. Gash said to Amy as the infant's head protruded.

A tray table with the needed medical supplies were next to Caleb. His attending gestured toward the episiotomy scissors.

"No anus is tearing under my watch," Dr. Harvey said.

Annabel at least understood what he was talking about, but had to laugh at his remark. At least when things were going as they should, she thought, there was room for humor in the delivery room.

Caleb picked up the blunt-tipped episiotomy scissors. He used them to make an incision to the perineum to widen the vaginal canal for delivery. By cutting the muscle between the vagina and rectum, he would prevent the vagina from tearing.

Amy concentrated deeper than before. She pushed with all her might.

The bottom of her was on fire. What felt like a basketball popped out as everyone in the room saw a giant head pop out. But her temporary relief was fleeting as the second round of pain finished her off. The baby's shoulders followed.

Under the mask, Caleb was as proud as the father. He didn't mind that he held a slimy newborn with a big cone head. Everything had gone well, and when that happened, it was the best thing about OB.

Wearing a huge smile, Amy grasped her husband's hand to the side. She lost track of time as the doctors continued with their afterbirth chores. But after all the "awwws" about baby Bobby, Caleb picked up suture material and began sewing her vagina back up.

"I never realized how much easier a C-section is," Amy lamented. She winced with pain.

"Now Susan and your dog Blue will have Bobby to play with," Annabel said, trying to distract her. "My friend and I bit the bullet and adopted the dog we were thinking about."

Amy nodded and managed to smile. "What did you name him and is he adapting to his new situation?"

"We named him Oliver. He has two new homes and he'll have so much love in his life, he's going to blossom like a rose."

With excellent Apgar scores, newborn baby Bobby was taken over to the nursery. Caleb wrote the notes that were needed in Amy's chart and the electronic medical record, and then Roosevelt congregated his resident and student in the hallway.

"Nice job," Dr. Harvey said. "And we can pat ourselves on the back. With Mrs. Wagner's help and cooperation, we pulled off a successful TOLAC."

Dr. Harvey looked at his wristwatch. "The hours are flying by. What do we need to put next on the top of our list?" He pushed his coat to the side, shoved his shirt in, and looked at Annabel. Caleb was still wearing a silly grin from his flawless delivery.

"I have all the pending labwork on patients," Annabel said. "Nothing was abnormal. May I suggest we visit Bonnie Barker and discharge her if nothing has changed after her transfer?"

"Excellent idea."

They headed towards Bonnie Barker's old room before her ICU experience. If Annabel was any judge of character, she could swear Dr. Harvey was enjoying himself a lot more than usual ... maybe with the sense of vigor like the old days when he was a resident.

CHAPTER 21

Bonnie Barker, nestled deep into the chair, held Sam with a baby blanket wrapped around her. After allowing her to nurse to her heart's content, she lowered the baby to her lap and adjusted her top. Tony enjoyed watching them and was ready to help her out in any way he could. Bonnie glanced at him.

"It's your turn," Bonnie said. "Would you like to hold Samantha?"

"More than anything." He crouched over and tenderly picked up his infant. He rocked the baby in his arms while Bonnie grinned.

"You're amazing," Tony said.

"She is, isn't she?"

Tony shot Bonnie a glance. "Sam is amazing, but I was talking about you."

"Oh. So are you."

He disregarded her remark. "I don't know any medical stuff, or the junk that goes on in hospitals, but seems to me you have had a horrid time of it since you got here and you're brushing it off with a smile."

"What else am I supposed to do? Cry? Look at the result. I'm okay and, despite Samantha having this fragile bone problem, she's going to be okay too. She has two parents who are going to see to it."

Tony half-closed his eyes and his lips trembled. That may be the case, he thought, but they'd be better off married. He sighed and continued to sway the bundle in his arms.

Bonnie scooted forward and turned to the side, facing him fully. "Did you really mean it when you alluded to us getting married in the past?"

"I did. I still think it would be best for us all, but I'm not going to belabor the point; otherwise, I would never find out if you really cared about me if I pressure you into it."

"Tony, I'm sorry. The best guy in the world has been right in front of me and I was too stupid to see it. In and out of my narcotic slump, all I did was think about you. All I did was want to reach out and tell you that I love you. Does the offer still stand? For us to tie the knot?"

He stared at her, a warm feeling growing in his heart.

"For us to get married," Bonnie added. She thought she was clear, but he sat there with his lips clamped like an oyster.

"Hallelujah! There is a God. Absolutely. I love you too." He held Samantha with his right arm, rose from the bed, and put his hand behind Bonnie's shoulder. They kissed and he crouched down next to the chair. They both peered down at their baby, Samantha's eyes glued on Tony.

"Maybe her bones will be sturdy enough," Bonnie said, "and you can teach her how to play soccer."

With the obstetric medical team down to three, they slipped into Bonnie Barker's room. Maintaining his balance on his sneakers, Tony was hunched down next to Bonnie's arm chair with Samantha in his arms. Annabel's heart warmed at the sight. They were wrapped up in their own world and didn't notice the team's entrance until they were practically on top of them.

Dr. Harvey cleared his throat and Bonnie looked over. "I made it back to where I started," she said, "thanks to all of you, and Dr. Watson."

Annabel didn't mention that she would not have gone to the ICU in the first place if Dr. Watson had practiced careful penmanship. She was only in training, but it amazed her the things that patients did not know ... like what went on behind the scenes.

"And we have an announcement to make." The sparkle in Bonnie's eyes became brighter. "Tony and I are getting married."

"Congratulations," Dr. Harvey said.

"When's the big day?" Caleb asked.

Bonnie and Tony shrugged. "We haven't gotten that far yet," Tony said.

"Hopefully, as soon as possible," Bonnie said.

"This is terrific news," Annabel said. "Congratulations."

Dr. Harvey scanned Bonnie's bedside chart, which had a new set of vital signs. "How are you feeling?"

"I'll live, despite a little sore throat and being tired."

"You had a breathing tube in your windpipe, so that is understandable. Your irritated throat will get better. And your blood count is improving after that hemorrhage, so in the coming weeks, you will feel perkier."

Roosevelt turned to Annabel. "What are her lab values?"

Annabel rattled them off from her card.

"All are within normal limits."

"Dr. Harvey," Bonnie said, "the pediatrician said we can take Samantha home when you discharge me, if we closely follow her up in the clinic within a week. Can't you send me home? I'm ready. I'm sure of it."

Roosevelt laughed and raised his sagging shoulders. "I couldn't deny that request if my life depended on it."

"You're just saying that," Bonnie chided back. "You wouldn't send me if I still had medical issues."

"So true. How about this? We'll coincide an obstetric out-patient clinic appointment before or after Samantha's appointment and we'll discharge you today. It's getting late, but Dr. Gash, your nurse, and the unit secretary can hustle for you."

Bonnie's face lit up like Christmas lights at Opryland and Tony stood and twirled around once with Samantha. The team advanced to the doorway.

"We wish you the best," Annabel said.

"We'll send you in a throat lozenge while you're waiting," Dr. Harvey said.

Annabel chuckled.

"What?" Dr. Harvey asked her.

Annabel shook her head in the hallway. "They love you too."

"Speaking of love, congratulations on the new pet. You're a brave woman to take on the added responsibility during medical school, but it sounds like you have it all figured out."

"Yeah," Caleb said, "a dog sounds like super companionship while studying. I wish I was organized enough to take care of a another living being besides myself. Maybe I can borrow him sometime."

"Maybe Bob and I can rent him out while either or both of us are on vacation, away, or whatever."

Bob tucked the vet's bill into his pocket and left their office with Oliver on a leash. The dog had been a big hit with their staff due to his affability and beautiful coat, but Bob snarled at the price of the bill as he started the car. He glanced in the rearview mirror and acknowledged to himself that he was already quite fond of the dog. Even if he had to scrimp with his monthly budget and deprive himself of an occasional fancy coffee from the hospital, he would do so. They were too expensive anyway, he thought.

He never asked his folks for money. His mother was a nurse in a physician's office and his dad was an electrician who had cut back on his hours due to chronic back pain. They supported him emotionally and were super proud of him, but they could not help him out financially. In essence, he hoped someday he would be able to kick in some of his salary for their golden years. Maybe his dad could retire altogether.

It was different for Annabel, he thought. If she had a pinch with money, all she had to do was ask her dad. He even covered her credit card for her Uber habit, which was actually a smart idea since she lived with a parking problem for her SUV. He was glad for her fortunate circumstance and also admired her for never taking them for granted. He had loved meeting them in Nashville and hoped the opportunity would present itself again.

Each day, Bob felt his tiredness dissipating. He was beginning to look forward to getting back to the wards in a few days and finishing up internal medicine as well as spending part of tomorrow morning with Annabel. He looked again in the mirror. Oliver stared back, his paws on the top of the back seat.

"When we arrive home," Bob said, "let's see how smart you are."

Bob let Oliver pee by the parking lot and hustled him into his apartment. He grabbed a few biscuits in his hand. Oliver already knew how to sit on command, but Bob wasn't sure if he could give his paw.

After the dog sat before him, Bob said, "You are the politest sitting dog I've ever seen." He extended his hand, trying the command without a biscuit. "Gimme your paw, Oliver."

Oliver kept eye contact; his tail swooshed on the hardwood floor.

"I guess not." Bob cupped a treat in his hand, held it out, and repeated his command. Oliver nuzzled his fist. Bob tried it again, putting a bit more space between them and picking the dog's leg up himself.

Finally, the dog picked up his paw on his own and extended it.

"Good dog, Oliver. Way to go." He opened his hand and Oliver took the treat politely. After a few more of the same, Bob switched to "Gimme five," and Oliver cooperated.

"First attempt to teach you something, and you catch on like a champ. Good boy." He gave the dog a hug, but Oliver tried to pry himself loose.

"So you're not the hugging type. I'll try and respect your wishes."

He asked for another "high five" and the dog raised his right front leg exuberantly.

"Wait till Annabel sees what you can do."

His iPhone dinged on the counter, alerting him to an incoming message from Annabel with the name of the funeral parlor.

Why don't we go together in my car? he responded. *I'll pick you up and, later on, drop you off at the hospital.*

Sounds good, she wrote. *I won't need a car service. Don't forget our companion!*

He's been 'vetted,' so I'll fill you in. And there's no way I will forget him!

Annabel left the hospital at the end of the day in the best spirits she'd had since starting the rotation. Even though her scut work had increased, she had managed some study time in the lounge; she found out she could also hunt down Caleb or Roosevelt if they were nearby and ask them questions.

She arrived home to her apartment by 6 p.m., scrambled together breakfast food for dinner, and started studying again. Choosing to sit at her desk, she avoided the temptation to be more comfortable and possibly fall asleep in her bed or her easy chair.

She opened up her textbook to the subject of ectopic pregnancies, which were pregnancies occurring outside of the uterus, most commonly in a fallopian tube. They had an incidence of two percent of pregnancies in the United States, she read, and a woman could die if it ruptured and caused a hemorrhage. She studied the table of risk factors.

If a woman came into the ER or a doctor's office complaining of abdominal pain, she read, lack of menstruation or amenorrhea for four to six weeks, and irregular vaginal spotting, that would raise a high index of suspicion for an ectopic pregnancy. In particular, she must remember that for any future time she spent in the OB/GYN clinic.

She glanced out her desk window to the dull view of the house next door, so she rolled forty-five degrees to her front window. The tree she loved had buds all over the branches and the squirrel's nest was becoming a bit more camouflaged.

From out in the kitchen, Annabel's phone rang, so she padded out and answered.

"Hello, gorgeous," Dustin said.

"You're in a fine mood. You've never called me that. Plus, how do you know? I may be standing here with bags under my eyes, pillow hair, and chapped lips."

"If that were the case, you'd still be gorgeous."

"Whatever you say. I won't stay on long because I'm buckling down to study, but how was your day?"

"Then I won't waste your time on the phone. Why don't you come over later and sleep here? And if you didn't eat yet, I'll bring in take-out." Now wasn't the time to share his frightful close call at the diner.

Annabel hesitated. Since she had leeway in the morning before going to the funeral service, his idea had merit. "All right. Let me study some more and I'll be over later. I ate a hodgepodge of a dinner, so how about dessert?"

"I'll whip us up something."

"No you won't."

"You're right. I'll go buy something."

"I can stop on the way."

"No way. I'll see you later."

Annabel hung up. She committed herself to not being sidetracked and finished a thorough once-over of ectopic pregnancies. She packed a flattering silhouette nightgown, toiletries, and an outfit for the event in the morning. She headed out, aware that she must drive back to her place in the morning so Bob could pick her up.

The night was lighter than normal on her drive to Dustin's. A full moon hung like it was the only act going on in the sky. She cracked her windows and enjoyed the fresh air. She changed her car channel to her iPhone and started a medical podcast. It was amazing these days to be able to learn important subject matter from a phone instead of a book and learning while on the go.

Annabel pulled behind Dustin's vehicle in his car port and rapped on the front door. "Hey," he said, opening the door and flashing a smile. His two-story house was small and she followed him to the kitchen.

Annabel put her bag on the counter while Solar bobbed his head from his nearby cage. "What have you been up to?" Annabel asked the bird. "You're quiet tonight."

Dustin rolled his eyes. "Just wait. He's driving me crazy."

She turned back to the counter and now noticed an open cardboard box with a full, delectable-looking cake. An iced orange carrot stretched across the cream cheese frosting.

"What a huge dessert, Dustin Lowe, and it looks scrumptious." She glanced at him. He was staring at her instead of the contents of the box. "My mouth is watering. Where'd you buy this at this time of night?"

"The best and closest restaurant around here."

He reached for plates and grabbed utensils while Annabel took it out of the box.

"I should put candles on top just to make it special."

"Hell, it already is special. Is there an occasion going on here that I don't know about?"

Dustin pushed down on the knife and slithered two chunks on their plates. The slices left a trail of flaky, moist crumbs on the counter.

"I had an eventful day. Sean and I were grabbing something to eat at *our* diner and a man came in with a firearm. He wanted to shoot the manager, missed, and grazed another employee."

Annabel bit her lip. "Are you and the employee unharmed?"

"Employee is lucky. He only suffered a local injury to his arm. Sean and I took down the man with the gun. He'll need more medical care, but nothing serious."

She flinched. "But you didn't get hurt, did you? You're not hiding a bulky bandage under those clothes, are you?"

"I tell you what. Why don't we eat our carrot cake and you can hunt under my clothes in a little while to find out."

She grinned. "In their haste, I bet the paramedics forgot all about you."

"And I need a physical."

She playfully tapped him on his chest and carried her plate over to the table.

Dustin followed. "And what can I get you to drink?"

"Wine?"

"Really?"

"Don't fill it to the top and only one. I'll splurge for a week night. Because I'm with you."

He put down her wine and sat on the side of a chair watching her sample the cake.

"This is so delicious, it's crazy. We need to go to this restaurant."

"I thought the way to a man's heart was through his stomach. I didn't know that went for the opposite sex."

"That's because I'm not like the average woman my age who wouldn't dare eat this chunk of calories you put on my plate, especially at bedtime."

"No, you're not average. Of that I'm certain."

CHAPTER 22

Even though Dustin's blinds were half closed, the moonlight pierced his bedroom. He purposely left the room's lighting to the moon. The ceiling fan twirled on low, making the air stir and the border threads ripple on a crocheted afghan his mother had made him, which was draped on a chair.

Annabel only had a few seconds to admire the usual tidiness of his room, the queen bed made as if it was in a five-star hotel, and his nightstand neat as a pin. He wrapped his arms around her from the back and brushed her hair away from the right side of her neck. Kissing her there sent warmth all over her body and she closed her eyes for a moment. Still standing, she turned around and placed her hands on his strong back and felt the ripples of his musculature under her fingers. His mouth came down on hers. Their embrace tightened.

Dustin wore a V-neck nylon T-shirt and they both insistently pulled it over his head. She was in love with the shape of his chest, which was well defined with the nomenclature anatomy she studied so well from medical school. He was toned and ripped perfectly, she thought, like an active policeman should be.

Dustin scrambled to help Annabel pull out her tucked-in ruddy top from her cargo pants. When it was freed, they both yanked it off. They kissed again in a frenzy and moved a few steps closer to the bed. Annabel flexed a knee and pulled off one shoe, but Dustin broke from the deep kissing, grabbed off each of his shoes, and tumbled them to the side.

On the way up from leaning over, he pushed his head into her abdomen, put both hands on her, and tackled her to his bed. She laughed while he unsnapped the top of his pants, unzipped his fly, and yanked off his pants in one fell swoop.

Still on the carpet, Dustin could barely control himself as he grew harder by the moment watching her slither out of her own pants and underwear. He shoved them off the edge and planted his knees on the bed, joining her. She wiggled under him to the pillows near the headboard and giggled because he still needed to remove his Jockey underwear.

He grinned at her, ripped them off, and met her face-to-face. The fan cycled with a peaceful hum as Annabel wrapped her legs around him and the two of them joined and thrusted in a frenzy.

"That was crazy," Annabel said later. "Is your middle name Casanova?" She pulled the creamy white sheet over her hip as she lay on her side facing him.

Dustin slid the hem up over her shoulder. "Dustin Casanova Lowe. That has a ring to it, but no. There is nothing like dangerous police work, like today, to make me totally appreciate the finer things in life." He traced the side of her face with a long index finger.

"What made you become a cop? It's not like you're following in your father's footsteps."

"Honestly, it wasn't only because I like to help people. I yearned to look cool in a uniform. I'm a stickler for precision, so I thought the training would be right up my alley, and I thought I'd enjoy firearms training and the physical skills needed for the job. A combination of things drew me to police work."

"I bet your mom was worried."

"She still is. And my dad never knew what I went into because he died while I was in college."

"What did he die from?"

"A ruptured brain aneurysm. He was alone for the weekend and my mom didn't find him until Sunday night when she'd gotten home from a trip. If he'd gotten to a hospital, maybe someone like your dad could have saved him."

"I'm sorry. That must have been difficult."

"I often think he caused it himself. He chain smoked like nobody's business. They told me his arteries thinned because of it. That's why you becoming a doctor and preaching to people about not smoking is important."

"No one in my family smokes. I'm fortunate. And I hate the stuff."

"I've been exposed to enough second-hand smoke growing up that I'm lucky my lungs are as black and white and disease free as they are on chest

X-ray. I will brainwash my own kids that if they puff once, Dad will arrest them."

"A tough love kind of dad."

"I think of parents as being their son or daughter's guardian angels."

"Nicely put. So how many kids are you going to have?"

Dustin held his tongue as he almost answered, "As many as we'll make together."

"Come on," she prompted. "You can tell me. I won't tell some future-wife-to-be of yours that you intend to keep her pregnant all the time." She put her fingernail in his impish, alluring dimple and circled it around.

Dustin swallowed hard, not liking to hear her words. "At least two, I suppose. How about you?"

"While in training, I can't think that far out." She glanced up at the swirling fan blades. "As a matter of fact, this rotation is scaring me to death. I never guessed the possibilities ... how pregnancies can end up like time bombs. There's preeclampsia and post-partum hemorrhages to worry about. There is danger delivering vaginally after a C-section and possible ectopic pregnancies to worry about. There is fetal distress and kids born with rare diseases, malformations, and ..." She looked at Dustin, who wore a puzzled expression.

"Oh, sorry. I'm talking shop. Anyway, there is more to worry about than simply the number of kids a person wants." She leaned over and kissed him. "Do you mind if I jump in your shower, put on my nightgown, and fall off to sleep with you?"

"Make it fast."

"Thanks for the best carrot cake I've ever eaten," Annabel said when she came back.

"Is that all?"

"It was almost as spectacular as the sex, but not quite."

He smiled and gave her one more kiss before their eyes closed.

"I'm using your bathroom to throw on some makeup," Annabel said as the daylight broke into the bedroom.

"Be my guest," Dustin said as he rolled over to watch her sit up. He pulled her back down. "But only if you can get away from me." He lightly pinched her arm and then let go. "I'd better get up too. I'm regular early shift today."

"I'll be out of your way, but fortunately, my schedule has a little leeway this morning." She stepped into the bathroom and fumbled through her bag for her clothes. Her items were wrinkle-free and draped her body like a charm. When she made it downstairs, Dustin was in a T-shirt and his underwear pouring them both coffee.

"You look nice," he said.

"Thank you. I'm going to a funeral parlor this morning. Not good; it was a patient of ours."

"I guess you meant what you said last night about the complications of child birth."

"Exactly. But at least I'm going to see Oliver. Bob is bringing him in his car."

"I thought he was not with you on OB/GYN."

"He's a dog. Of course not." She kept a straight face, although she was messing with him.

"I mean Bob."

She broadly smiled and took the mug he extended to her. Dustin shook his head while Annabel looked up at Solar. "The cat's got your tongue this morning."

"What's your problem?" Solar chirped.

"Oh, please don't start him," Dustin said. "He's imitating me more, ever since I brought an Alexa into the kitchen."

"Alexa, what's the temperature?" Solar asked.

Alexa ranted out the day's weather forecast and Annabel's jaw dropped.

"See. I told you he started something new. I don't know who's smarter ... Alexa or Solar."

They both nodded. "Solar," they chimed.

Annabel poured flavored creamer into the rich coffee and stirred.

"So is your friend Bob back on the same rotation?"

"No. He's coming with me because two students are better than one and he's free to do so. Plus, I'll get to see Oliver."

Dustin took a deep breath to detach himself from a tinge of anxiety in his gut. "The dog must be handsome. You'll have to show me a picture of him one of these days."

Annabel recalled the pictures Bob had sent her. On one hand, she wanted to show him the photo of her and Oliver, but her instinct told her not to show him the other two. For the selfie of her and Bob and Oliver, they had huddled very close together. To Dustin, it might appear like an intimate couple with their dog.

"What?" he asked, noticing her quietness.

She pulled out her phone and carefully scrolled to only the picture of her and Oliver. Careful not to let go, she showed him.

"Wow. He's a beauty. Congratulations. I can't wait to meet him."

She pulled her arm back to her side, slid away her phone, and focused again on her steaming beverage. "Does Solar behave himself with dogs?"

"I guess we'll find out. Better yet, does Oliver like parrots?"

Annabel drove home to the pick of parking spots on her block. Young professionals had left for work and she parked across the street. She still had time to kill in her apartment. At her desk, she opened her computer and began setting up a Power Point presentation for next week's grand rounds. She worked an hour and closed down. Bob would be by soon and she needed to update her father about the day before.

She went to her phone, skipped texting either of her parents, and called the home number to leave a message.

"Hey, it's Annabel," she talked to the recorder. "Dad, thanks so much for your advice yesterday. I asserted myself with my attending and told him what I needed about me having little to do with the patient's narcotic order. The rest of the day went much better. No more news for now, except that I'm going to see Oliver and Bob this morning. I don't go in to the hospital until this afternoon. Have a great day. Love you."

Footsteps sounded in the hallway and Annabel immediately flung open the door. Bob's hand was midway in the air, ready to knock. Oliver was beside him.

"Surprise!" Bob said with his usual cheerful expression. He wore black pants and a subtle plaid shirt. He let go of the leash and Oliver bounded in.

"Don't acknowledge me, Oliver. Make yourself at home."

Bob closed the door behind him and, inside, Oliver scouted around

Annabel's big room. He circled her furniture and popped his nose into her waste basket. She grabbed him, circled her arms around him, and squeezed. He gently pulled away and sat.

"He's not into hugs," Bob said, "but we do have a surprise."

He stood next to Annabel, who was crouched down. "Ask him to give his paw, or ask for a high five."

"Oliver, high five." She stuck out her hand and the dog popped up his paw.

"Wow! Good boy." She stood and narrowed her eyes. "Did he know that trick or are you Cesar Millan?"

Bob beamed. "I taught him."

"Sweet."

"And he had his first vet visit. Like being in a pediatrician's office, he was inoculated for every malicious threat for disease. He was also started on flea, tick, and heartworm prevention and I had him microchipped."

"Thanks for all that. He's worth it, isn't he?"

"You bet."

"And what do I owe you?"

Bob slipped a copy of the bill out of his pocket and laid it on the counter. Annabel wrote a check for half and handed it to him. "By the way, you look handsome."

"The same goes for you; too pretty for a funeral, but you can't help it."

He glanced at her Keurig machine on the counter. "Are you getting good use of that?"

"Thanks. I am. I haven't used it today. Would you like one for the road?"

"No coffee yet? That's not like you."

"Well … I just came in from Dustin's. I had coffee there." She averted her eyes to the machine and walked over.

"Oh." Feeling dispirited, his heart squeezed in his chest.

"What flavor would you like?"

"Please don't bother."

She put her hand on her hip. "I'll make you hazelnut."

Bob nodded.

"I have so much more to tell you about the rotation. You won't believe it … things are happening in a New York minute. And Dr. Harvey has assigned me with giving next week's grand rounds."

Bob's ears perked up. "You're kidding."

"Nope. You'll be on medicine next week, but maybe you can come."

With a fresh brew in Bob's hand, they took Annabel's things for the day, as well as Oliver, and left for the funeral service. Bob became pensive, mulling over her sleepover with Dustin. She must like him a lot, he thought, to break away from the demands piled high on her plate.

A somber mood fell over Annabel and Bob as they entered the first door to the left inside the great white arched funeral home. They signed into the official guest record book and put "medical student" after their names.

To not belabor their sadness, it was the only day the family allotted to commemorate their daughter. The room had no space to spare. Individual groups of people clustered in the middle and side aisles and individuals crowded the tables in the front and back of the room glancing through pictures and memories of Mary Chandler that Kathleen and Mike Chandler had on display.

Since the young woman had been cremated, a solid urn rested on a pedestal in the front of the room. Wreaths, flower vases, and sprays of flowers on easels jammed up the space in a circular pattern to reach the display tables in the corners.

At least half the visitors were young people around Mary's age of eighteen. Most were probably previous classmates, Annabel thought. She waited patiently with Bob to express her condolences again to the parents, who were surrounded by others also waiting to do the same.

Two young women stood behind her facing two men about the same age. "We really don't know why she died," one of the girls said. "She was ready to have her baby in about two months and I heard somebody at the hospital killed her. Right through her IV. Ran a deadly drug right into her hand."

Moans and groans sounded behind Annabel and Bob and the other girl chimed in, "Who woulda thought. I'm not going to any hospital if I can help it. And poor Mary. She didn't deserve what she got. She was going to raise that baby all by herself. I heard it was that shithead Freddie Hogan that got her pregnant, but Mary never said a word. I don't think her parents even know him."

One of the young men spoke up. "I know a girl who went out with that loser; she said he tried to rape her on the date."

"You're kidding me," the first girl said.

"No. And she's not one to make up stories."

Annabel stared at Bob with disbelief and shuddered. He heard every word as well and shook his head.

"Speaking of the devil," the other man said behind them. Annabel glanced back at the group of four. They stood with respect and mournful expressions. The man talking nodded toward the back corner where one young man stood alone tentatively scanning the room. He nervously rubbed his hands together and wiped the sweat off his forehead.

"Over there," the man alerted his friends. "That's Freddie Hogan."

All three heads turned. Annabel and Bob couldn't help it either and turned to check him out.

"But why would he dare show up here if he really was the father of Mary's baby and didn't want anyone to know?" one of the girls asked.

"Closure," one of the guys said.

"Or like a criminal returning to the scene of a crime," the first girl added.

The space opened up a bit to speak to the parents and Annabel tapped her elbow at Bob. They slipped in front of Kathleen and Mike and Annabel introduced Bob.

"We are humbled to come this morning," Annabel said, "to both celebrate your daughter's life but also to grieve her early passing."

Mrs. Chandler first took Annabel's hand and squeezed, but then pulled her in and gave her a hug.

As they wandered out, Annabel paused in front of Freddie Hogan and gave him a piercing stare. She didn't know if the story about him was true, but based on his cowardly stance in the back of the room, and what she knew of Mary, she believed it.

CHAPTER 23

"Do you have time if we go across the street to that mini-park and walk Oliver?" Bob asked Annabel outside the funeral home.

"I do now."

They opened the back of Bob's car, Annabel fastened Oliver to the leash, and he jumped down. They crossed the street and landed on a circular path with a small field and playground in the middle.

"This is perfect," Annabel said, "if the pollen blowing around doesn't cause us to have an allergy attack."

"A little walk will help tire me out before taking a nap when I get back home." He looked at the dog. "If Oliver doesn't demand any attention."

Annabel let the dog sniff to his heart's content and they walked. "I have off on Sunday. Why don't I take him then? You can have more time to yourself before going back on Monday."

"Sure. It will be your turn to enjoy him anyway."

Two trim young men dressed in running gear slowed their pace. "What kind of dog is that?" one of them asked. "He's gorgeous."

"We're not absolutely sure," Annabel said. "We just adopted him from the shelter."

"DNA will tell you. Have a nice day."

The two men sprinted off and Annabel admired their pace. "We better spring for the kit so people stop telling us to do that. I'll buy the kit and we'll find out once and for all what Oliver's ancestry is. That's right, boy. Are you like Bamse, the famous Norwegian dog, or Balto, the famous Siberian husky?"

"Or the famous collie, Lassie?" Bob pitched in.

Annabel patted Oliver's head. "He is walking like a charm. I bet he's grateful that he is with us and lives in a place that he can call home; he's being extra polite to please us."

"I agree." Bob glanced at Annabel. She wore a smile as she walked the dog. She needed for this to happen, he thought. He did too. Something from the natural world to focus on while away from their four-walled routine and stress ... besides seeing each other like he planned.

"So what is the topic for your grand rounds?"

"Medical errors and physician burnout."

"No way you can cover all of that."

"Dr. Harvey expects me to only hit the highlights. There's not enough time to do justice to both topics nor do I have the time to prepare so much."

They neared the end of one whole loop and Annabel stopped. An elderly couple passed them single file and patted Oliver on the head. He wagged his tail and sat down. Annabel jimmied the zipper on her shoulder bag, reached in, and pulled out the chocolate-covered blueberries she previously bought for Bob.

"Here you go."

His rich blue eyes sparkled as he took the box and tore it open. "Thanks, what a treat. I'm glad you didn't buy the expresso beans since I should stay away from the extra caffeine."

"You're welcome."

Bob shook some into his hand and rattled them towards her. He poured a few out for her as well. Oliver watched.

"Don't give us that sad expression," Annabel said. "These would be a double whammy for you. Chocolate and blueberries aren't good for dogs."

"I'm glad you know these things. I'm more of a novice than you."

"I learned a lot from my dad inheriting Dakota. Come on; you should go relax and I need to go show up on the baby-birthing rotation."

Bob curtsied in jest. "At your service, ma'am."

He dropped her off at the front door of the hospital. It was a beautiful morning with her and Oliver's company, he thought, even though he was second fiddle to what he was sure was a romp in the sack with Dustin the night before.

Annabel took a gamble that it would be all right with Dr. Harvey, so she stopped in the cafeteria and bought lunch. Since she had eaten nothing at Dustin's or her own apartment, her stomach growled.

She met Emmett pushing a wheelchair towards the elevator as she towed along her backpack, shoulder bag, and sandwich.

"Dr. Tilson, we missed you all morning. I'd help you carry something but, I'm headed downstairs with this. The place is jumping up here."

"You're thoughtful, Emmett. I suppose I'll find out for myself."

"That you will." He clunked the wheelchair over the lip of the elevator and was gone.

At the nurses' station, Annabel stopped to let her presence be known. Roosevelt did a double-take. "You're here earlier than I anticipated."

"Mission was accomplished, Dr. Harvey, and Mary Chandler's parents appreciated the visit. I'm glad you recommended it and that I went. I did stop downstairs for a sandwich. Do you mind if I eat?"

"By all means. And since you're dressed so nicely for the potentially messy business of being on the labor and delivery ward, change into scrubs."

Caleb stood behind Roosevelt's shoulder. She scrambled to the table inside and dug into her hot barbecue sandwich. Roosevelt and Caleb followed and discussed the information on the board.

"We have admissions," Roosevelt said. "Annabel, when you're finished, ask Dr. Fleming if you can tag along while she puts in an epidural on Laverna Santana." He tapped on her name listed for Room 2. "She's a twenty-nine-year-old obese G2P1 woman. And Dr. Gash, we better go get a bite to eat too."

Caleb glanced down where Annabel struggled to keep from making a mess, especially with good clothes on. "Does that bun hold more barbecue sauce or brisket?"

"Whichever it is," Annabel said, "this barbecue is competitive enough against the downtown joints on Broadway in Nashville. For the hospital cafeteria, a miracle must have happened." She shook her head, wondering about her fortunate cake last night and now her sandwich. Or maybe it was the men in her life spicing everything up.

"I'm headed that way. Annabel, mind the shop." Caleb raced to catch up to Roosevelt, who beat him out the door.

Annabel scrunched up the trash, washed her hands, and changed in the female locker room. She hunted for Kristin Fleming and found her already in Room 2. Inside, she approached the patient first. "I'm Annabel Tilson, a medical student doing obstetrics. I'll be asking you questions for a history and physical when Dr. Fleming is finished."

Laverna Santana had a sizeable pregnancy protruding in front of her, but the rest of her was pretty big too. Dr. Harvey was correct with his "obese" terminology and Annabel wondered how much weight gain she had amassed during the last nine months or if she started out with a husky size. She had heard that some women go nuts and "eat for two" and wondered how much their doctors advise them not to do that.

The woman shrugged her shoulders. "I'll be comfortable by then and won't mind your questions because Dr. Fleming will be giving me drugs."

"An epidural," Kristin said to clarify.

Laverna grimaced and looked toward Jed, the man sitting on the windowsill. He wore a baseball cap and a five o'clock shadow.

"Yeah." Laverna said. "The sooner you get that epidural in, the happier I'll be."

"Is it okay if I watch?" Annabel asked.

"Absolutely."

Jed jumped off the sill. "I'm outta here. I can't stand needles." He rubbed his hand on Laverna's shoulder and went out while a nurse came in.

"Adios." Laverna shook her head. "Afraid of needles!"

"I'm Pam," the RN said. "I'm going to help Dr. Fleming. Let's move you to the side of the bed with your feet dangling and, when the time comes, we'll ask you to bow your back out."

Laverna scooted as she was told and faced the door while Kristin stepped to the window side and rolled her cart close by. The red cart held everything she needed.

From what Annabel had previously observed watching anesthesiologists, she already liked the field, so she paid strict attention to Dr. Fleming. Kristin settled her wide-rimmed glasses firmly on her nose and prepared an epidural kit on the side table, making sure to not touch anything inside. The blue drape it came in hung over the sides and she peered at the contents of the container as if she was running a checklist off in her head.

"I'm going to wash your back off," Kristin said, "with an antiseptic."

"This will feel cold," Pam said with a husky voice as she stood in front of her large patient. She adjusted the open back of Laverna's gown to the side.

With a sterile technique and wearing gloves, Kristin finished and then laid another blue drape from the kit on Laverna's exposed back. She prepared her syringes and then felt along Laverna's midline vertebrae.

"Arch your back like you're in the fetal position," Kristin instructed her. Pam gave Laverna a demonstration and the doctor and nurse glanced at each other and frowned. Due to Laverna's large size and compounded by her big belly, her ability to push out her back was limited ... which would make it more difficult for Kristin to access between her intervertebral spaces with the large epidural needle.

After palpating some more, Kristin selected the skin spot between the second and third lumbar space and injected a bee sting of local anesthetic. She hooked a glass epidural syringe on the large-bore needle and inserted it to no avail because all she hit was bone. Her aim was to ever so slowly advance the needle to the epidural space, the area between the dura, which was a membrane, and the vertebral wall. The dural sac would be filled with cerebrospinal fluid and the nerve roots. The real trick was not to go too far and puncture the dural membrane. Otherwise, spinal fluid would drain into her needle and would be a "wet" tap, most likely causing a headache ... possibly a severe one.

Kristin hated when an accidental wet tap occurred. Laboring patients were already in pain, but that headache was a real burden in the postpartum period when a mother should instead be enjoying her newborn baby.

Kristin was also slick at the paravertebral technique, so she numbed off to the side of where she'd been and went in at an angle. She advanced the needle gingerly and also pressed her finger on the end of the syringe, which was filled with air. Since Kristin was lanky and trim, she had to work at her maneuver to get through Laverna's back. After a few moments, she encountered the correct epidural space and her syringe encountered a loss of resistance and she tapped a few cc's of air into the space. No wet tap occurred and Kristin sighed with relief.

The anesthesiologist took off the syringe from the end of the needle and uncurled the thin, long catheter from the plastic kit. She threaded it into the needle and advanced it correctly and then removed the needle over it.

"You can relax just a bit," Kristin said as she adjusted the end of the catheter to the pieces where she could deliver drugs. She secured the epidural catheter on Laverna's back with a see-through bandage and gave Laverna a test dose of local anesthetic which contained epinephrine. Since her patient was hooked up to monitors, her heart rate would increase if the catheter was incorrectly placed and the epinephrine raced into a blood vessel.

Everything so far checked out perfectly and Kristin's job was now to dose the epidural. She began opening the drawers of her cart. "You can settle back on the bed. Worst part is over."

Annabel pitched in to help while Laverna wiggled on the mattress to the top of the bed. Kristin opened and shut drawers again and frowned. She tinkered with the two sets of earrings on her right ear lobe.

"The anesthesia tech restocked those drawers this morning," Pam said, noting Kristin's displeasure. "Is there something missing?"

"I heard the drug shortage of local anesthetics is getting worse. Do me a favor and call the tech. Only thing in here is the stronger concentrations of bupivacaine. Ask her if she has any 0.125% bupivacaine."

Pam called the front desk to send in the tech and the woman soon poked in her head.

"What's going on with an eighth of a percent of bupivacaine?" Kristin emphasized her discontent and threw her arms in the air.

"Sorry, Dr. Fleming. I double checked with the FDA website this morning, so I know that Ohio is not being singled out. There is a national shortage of what you want and not much of the .25% bupivacaine left in our carts either."

"Thanks. It's not your fault."

Kristin shook her head. This was a situation she had no control over. "These shortages of drugs, which has been going on recently, affects more than anesthesia. Outpatient caregivers and patients have to seek out other methods of pain relief, which, I believe, worsens the opioid crisis. And in the hospital, surgeons can't use the numbing drugs at surgical sites, which again ramps up the need for injectable opioids like fentanyl and morphine."

She tapped her foot. Laverna squirmed and pleaded with her eyes for some pain relief.

"Usually I give a bolus dose of ten cc's," Dr. Fleming added, "but I'll give less and do my usual short increments. We don't want Mrs. Santana to get a heavy motor blockage with the higher dosage. What we normally want is a sensory blockade with little motor deprivation."

Kristin aspirated from the catheter to make sure there was no blood on return and then injected three cc's of the .25% concentration. After four minutes, she injected another three. She wrote an order for the pharmacy to make up a bag of a bupivacaine solution with very low dose fentanyl so they could put it on a pump and infuse it into the catheter.

"My pain has eased. Thank you," Laverna said after a while. "Anesthesiologists are angels that fly down from heaven when a woman goes into labor."

"Hmm. I've never been called that before." She cleaned up her mess and looked at Annabel. "Are you staying to do Mrs. Santana's H&P?"

"Yes, and thanks for letting me watch."

Kristin glanced at the fetal heart rate monitor and cycled Laverna's blood pressure cuff one more time. Satisfied, and with a spring to her step, she headed out.

CHAPTER 24

Annabel finished asking Laverna about her past history, surgeries, and previous pregnancy. The twenty-nine-year-old had no problems from the past that should pose a problem for this delivery. So far, that was what she liked about obstetrics. The patients were young and mostly healthy, unlike internal medicine, where cardiovascular disease, COPD, and diabetes was rampant in most patients who walked through the door.

But for the last few minutes, Laverna grew paler. "I don't feel so well," she mumbled.

Annabel cycled her patient's blood pressure cuff and at the same time noticed the fetal heart rate monitor, where she detected evidence of fetal distress. The baby's heart rate did not seem to change in response to Laverna's contractions and the rate was slowing down from the brisk hundred and forty beats per minute that he'd been exhibiting.

The pressure registered on the bedside monitor as 96/68. Annabel stepped to the doorway and glanced up and down the hallway for Dr. Fleming. The room was close to the nurses' station, so she called out for the anesthesiologist.

Kristin stopped what she was doing in the supply room and came running. "I learned that a hollering medical student is to be taken seriously!" she exclaimed as she surmised the entire situation with one scan of the room.

She took Laverna's blood pressure again, with the same result as when she came in the room. She popped out a vial and a syringe from her anesthesia cart and drew up a concoction. She injected it into Laverna's IV.

Kristin moved her patient's gown off her belly and took a dull needle and poked it on her skin at various spots above and below her umbilicus. "Do you feel this?" she asked each time and asked her to differentiate how much numbness she felt from the epidural block she had placed.

Jed burst into the room. Some soda splashed out of the paper cup he held, so he slowed his pace. "I was in the cafeteria and overheard a conversation about recent life-threatening situations happening to unsuspecting patients on the OB ward. And then I get to the floor, and a nurse tells me to hurry in here!"

Kristin eyed the monitor. The baby's heart rate had picked up; otherwise she was two seconds away from calling the obstetricians stat. Laverna's pressure was also better. She took in a deep breath.

"She had a spell of hypotension, low blood pressure," Dr. Fleming told them. "How do you feel now, Mrs. Santana?"

"Not like I'm going to faint anymore." She glanced at her husband's paper cup. "Don't drink that in front of me. I'm dying for something to eat or drink and you're making the temptation too great."

"I think she's feeling better," Jed said. He turned around and sipped the rest of his cola and tossed the cup. "There, that should make you happy."

"Really? The only thing that would make me happy right now is for you to be having this baby and me standing there watching you."

He rolled his eyes. "You've turned into someone I never knew existed."

Annabel followed Kristin back to the supply room, where Annabel chuckled. "Some of these couples are hilarious. Seems like a lot of women get testy during labor and take it out on the guy."

"Sometimes keeping a straight face in the rooms is quite difficult."

"So what went on in there?"

"It can happen ... a more intense sympathetic nervous system block than anticipated. In this case, it may or may not have been due to the concentration of the bupivacaine that I used. In any case, medical drug shortages are another problem to deal with. During my training, it appears like they are increasing in frequency, but imagine being a patient waiting nine months and then being told she can't have an epidural because the anesthesiologist doesn't have the correct drug?"

"I guess I wouldn't want to be on the receiving end of that statement."

"Me neither."

Besides doing scut work and seeing two other patients, Annabel managed to study for an hour. She was out of view from the nurses' station because she huddled at the end of the couch. Traffic increased into the lounge as some nurses changed shifts and reassigned their names on the board and Caleb came in twice to change the status of patients' stages of labor.

She managed to read a synopsis of gestational diabetes, which was a different affair than what happens with a non-pregnant person. An extra consideration was how it impacted the fetus. She slipped the open book down to her thighs and stretched out her arms as Dr. Harvey walked in.

"Annabel, I know the answer to my question because I read over Mrs. Santana's clinic record. I'm wondering how astute you were with her history? Did you ask any questions about her weight?"

"What kind of questions?"

"Was she already obese before her pregnancy? Did she also lump on excessive weight gain during her pregnancy ... which would be over thirty-five pounds?"

"We talked about her weight gain. She gained forty-seven pounds. And she weighed in at two hundred twenty pounds on admission, which did make her obese before her pregnancy. Before, she must have been around one hundred seventy pounds."

"Very nice. Which means you did a very thorough history and it also means she is positive for both those factors. Now there is another additional risk factor. She's having a prolonged second stage of labor."

Annabel moved her book to the couch as Roosevelt added, "We didn't want to call you before, but now is the time to be in Mrs. Santana's room."

"Thank you for letting me study. The risk factors you're referring to ... what is the possible problem?"

"Shoulder dystocia upon delivery of the fetus."

She furrowed her brow with only a vague impression of what that meant.

"You're coming with me."

In Room 2, Laverna was in full lithotomy position, working hard at her delivery with her husband and nurse nearby. Jed might not like needles, Annabel thought, but apparently he had no problem with childbirth. Caleb was in blue attire at the bottom of the bed and his tense facial muscles relaxed when Roosevelt came beside him.

Laverna had a moment between contractions. She spooned an ice chip into her mouth from a paper cup and grimaced up her face like she was in agony. "What the hell is wrong with these? Jed, get me new ice."

Jed sighed and hustled out of the room. Laverna's pain was much diminished from the epidural but there was still some to contend with. She accepted the fact that a solid block of numbness would render her unable to push, but she still voiced her complaint.

"Make me ..." she screeched with pain, "knocked out ..." she yelled, "or numb ..." she squealed, "like my body's got no nerves in it."

Jed walked back, his eyes going from one person to the other. He handed the cup of ice to Laverna. "Just don't throw it back at me."

"You're not funny. Besides, didn't your mama teach you anything?"

Jed kept his lips plugged together. No way was he touching that remark.

"Men die in battle ..." she panted, "and women lose their sense of humor in childbirth."

After Laverna had her way with words, Caleb gave her a big nudge. "You can do this," he said. "Next contraction, give it all you've got."

Lucky for Dr. Gash, Laverna gave him no back talk and did as he requested. With a mighty push, the soft skull of the fetal head popped out.

But the baby's head did not keep sliding forward. It retracted back towards Laverna's vaginal opening.

"Let's push some more," Dr. Roosevelt said.

"Whaddaya mean by 'let's'? There's no 'us' in my pushing."

"Sorry, Mrs. Santana. You are right about that."

"Of course I'm right. The customer is always right."

Annabel heard Roosevelt exhale in a puff. Another contraction came quickly and Laverna pushed. Caleb glanced up at Dr. Harvey. The fetal head was still retracted back toward the maternal introitus and the fetal shoulders were not being delivered.

Annabel realized, like many attending doctors, Dr. Harvey had years of experience. After seeing so much in his career, he anticipated this as a problem. Laverna's risk factors were his first clue. She shuddered for the unborn baby, the mother, and the two doctors next to her and wondered how they would solve the problem. She figured an emergency C-section was always an option.

"Mrs. Santana," Dr. Harvey said, "there's a problem. The top of your baby's head is here, but the rest of him is slow to follow."

Jed stood and took a spot next to Annabel. Laverna pushed again.

"Or will not follow," Dr. Gash mumbled.

Jed's eyes bulged. He had watched their first baby be born, but this one was not proceeding as it should. He backed up next to his wife.

"To clarify," Roosevelt said, "your baby's anterior shoulder is impacted behind the symphysis pubis. Dr. Gash and I will try and free it up."

Roosevelt signaled to the nurse to help him and he gowned and gloved like Caleb. He motioned for the resident to change place with him. Annabel figured he would only take over if it was an emergency and his proficiency was needed. Caleb went to the side of Laverna's leg while Roosevelt wrapped his hands on the fetus's head.

Caleb placed his right hand on Laverna's right foot. He hyperflexed her hips onto her abdomen. With his other hand, he applied suprapubic pressure and checked for visual clues from Roosevelt if his technique was correct.

"Dr. Gash is trying to push your baby's shoulders into an oblique plane," Roosevelt said to Laverna and Jed. He gazed at Annabel. "I'll explain the McRoberts maneuver later."

Annabel felt like her heart was paused while she observed the situation unfold. Caleb pushed downward or laterally, trying his best to manually push the fetus's shoulder into an oblique plane. Dr. Harvey struggled at his end.

"Call peds," Dr. Harvey said.

"I did a few minutes ago," the nurse responded.

Roosevelt nodded.

Caleb exerted pressure downward again while pushing Mrs. Santana's hip up as much as he could. The woman's large size made it that much more difficult to obtain a good flexion. As he did so, the baby's head began to further descend with Dr. Harvey's hands wrapped around it. The shoulders miraculously turned appropriately and slid out behind the baby's big head.

Dr. Harvey now held a full length, moist, slippery neonate. With a suction bulb, he suctioned the baby's nose and mouth to clear secretions and then rubbed his back. Baby John Doe took his first breath and began crying.

Jeb popped up. He mimicked talking on the phone with his right hand. "Houston," he said, "we have a baby!"

Roosevelt continued working and handed the baby to Dr. Thomas, who had sneaked in during the emergency. He stepped to the warming unit, where he dried off all the moisture and sought to minimize the infant's loss of core temperature. After five minutes, he announced the newborn's one and five-minute Apgar scores.

"Here's your baby boy," Dr. Thomas said, holding him over his parents. Laverna's eyes moistened and she tapped her finger on his button nose. "Welcome to the world, you little troublemaker."

"Can I hold him?" Jed asked.

"He half-battled his way out of your wife's birth canal, so as a precaution, we better bring him right over to the nursery to the warmer and finish our pediatric evaluation. There'll be plenty of time, and years, ahead for all of you to be together."

Annabel waited in the lounge as Dr. Harvey and Dr. Gash discussed and documented Mrs. Santana's delivery outside. She frowned at the muddy coffee in the pot, dumped it in the sink, and began a fresh pot.

"How'd it go in there?" Emmett flashed his usual broad smile. He opened the cupboard and reached for Styrofoam cups for both of them.

"Another crazy delivery for which I have more questions for Dr. Gash and Dr. Harvey than answers." She took the cup he handed her and turned her back to the counter. "I bet over the years, you saw and observed so much, you could answer some of them too."

"Maybe." He beamed with enthusiasm. "I read a lot over the years too. Been in a few situational experiences as well."

"Situational experiences?"

"Yeah. I could call it that. Like a year ago, I transported a lady up the elevator in a wheelchair. She was one of them multi-multiparous pregnant ladies that end up plopping each baby out easier'n easier. The baby started coming. I got the elevator stopped on this delivery floor and yelled for one of the docs. It was me that stood guard at the elevator door blocking the view so visitors couldn't gawk at her while the senior resident caught that baby in the elevator. I never want that to happen again. Later, it was me who had to mop and scrub out the elevator!" He laughed and added, "But it turned out okay. Guess what she named her baby girl, her fifth kid?"

"Tell me."

"Ellie, short for elevator."

"Oh no! So, back in the day, did you ever think about going into medicine?"

"Wouldn't have never been able to afford all them big tuition bills. Nowadays, it's different. There's money to be had with easy, available loans and free money from grants and scholarships. The doors are wide open for young people of all ethnicity and backgrounds, and whether they're rich or poor. No excuse to not make something of yourself these days."

"I think you're right, Emmett. Ever think about changing anything now?"

"Nah. I'm better than okay with my simple life and what I got. I love my routine and making changes makes me uneasy like a bear watching a bulldozer knock down his forest. Hands-on medicine is for other folks. You know, everyone has a place in this world. I'm lucky I found mine."

"I'm glad you're content. Living with less stress is good for your health." The coffee stopped dripping. She poured him a cup first and then herself. He handed her a flavored creamer, guessing she wanted one. She dumped it in and tossed the container in the trash.

"I'd better chug this down fast," he said. "Rarely do I drink coffee in here."

"I'll stand right here with you. We'll enjoy it together until the other two docs arrive and then I'll be summoning up my nerve to ask my naïve questions."

CHAPTER 25

Emmett passed Dr. Harvey and Dr. Gash in the doorway as he left to finish his shift. Roosevelt patted the resident on the shoulder as they came in.

"Dr. Annabel," Roosevelt said, "you witnessed a perfect outcome for a shoulder dystocia delivery." He jockeyed his shirt into his pants with a shove and beamed his love for obstetrics all over his face.

"I don't understand why you didn't apply fundal pressure like I've seen in other deliveries. Wasn't that the problem ... getting the baby out?"

"You noticed the difference. We absolutely avoided that maneuver in this situation since it's associated with an increased incidence of neonatal injury. We performed, and you witnessed, the first-line treatment ... which is the McRoberts maneuver. Most cases of shoulder dystocia are relieved by doing it but, if not, there are a host of other named actions which can be used. You should look them up: the Zavanelli maneuver and the Wood's corkscrew.

"The delivery can be fraught with trouble," Roosevelt added, shaking his head. "The longer the delay from the delivery of the head to the body, the greater the risk for significant fetal hypoxia. Other complications for the fetus are things like brachial plexus injuries, clavicle fractures, or even death."

"And the mother," Caleb said, "can suffer consequences too. Like lacerations to her vagina or perineum, or a postpartum hemorrhage similar to the one you witnessed the other day."

"Studying this subject will now be so much easier," Annabel said. "Thanks so much." She turned to the counter and pointed. "I made fresh coffee."

"We'll help ourselves," Roosevelt said. "We'll round on patients, update the board, and then you're out of here. And, Caleb, you give report to the night team."

Annabel decided to go home wearing the hospital scrubs she had on, so she folded the nice clothes she wore for the funeral service that morning into her bag. She booked her ride home using her iPhone app, waited in the lobby, and was soon in the back seat of a minivan.

The driver, clean shaven and crisply dressed, fiddled with his GPS app and then pulled forward. A small picture of him and a woman was stuck on his vent and a shark's tooth dangled from the mirror.

He turned his head. "How are you doing today?"

"Not bad for a long day. How's the rush hour traffic on the interstate?"

"Moving like a stream down a mountain." He glanced into the rearview mirror. "Hospitals must be interesting places to work. Are you an X-ray technician or a nurse?"

Strike one, she thought.

"What if I told you that female medical students now outnumber male medical students?"

"That would be crazy. Then sooner or later, there will be a glut of family practitioners."

Strike two, she thought.

"Why do you think that?"

"Because females don't possess the physical strength of a man. For instance, to do orthopedics. Those surgeons ream rods into bones, like hips, or reset fractures. Stuff like that."

Strike three, she thought.

"Even if that were true, there are many other specialties."

"Yeah. Like heart surgeons. My uncle had open heart surgery and the *male* surgeon used a saw to cut through his sternum. You know ... the breastbone. A woman can't do that." He laughed. "At least I wouldn't want to be the patient under a woman coming at me with a power tool. She'll miss and split open my heart."

Annabel rolled her eyes. At least the updated rider service gave the customer a chance to leave a tip. She would have the last laugh then. She didn't equate his ignorance with his occupation, however, because his views probably represented a minority of men in any field outside of medicine. She took a deep sigh.

After a spell of silence, he turned on Annabel's street.

"So what nursing unit do you work on back at the hospital?" he asked. "You may take care of me someday."

"I hope so. I'm a medical student, so someday I'll be your

cardiothoracic surgeon. You'll be asleep with anesthesia and I'll be above you wielding my power tool."

He jerked his head around to look at her. After creeping along to her address, he stopped and she jumped out with her bag.

"Thanks," she said, closing the door. He totally lost his tongue as she stepped on the curb. In the staircase, she took two steps at a time to her apartment. She felt bad after saying those things to the driver, but apparently, she couldn't help it.

Annabel hung up her dress clothes and stood at her window. Over the last week, the usual squirrel had reinforced his nest in the front tree and it busily nibbled away at an acorn it held in its paws. She needed to buckle down for the night; the pressure to study and work on her Power Point presentation weighed down on her shoulders. Yet she was overdue for some exercise.

She donned running clothes and lightweight sneakers and hit the sidewalk. After passing the garden around the corner, she zipped down half the staircase, over the major road off the interstate, and to the path by the Ohio. She picked up speed but didn't fail to notice the spot where Bob had sat down while running with her and had picked up the tick which had made him ill. Next time she ran or walked the path, she thought, Oliver would be with her. Just thinking of the dog trotting at her side put a smile on her face.

The moon reared its majestic white ball in the sky rising up over the bridge from the Ohio to the Kentucky side. It looked like it was going to be full. Maybe Emmett was correct about the effect on pregnant women and the ward would be jumping overnight.

When she slowed her pace in front of her apartment house, she kept going up the block. Needing to eat something, she rationalized a trip to Pete's Café. She swore to herself that she'd work the rest of the night like a fiend.

She stood in front of the coffee shop counter and Pete turned around.

"Annabel, nice to see you. Which of your male friends will be joining you tonight?"

"I'm solo, Pete. Heck, you're making me wonder why I don't have any female friends."

"I'll ask the question, then. Why not?"

"Except for sleeping, ninety percent of the time I have is for medical school and whatever rotation I'm on. The people I hang with come from whoever's with me on the wards. Of which, there was one female who is gone now, but she couldn't befriend a woman if she tried. My most precious time is spent with either a boyfriend or a best friend." She eyed the menu on the blackboard. "Of course, you've met both of them."

"Sometimes I'm not clear which one is which, however."

She narrowed her eyes and twiddled with her hair. "Dustin's the cop. He's the boyfriend."

"Oh. Okay. I'll try to remember that. Ah-ha, he's the one who picks up the bill more often."

"That's him."

"So what can I get you?"

"A fried green tomato BLT and cole slaw and an iced tea with caffeine, which will give me zip for the work I'll be doing tonight."

"Coming right up darlin'."

"And Pete, may I borrow a pen and paper? I can scribble notes while I wait."

He reached under the counter. "Here, keep them instead of borrowing them."

Annabel selected a booth against the wood-paneled wall. She jotted the major topics of her grand rounds lecture and began scribbling in highlights of her topics that she already knew. As the waitress bused over her drink and food, she came up with more and more points and made notes of what she still needed to research. Finally, she bit into her sandwich.

"Annabel," Pete said. She glanced over while noticing she was the last person in his café. "We're closing in five minutes. I'd give you more time, but this place opens at 7 a.m., so I have a quick turnaround."

She looked at her iPhone. It was eight o'clock. "Sorry, Pete. Nothing like being absorbed with what I'm doing. The time also passed quickly because of your tasty sandwich. "Thanks a lot," she said after paying her bill and folding her notes.

"Come back soon."

Back at her apartment, she lined her notes next to her computer, ready to be integrated into slides. Taking a break, she texted Bob.

How was your day with Oliver?

He's the reason I went out two more times after our walk in the park this morning. And he's a hit around here. The schoolkids are going to be knocking at my door to give him biscuits!

Awwww. Sweet.

How were things on the ward?

OB is so unpredictable! Saw a complicated delivery ... obese patient with a 'shoulder dystocia' fetus. Good news is that the attending is teaching me like crazy.

Sounds interesting. I'll look that shoulder thing up.

I'll still see you on Sunday, right? We'll swap Oliver?

For sure. I'll miss him.

I'm ordering his DNA kit tonight.

You're busier than me. I'll do it.

Wow ... thanks. I'll reimburse you. Better go.

Hope all's well on OB tomorrow.

I'll keep you posted.

Annabel tossed her phone on the bed. She wondered how Dustin's day went. Yesterday had been a scare. She needed to trust the fact that he was a skilled police officer and totally adept at taking care of himself. After tucking her legs cross-legged on her bed, she grabbed a textbook, ready to study OB for another hour or two. She could catch up with Dustin in another day or two.

Exasperated, Dustin Lowe rubbed his hand along the side of his face and into the tight ringlets of hair from his ear to the top of his head. He stood on an exit ramp of the interstate way too long, taking a report and waiting for a wrecker to take away the two vehicles smashed up in an accident. Only one passenger had zoomed away in one of the two ambulances that had arrived and the other adults stood around giving their version of what happened. Probably a moot point, he figured, since the driver of the second car undoubtedly hit the vehicle in front of it. Most likely, in too much of a hurry to get off the interstate.

Although he was working a late shift, he already craved some caffeine.

This was his second vehicular accident in a few hours. He noted the rising full moon over the city, which was never a good sign. Based on his experience, with no data to back up his theory, people had some kind of circadian rhythm during a full moon. They stayed out more and were like non-thirsty vampires roaming the streets in cars and on foot. Getting hit by cars went for pedestrians as well. Which was why he made sure he stood well away from the occasional cars getting off of I-75, almost all with rolled down windows and drivers gawking at his accident scene.

He was parked next to the two damaged cars with the stop sign in front of his patrol car. He held his clipboard and figured most of the immediate paperwork was done. Soon he'd be back at the station to tie up the loose ends, but maybe he could meet Sean somewhere for coffee and a dinner break. His colleague was still ribbing him about getting more serious with Annabel. Sean sensed he was successful in putting the bug in Dustin's head and now used terms like "tying the knot."

"Exactly," Dustin had replied. "Marriage is a knot. You're laced up in a tight shoe and you can't flip sandals on or off anymore and wiggle your toes in the sand."

But Dustin knew better. He was just trying to dampen Sean's remarks. He *was* thinking about proposing to the medical student who'd gotten under his skin.

Dustin went to his vehicle, slid into the driver's seat, and placed his clipboard on the passenger seat. His police radio blurted out an incident in a shopping mall as he reached for his cell phone to call Sean. As he anticipated his buddy to answer on the third ring, a large thud sounded from the back as his vehicle jerked forward and slammed into the pole with the stop sign.

Dustin pitched forward as well. His chest slammed into the steering wheel. His momentum, as well as the car, stopped. In a momentary daze, his shook his head. Son of a bitch, he thought. His chest felt like it was on fire and his heart palpated in a flurry.

"Officer, are you all right?" A paramedic from the second ambulance yanked the cop car's door further open. His female buddy was right beside him.

Dustin nodded. "I'll be fine. Nothing like a punch to the chest. What the hell happened?" He swung his legs around and put them on the ground. The paramedics helped him out.

He gazed at the rear end of his vehicle, where another third car had rammed into him. "What the ...?"

The paramedic team looked at each other. "Emily and I need to check you out. We think you should go to the hospital."

Dustin grinned. "What for?"

"For the direct blow to your chest from the steering wheel which we bet on our next bacon and eggs that you suffered a blunt cardiac injury. You know, the force to your thoracic wall compressed your heart between your sternum and spine."

"I get it," Dustin said. "You're just doing your job." He glanced back inside the vehicle and picked up his phone on the floor. He put it to his ear. "Sean?"

"What the hell is going on there?"

"You or some other officers need to come over to my accident scene because there's been another one and they're taking me to the hospital."

Dustin read the paramedic's name tag. "Richard, which hospital?"

"University," he said while Emily went to get the stretcher.

"Sean, they're taking me to University. Don't worry, I got rear ended and my chest slammed into the steering wheel. It's not like I'm bleeding to death."

"Some of the worst things happen that are hidden," Sean said, "so just do as you're told."

"Who would have thought that you need to wear a seat belt when you're stationary in your car and not driving?"

The two paramedics placed the stretcher next to him.

"I'd better go, Sean. I'll update you from the hospital."

"I'm almost at your exit ramp. Don't worry about a thing."

The driver from the vehicle behind Dustin's stood watching the paramedics haul him off.

"You're sure you're okay?" Emily asked the man.

"Not a bone broken." He stood against the stretcher nervously rubbing his hands in front of Dustin. "I'm sorry, man. I can't believe I banged into a police car."

CHAPTER 26

Dustin answered one question after another in the ER from a skinny, medium tall doctor with a facial tic. The man proceeded to give him a fast, yet thorough, physical exam. He proceeded in a business-like manner and was glad to be of service for a team player on the city's "stellar police force."

Dustin rubbed his chin while a technician slapped EKG pads on his chest. The machine scratched out a squiggly tracing and the tech handed it to the doctor standing outside the drapes.

Dustin assumed that his heart had settled down after the ambulance ride. It no longer made jump starts like he was running sprints. He felt sore and uncomfortable all over his breast bone and on either side of it. Most people, he thought, are accustomed to bangs on their arms, legs, or other places on the bodies except for a direct hit to their chest. That area was like the door to someone's heart and a steering wheel had just tried to open his.

He observed the monitor to the side of the stretcher. The distinct wave form, which read ninety-nine percent, came from the clip probe on his finger. He had figured that out because when he took it off, the tracing disappeared. In any case, he realized that was an excellent score for *something*. He must be just fine.

The next person who hastened into his room was a woman with a navy shirt and an white tag announcing her position as a laboratory technician. She took his arm, no longer clad in his uniform, only a sleeve of a cotton gown, and began siphoning out blood from a vein for a cluster of vials. He sighed when she left and sank his head back in the pillow.

Now Annabel cluttered up his mind even more. He argued with himself whether he should call her and decided to not inform her of his circumstance. She would be home tonight after spending her whole day in an environment like this. Plus, she was none too happy when he told her about the diner shooting.

Another person came to mind. No way would he tell his dear mother, who lived forty miles away. Knowing her, she would jump into her car and be next to him by midnight.

The ER doctor came back in with another doctor. "This is Dr. Singh, a cardiologist," he said. "He has all the information gathered so far."

Dustin tolerated another history and physical with a smile. The man grimaced, which emphasized his heavy black beard. "I recommend an overnight admission so we can keep our eyes on you. Cardiac contusion presents as a spectrum of severity and you did take a forceful shove."

"Where do you think I fall as far as the spectrum you mention?"

"Apparently, you alluded to the paramedics you had some palpitations at the scene; they also noticed a short burst of an arrhythmia on their initial monitoring. Since then, there has been no new abnormal palpitations and I think the precordial pain you are experiencing is attributed to concomitant musculoskeletal injury. Also, your EKG shows only minor electrical changes. We'll monitor you overnight, I'll check the lab work we ordered, and run another EKG in the morning."

"Okay, but I wish I had a book to read."

Dr. Singh cracked a small smile.

After what seemed like hours, an orderly came in and wheeled him past the ER desk, where he picked up Dustin's chart.

"Thanks," Dustin said to the ER doctor. "By the way, my girlfriend is rotating through the hospital as a medical student."

"What's her name?"

"Annabel Tilson."

"She's a bright one. We'd love to have her here if she decides to go into ER medicine."

"I'll pass that on," Dustin said, and wondered what specialty his possible future wife would go into.

Annabel woke with a start and a scare. She pressed off the alarm clock, which fully snapped her out of an OB dream ... a dream of her having a baby, but she was plagued with the complications she witnessed on her rotation and doctors were manhandling her ... so much so that it felt like an ambush against her privacy. She shuddered. How did millions of women go through this experience of childbirth, with or without the sometimes necessary manhandling?

She put a one-cup coffee container into her machine and drank the result as she dressed. During her ride to the hospital, she said little to the morning driver. She didn't want any type of repeat conversation like last night. When she arrived on the OB floor, Emmett wheeled a cart by on his way to the supply room.

"Where is everyone?" she asked.

"They went back a little while ago to take over a C-section from the night team because they're leaving. You should probably go back there."

"Thanks, Emmett. I'd better hurry and change into scrubs."

"By the way, I heard from the ER group downstairs that your boyfriend showed up there last night. Nice to hear you have a boyfriend, but I hope he's okay."

"What? Are you sure?"

"You didn't hear from him? The ER doc said he is a cop. Is that true?"

Annabel reeled from the news. "That's him. Did they tell you anything else?"

"Nope, except that they put him in the hospital."

"Oh my God," Annabel said, thinking the worst. "He could've been shot two days ago. Now what?"

Annabel changed into scrubs. As soon as she got out of the surgery, she figured, she needed to find out where he is. She stepped out of the locker room and bumped into Stuart.

"How's it going, Stuart? Were you in on that C-section?"

Stuart nodded while Annabel noted he needed a smaller size scrub set; another person could fit into the ones he wore. "We started not too long ago. The baby's out, so you've missed that part. The fetus showed signs of distress in the labor and delivery room, so the senior resident took the mother back to the OR." He spoke softer. "I'll still be glad when this rotation ends. This is not my thing."

"Things have improved for me, Stuart. The chief resident isn't with us anymore and the attending is doing some teaching."

"You're lucky. Maybe I'll see you tomorrow morning. I'm going home to bed."

"Hang in there and get some sleep. And, by the way, I've been assigned to give the next grand rounds. I hope you don't miss it."

Stuart's face showed more expression than Annabel had ever seen on him. He stared straight at her. "A medical student? I'd be scared to death. How did you pull that off?"

"I fell into it."

"When you fall, you fall hard."

Annabel grimaced. "We'll see. More importantly, I'd better pass the OB exam."

"Goes for the two of us."

Annabel frowned, watching her brainy fellow colleague go into the male locker room. No matter what, Stuart always pulled off the top grades in the class. She donned blue booties over her sneakers and realized she was going back to her first C-section.

Annabel scurried into the OR. At the top of the table, Kristin Fleming had the patient under a general anesthetic and worked at a frantic pace since the case was winding down and she had lots of catch-up to do. Since a C-section's blood loss was double the amount of a normal vaginal delivery, Annabel noted the bloody lap sponges. The RN counted each one of them to make sure none were left in the patient and Dr. Thomas was on the side doing the newborn's assessment.

Dr. Harvey glimpsed at Annabel. "Not much going on here now. Too bad also that it's not an open abdominal case like you'll observe doing gynecology. Then your attending will interrogate you about pelvic anatomy." He looked carefully at the closure of the uterus, stepped back, and snapped off his gloves, which meant he was letting Caleb close the skin.

"Make a note," he continued to Annabel. "If that is the case, you may need to point out the ovaries, uterus, and fallopian tubes to your gynecology attending. Also the patient's bladder, cervix, sigmoid colon, round ligament, pelvic floor. You must be familiar with the vascular structures, including the branches of the internal iliac artery; the uterine artery, utero-ovarian artery, and the infundibulopelvic ligament. Shall I go on?"

"I'm thinking back to gross anatomy. Also the broad ligament, cardinal ligament, and sacrospinous ligament."

His eyes sparkled at her; he enjoyed anatomy so much. "It appears you're ready for that. Perhaps you could go tell this patient's husband that his new daughter and wife are doing fine. Last name is Moran. And follow up with this patient in recovery. Get her post-op labs, etc." He turned his head away and went to the chart.

Annabel went back out, looked at the board, and went into Room 6. A man in sweat clothes and crumpled hair sat forward on the recliner rubbing his thumbs together. His five-year-old daughter twirled in circles. She wore a dalmatian pajama set.

"Good morning," Annabel said. "Mr. Moran, your new baby girl is testing her lungs back there in the OR and your wife is fine."

He jumped up. "Hallelujah, I was getting worried." He stepped forward, and before Annabel could brace herself, he gave her a hug. He crouched to his daughter. "Teri, your sister is here."

The little girl hugged her father and stepped back. "I can help take care of her, Daddy."

"I bet you will."

"What's your name?" the little girl asked.

Annabel leaned over and the girl tapped the pocket of her scrubs.

"I'm a student doctor. Annabel Tilson."

"I'm going to be a doctor when I grow up."

"Really?"

Teri bobbed her head up and down.

"There will be a lot to learn, and remember to ask questions."

"What kinda questions?"

"Like what do muscles do?"

"Walk. And move," she shouted.

"What do your lungs do?"

"Breathe."

"I'm impressed. What does your heart do?"

"Love."

Annabel rose. "Wow. You are going to make a spectacular doctor."

The little girl's face beamed and she scooted off into her father's arms.

Annabel rushed out to the lounge where she typed in Dustin's name on the computer and found his room number. She was still clueless why he was admitted, but she knew it was a privacy violation to check his electronic medical record. He was, however, not admitted to the ICU, nor was he in a regular floor room. His room number fell under intermediate care with monitored beds.

Dr. Harvey paused as he made his way to the locker room. He pulled a twenty-dollar bill from his wallet. "The coffee pot is empty. Would you mind going downstairs and buying the three of us extra-appreciated coffees from the lobby?"

"No problem. What kind?"

"Three flavored cappuccinos or their special coffee of the day."

"Dr. Harvey, would it be a problem if I first stop by to see a patient that I know?"

"No," he said, waving his hand for her to leave.

Annabel scrolled her iPhone as she rode the elevator and looked for any message from Dustin since last night. There was nothing. She worried that something had happened bad enough to land him in the hospital, but also saddened that he didn't call. Was she really his "girlfriend?" Was he possibly seeing someone else? Her gut told her no; he was sincere and trustworthy. He was secure in his attitude towards his job but also with her. His personality reeked of composure and confidence. She admired his self-reliance and his thoughtfulness, and how many guys could attempt to keep an exotic pet and care for it with the same TLC that Dustin did? He was pretty amazing.

She stepped off the elevator, put her phone away, and landed outside his room, where she gently knocked.

"No need to knock," Dustin said. "Come in."

His jaw fell as she entered. Annabel put on the sternest expression she could. "Dustin Lowe, I'm furious you didn't tell me that you're here but, on the other hand, I'm ecstatic that you appear to be okay from whatever it was that you didn't tell me!"

Dustin covered his eyes with his hand and then peered out from under it slowly. Hooked up to the standard monitors, he was relegated to a thin hospital gown like her patients. "I didn't want to bother you last night. I was going to let you know today. Besides, the cardiologist hasn't been in yet this morning, so I don't have a clue if he's going to spring me."

"Cardiologist?!"

She sat beside him on the mattress. He brushed his hand along her long fingers and then wrapped his palm around them. "I'm sorry I didn't call, but you need to focus on your situation. Everything has been under control,

I promise. I was working an accident last night and was rear-ended by another vehicle while I was sitting in my car and catapulted forward into a pole. Paramedics chaperoned me in because of a cardiac contusion. They wanted to monitor me overnight, that's all."

She squeezed his hand. "There are two kinds of patients. The first kind screams bloody murder about pain if they get an invisible scratch on their skin. The second type of patient can have a limb fracture or a huge gash requiring twenty stitches and they barely complain."

He twisted his lips. "I'm the second one?"

She tapped his biceps. "You know damn well you're the second one." She leaned over and kissed him. He pulled her in and kissed her again quickly.

"So how bruised are you?"

He jockeyed up his gown and showed her.

"Ouch."

Annabel turned to the heart monitor and watched the tracing. Then she put her fingers on his pulse at his wrist. "Are you feeling any heart palpations or irregularity?"

"No, doctor."

She hit him again. "As far as I can tell, your heart rhythm looks good. But I'm no cardiologist."

"Yeah, what the heck. The heart serves two purposes anyway. One is to beat and one is to love. As long as I have most of the first, but all of the second." His eyes fell on hers and didn't deviate.

She glanced down; she could swear her cheeks were reddening. "Funny you should say that because an astute little girl just related that very idea to me."

"She must be very smart, like you."

"Let's get back to you," she said with a roll of her eyes. "But I do need to go because I'm almost due back on the ward. Text me as soon as you know something. You do have your phone, don't you?"

He nodded towards the night stand.

Annabel rose, leaned over, and hugged him. "I'm glad it wasn't worse. You could have gotten killed. Your week has been one thing after the other."

"You don't tell me everything, but I suspect your weeks are as bad."

She raised her eyelids and turned to leave. "You're right about that."

"By the way, you're a knockout in that white jacket."

CHAPTER 27

Annabel gripped a take-out container with the hot cups, and after going back upstairs, she snapped off one of the lids. Kristin walked in the lounge untying the blue mask that dangled off her neck.

"Mrs. Moran is all tucked into the recovery room. Your resident is still in there." She tilted her head over Annabel's cappuccino. "Mm. I could do with one of those."

"Had I known, I would have been happy to bring you one."

"I'll put coffee on. I can sit for a short time because, right now, no patients are due for an epidural or they already have one."

"What are your plans after residency?"

"I'm staying here at the University and I'll be an anesthesia attending. At least I can start paying off some bills."

"Good luck. You must like teaching."

"I do. And I notice you've been writing notes when you're in here besides reading from the OB manuals."

"Dr. Harvey gave me the task of preparing grand rounds for next week. I'm covering a few topics: physician burnout, medical errors, and maybe drug shortages. He wants it succinct and short, not like what the department would expect from a doctor like you."

Kristin gave her a questioning expression from the counter. The water stopped dripping and she poured.

"I guess you're wondering," Annabel said. "Ling was taken out of residency, so I was put in her place for the talk."

"Would you like a little help? I could fork over some information to you today, each time we get the chance."

"Would you? I'd be so appreciative."

"Drug shortages are a real and present danger. Remember I had to substitute a local anesthetic for an epidural? Those bullet points would fit into your talk very nicely and doctors in training should be aware of the problem."

Annabel became more excited about her lecture. "I'll be in here as much as I can. I'll even bring lunch up later."

"Okay, then, that makes two of us."

Annabel stirred her drink and heard a familiar voice.

"Well, did you get to see him?" Emmett asked, popping his head in.

"I sure did," Annabel replied.

"Is he okay?"

"His chest smashed into his steering wheel at an accident site. That man works a dangerous job. I think he'll be fine and, hopefully, the cardiologist is discharging him today."

Emmett's smile grew wider. "Happy to hear that."

"And, Emmett, thanks again for letting me know."

The orderly waved and ducked back out.

"Somebody dear to you?" Kristin asked.

"My boyfriend. He's a police officer. He didn't even tell me he was taken to the hospital last night. I found out through Emmett."

"Emmett's the first to find out about anything around here. Sounds like your boyfriend doesn't just protect the public. He shields you from worrying about him."

"That's his nature, I suppose. He'd do that with anyone he's dating."

"But you're the one he's chosen to date."

Annabel nodded and raised her beverage. Kristin reached over for a sugar packet.

"What's your status as far as dating?" Annabel asked.

"I'm married. Only for a year. Don't tell anyone, but I'm two months pregnant." Her face lit up like a young girl in front of a birthday cake.

"Congratulations. At least you know from working here what you're getting into." The two women giggled and Kristin leaned in.

"When the time comes, however, I'll steer clear of this place. I'm not baring my anatomy to my colleagues!" They laughed again.

"I don't blame you."

"Grab a notepad. Let's start working on your notes."

Annabel checked on Mrs. Moran's postop labs and found that her patient's hemoglobin barely budged from her preop value of 14 g/dl. It was a tribute to how skilled Dr. Harvey was as a surgeon and also how healthy her patient was.

Kristin may be having her baby months down the road at another hospital, Annabel contemplated, but there were many skilled attendings who stayed on board at teaching facilities. She thought back to her other rotations. Her psychiatry attending, Dr. Keeton, had been one of her favorites. But Annabel saddened when she thought of the woman's tragic fate, which would have never occurred except that she loved her specialty.

It was amazing all the things she had witnessed, the patients and physician teachers she worked with, and all the things she had learned since she began the third year of medical school. That realization warmed her heart.

Since Mrs. Moran was out of the recovery room, Annabel went back into Room 6. Teri sat in the big chair kicking her feet up and down and her father sat at the bottom of the bed.

"You just missed our baby girl," Mrs. Moran said.

Andy nodded and said, "Glad you had that mother-daughter bonding."

"And Teri held her."

"I bet your heart is welling up with that love you told me about earlier," Annabel said, looking at the little girl.

Teri stuck out her arms and widened them. "This much," she said.

Annabel turned her attention to her mother. "Dr. Harvey is most likely going to ask me to give a medical presentation on you, Mrs. Moran. You were previously in the OR, so I didn't yet do a history and physical on you. Do you mind if I ask you questions?"

"Not at all, especially since my pain is still under control since the recovery room."

"Thanks to Dr. Fleming and the nurses."

Two hours later, Dr. Fleming tugged at Annabel's coat sleeve in the hallway. "I can run downstairs and bring us back lunch, if you'd like."

Annabel glanced up and down the corridor looking for Dr. Harvey and Dr. Gash. "That would be perfect because then I could run over and see my boyfriend, who hasn't told me a thing."

The two women wasted no time. Annabel trotted down the empty upstairs corridor into Dustin's room. His curly hair was more kempt than before and he wore his uniform.

"I apologize," he said. "People have been coming and going and only now I was going to text you."

"They're discharging you?! I wish I could have hitched a ride to your place and brought you back street clothes to change into."

"No problem. No one will mess with me on my way home."

"The uniform doesn't seem to afford you any extra protection."

He shrugged his shoulders. "Maybe so." He closed the gap between them and wrapped his arms around her; she hugged him back and closed her eyes.

"What did the cardiologist say?"

"He said my heart checks out fine and there is no sequela except for the bruising and pain to my chest wall … for which he's prescribed pain pills."

"So you better take it easy."

"He wrote an absentee prescription as if I'm a little kid who needs to present it to my teacher so I can take off from school. Actually, seriously, he did, but I spoke earlier with Chief Erickson about the doctor's orders. I'm officially off for the whole weekend, not just Sunday."

Annabel smiled and wiggled her head. "Doesn't mean you can do anything exertional."

"Oh, I get it. Shucks. But it does mean we are going to kick back on Sunday. Whatever time you can parcel out for me."

"Besides the work I have to do, which includes studying *and* working on a presentation, we can chill together. Don't forget that my new dog is included in this plan too, and our two pet species are set for an introduction." She put her hand on her hip and pursed her lips. "And by the way, how are you getting home?"

Dustin pointed behind her. She turned to see a paunchy, middle-aged man wearing an officer's uniform, the same as Dustin's.

"Annabel, meet my partner, Sean. Sean, meet Annabel."

Annabel had met Dustin's last partner, Edgar Banks, but not Sean.

Sean extended his hand to Annabel. "Nice to finally meet you. Now I'll be able to visualize you when he speaks about you over diner dinner."

"Or breakfast, or lunch," Dustin said.

Annabel laughed and twisted her mouth. "You two have more interesting things to talk about than me."

Sean raised his bushy eyebrows. "You are …"

"All right," Dustin butted in. "Guy talk needs to stay in a safety deposit box shared between two guys."

Sean shrugged and hooked his thumb in his belt.

A nurse came in, followed by an orderly with a wheelchair. The RN handed Dustin a stack of paper she went over with him in advance. The orderly motioned Dustin into the chair.

Dustin looked up at his partner. "Don't worry. I'm not that frail. It's hospital policy to transport patients to the front door. They're covering their asses in case I trip on a floor tile."

"My," Annabel said, "you learned a lot while you were in here for one day."

They cluttered the corridor and the elevator and Annabel stepped out from the elevator on the OB floor.

"Hey," Dustin said before the door snapped shut, "we still haven't finished watching *Gone with the Wind*."

"We can finish it on Sunday!"

Kristin's arm was extended on the table, her head bent as she fiddled with her right topaz earring. For the OB team, rounds were finished and the day as good as done. Annabel's time with the anesthesia resident had proved fruitful and she extrapolated exactly what she would use for her "drug shortage" slides. Kristin was so helpful, however, that she continued talking even though they both could go home.

"The FDA plays a big part in this," the senior resident said. "They are the gatekeepers, protecting the public from potentially unsafe drugs products. They are the ones who discover a company's noncompliance with current good manufacturing practices or cGMPs. The reason may be because the company in question owns manufacturing equipment that becomes antiquated, or a sudden loss of personnel overseeing compliance issues, or a host of other reasons. In other words, they may not be intentionally noncompliant."

Annabel nodded. The FDA was a superpower and important to the public.

"Or, a manufacturing company may decide to close down a certain facility due to business reasons, or a subcontractor supplying products to the pharmaceutical manufacturer has a problem on their end. Think about it. What if the factory of the supplier of the local anesthetic bottle is hit by a hurricane? Even though the local anesthetic can still be produced, its availability will grind to a halt."

"Causing the cascade of problems we must deal with," Annabel said.

"At least my specialty has the American Society of Regional Anesthesia and Pain Medicine and they keep us current on drug shortage problems and suggest other methods of pain relief."

Annabel sat up tall. "Thanks again. I'm going home soon."

"And what's going on with your boyfriend?"

"He's home. We don't live together. The cardiologist instructed him to take the weekend off."

"Living together can have its advantages. My husband and I did it for a year before we married."

Annabel admitted to herself … she liked her own independence. She was growing closer to the police officer. Living together was something she hadn't considered, and with her hours, and with *his* shifts, that would probably be a certifiable psychotic idea.

It was so perfectly quiet in the lounge that Annabel procrastinated and figured she would work a few more minutes. Kristin had left. Dr. Harvey and Dr. Gash were gone too.

Pam came in and scribbled something on the board behind Annabel's back.

"Where are the night docs?" Annabel asked.

"Down in the ER." Pam cleared her hoarse vocal cords and went into the restroom.

That wraps it up, Annabel thought. Kristin had been so helpful that all she had to do was make some fancy slides at home with pictures, type in the bullet points, and her lecture would be almost ready. By tomorrow, it would be, she promised herself, and then she would have a few days to review it and be armed for any questions. Or at least some questions. She counted on Dr. Harvey bailing her out if someone stumped her with an impossible query.

She closed her binder and packed her bag. At the round table where she'd been sitting, she ditched her iced tea cup and napkin, and brushed off cookie crumbs. Looking down at her scrubs, she decided to wear them home and not change. It was easy to make a habit of that. If the driver tonight asked her a sexist question, she would change the subject. Inside the locker room, she folded her blouse and pants, and overstuffed her backpack, ready to go home.

Since she had off on Sunday, tomorrow, Saturday, would be the last day of her first week. She sighed with uneasiness because then there was only one week of obstetrics left before veering off into gynecology. At this point, was she as prepared as she should be as far as her test-taking?

She glanced at the board and saw Emmett's name down in the corner where the RNs usually noted which orderly was helping out. Pam had not written in the night orderly, but maybe he was running late.

At the nurses' desk outside the room, Annabel paused with her back pack clinging to her shoulders. She tore open a peppermint from the candy dish on the counter and popped it in her mouth as she contemplated. The day had turned out not to be as exciting as it had started. There just wasn't much obstetric volume and, for the only afternoon delivery, one of the RNs had chased her out of a room in favor of a "real obstetrician." Dr. Gash stayed oblivious to her absence, so she left it at that.

She dragged herself down the hallway, her eyes glued on the lobby, when a door flew open and Emmett tripped over an IV pole he was pushing. He righted himself and his bulging eyes fell on Annabel.

"She needs help! Come on!"

Annabel's anxiety rose in her throat and her pulse quickened. She didn't need board certification in obstetrics to figure out that her skills, or lack thereof, were needed. A young woman swayed back and forth on the bed inside like waves were rocking her in a boat. Her eyes were fastened on the skull of a head trying to exit her genital canal.

Annabel's legs were frozen to the floor.

"She needs you!" Emmett exclaimed.

"Me?"

Annabel and Emmett jerked their heads up and down the barren corridor, and then their eyes met. Yup, it was up to her.

CHAPTER 28

Annabel and Emmett sprang into the room. Annabel grabbed an OB delivery kit from the cabinet above the sink. Emmett scooted the rolling tray table near the end of the bed.

She ripped open the package on the table, exposing the drapes and shiny instruments. Emmett pulled the adhesive off another packet and Annabel rushed her arms into the blue gown and then gloved. The orderly tied her up in the back.

"I'm Annabel," she said, remembering an important point previous attending doctors had told her: "See one, do one." Besides the shoulder dystocia delivery, she had witnessed one full vaginal delivery from the beginning to the end. She better recall every last detail.

The woman gripped the side of the bed like she held the bow rail of the sinking *Titanic*. Her face grimaced with pain and she gritted her teeth. Perspiration matted her hair around her forehead and, for a second, she locked her imploring stare on Annabel.

Spared of dealing with the amniotic sac, Annabel saw that Mother Nature had ruptured it already. She put her hand over the crowning baby's head and it delivered nicely. Fumbling with inexperience, she lightly suctioned the baby's nose and scanned all around the infant's neck. She would stroke if the cord was wrapped around and between the head and shoulders, but the neck was clear.

Then her heart banged against her chest and her hand trembled. What if ... what if ... the baby had shoulder dystocia? She would be at a loss, or Emmett would need to assist her with the McRoberts maneuvers, which her team members had performed. However, she remembered a big risk factor for shoulder dystocia from her studies. Her patient was not obese, so, most likely, she need not worry about it.

In a flash, a shoulder went down and a shoulder went up, and a whole new human being slithered out.

Annabel placed the newborn baby girl with her mother and a smile of sheer joy replaced the woman's pained expression.

For Annabel, her dread was replaced with a pure magical moment. She clamped the cord.

"Emmett, how about cutting the cord?"

The imposing man widened his smile. His adventure with Annabel just kept getting better. He did as she asked.

"Can you please hunt down Pam, the RN?"

Emmett took off.

"I'm Linda," the woman said. A tear hung on the inside of her eye and she left it there with pride.

The baby's color looked rosy and she wiggled her little fists around in the air. No worries there, Annabel thought. "What's her name?"

"Wilma."

"Welcome, Wilma."

"What on earth?" Pam said as she rushed in with Emmett at her heels. "I'll page the senior resident."

"Can you first draw cord blood?"

Pam nodded.

With a curved clamp, Annabel held the umbilical cord, and ever so gently, gave a bit of traction. The placenta slithered out into a round pan.

She felt drained but nearly tearful like Linda.

After being summoned, the night resident came in to take over the minor remaining details and was impressed with Annabel's accomplishment. Before Annabel could leave, however, she needed to document the delivery. She felt like a senior resident performing such a chore, one she never imagined doing as a student.

She left the room different from when she went in: revitalized yet fatigued; ecstatic yet blue. She had done it. If she decided not to go into obstetrics, that might be the only baby she ever delivered.

She grabbed the patient's chart from the desk, but on second thought, placed it on the counter top for the time being. There was someone she really needed to see before leaving.

Annabel waited patiently for a few minutes and then Emmett strolled out of the male locker room.

"I'm sorry I dragged you into that delivery," he said, looking down at his shoes. "It's just that nobody else was around."

"Emmett, you had no choice. Thank you for grabbing someone ... I happened to be handy. I am so glad you yanked me in there. We made a great team. Can you believe it? We delivered a baby!"

He smiled wide enough to expose his chipped tooth. "I guess we did a decent job, Dr. Annabel."

"Not too shabby, Emmett. And we stayed over beyond our hours of duty. We both could have been out of here a long time ago."

"No gym for me tonight. This evening was enough excitement for one night."

"Me too. Good night, Emmett."

She burst with excitement as she rode home in a bright yellow Uber car in back of a woman with a ponytail sticking out of the hole of her cap, but all she really wanted was to call Bob and spill out the details. That would freak out her driver, she thought, so she stayed clammed shut.

Annabel shoved everything on the kitchen counter after running up the stairs as fast as she could. She whipped out her iPhone and called Bob.

"Hey," he said.

She had a difficult time composing herself, so she grabbed a deep breath and then puffed out quickly. "You are not going to believe it." The words raced out of her mouth.

Bob's interest piqued. "Did something happen while you were running?" He took a short cut through the apartment's pool area after Oliver's last walk, but stopped short, dropped down on a lounge chair, and held the phone with his free hand.

"Nope. I just got home late. It was like a female seal slipping out of the ocean and squirming onto a rock and I caught her! A baby!"

"What? Are you telling me you delivered a baby? The resident actually let you do that?"

"No. I mean yes. I mean nobody, nurses or the night team, was around. One minute I walk into this lady's room where she's in a pain score of eleven out of ten and her abdomen has this wave moving on top like a basketball is moving to her vagina. I went in there to clean white sheets on her bed and left behind the dirtiest linen imaginable."

"Wow. That is crazy. So what was it like? What did you do ... exactly? Was the baby okay?"

"There were no complications. Mother Nature took care of most of it."

"Still. Don't be so humble. You knew what you were doing. What about the afterbirth and all that? Details, please. What if I have to do the same thing before I even start OB? What if I have lousy residents like what happened to you the first few days?"

Bob leaned back and Oliver sat politely next to him, so he put the leash loop on the end of the chair. He listened attentively while she told him the whole story of her emergency obstetric care.

"I may not do that again," she said, "ever."

"Wow. In a way, you took a big risk. People are so litigious these days, but you had no choice. You may need to have an attorney write a new law for us - a 'Good Samaritan medical student law' protecting us from liability if unintended consequences befall us from rendering our assistance." He laughed at his legal jargon.

Annabel chuckled as well. "My poor dad. Maybe I should ask him for more money for legal counsel."

"I know. While you're at it, why don't you ask him if he wants to be a behind-the-scenes dog owner of Oliver and support his expenses?"

"Ha. I'd better not and I'd better get off the phone. My whole night is shot and I'm due on the wards tomorrow morning. One more day doing OB before I pop by your place and pick up Oliver."

"See you Sunday, but let me know tomorrow what your attending thinks about what you did."

"Okay, later."

Saturday morning, Dustin woke up with a loud grumble and made the analogy of what he perceived in his chest to a hangover. The physical discomfort on his chest wall was not from drinking alcohol and suffering a day-after effect to his head, but a steering wheel's day-after insult to his sternum. He grimaced as he swung his feet to the side and pushed off from his bed.

He contemplated his weekend off ... the only secondary gain of his stationary car accident. Not that he minded his job, but the weekend would serve a useful purpose. He would rest like they told him, however, he was going to implement his plan - his idea to ask Annabel to marry him. With no uncertainty, he cared for her more than any female in his life before. He must be in love with her; otherwise, he did not know what love was.

He washed and dressed and went downstairs gingerly. "Good morning,

Solar."

The bird bobbed his head when Dustin entered the kitchen. "What's your problem?" he chattered.

"I'm hurting, Solar, which is my problem. Be a good bird, be polite, and put up with me today. And for your information, I'm making an important purchase this morning."

Dustin spooned instant coffee into a cup, added water, and slipped it into the microwave. He popped a nonsteroidal anti-inflammatory pill into his mouth and chased it down with water. As much as he could, he was going to avoid the narcotic prescription sitting next to the fruit bowl. Every once in a while, however, he needed to pull a deep breath, and that was no fun. No fun at all.

He looked out the kitchen window to his small front yard. The sky was partly cloudy and the trees gently swayed. It would be a nice morning for his one and only excursion; a trip to the mall. He hated shopping, but this would be different. He would buy an engagement ring as fine and polished as Annabel.

"Alexa," he said, "what's the temperature?"

"Alexa," Solar mimicked, "what's the temperature?"

The Echo Dot device voice control became mixed up with the two questions asked one after the other. "I'm sorry, I don't know that answer."

"Solar," Dustin said, "let *me* ask the question."

"What's your problem?" Solar asked Dustin.

"For Pete's sake, Solar, butt out."

"Butt out."

Dustin shook his head. "I've created a monster."

At least Dustin had some knowledge about engagement rings. Searching the internet for reputable information about diamonds had proved fruitful. Advice he received from Sean helped too. More than that, he wished Sean could accompany him to render his opinion, but he was pulling an eight-hour day.

He strolled into the store with a generic title, "The Diamond Jewelry Store," which was a misnomer since they sold all types of jewelry. The see-through display cases were meticulously clean. Not a smudge on them.

When the salesperson came over, he thought he needed to speak the "language" of diamonds so he didn't appear to be a pushover for a quick sale. He at least knew about color, carat weight, clarity, and cut.

A very shapely female with puffy red lips headed his way from one aisle over inside the maze of cabinetry.

"May I help you?" she asked. "You have 'engagement ring' stamped all over your forehead."

The woman was so distracting, he had to rein in his thoughts about her figure. His visit here was all about Annabel and he was dead certain about his choice in women.

"Smart guess," he replied.

"How much would you like to spend?"

"My buddy told me the cardinal rule. I should spend two months of my salary on my girl's ring."

"The trend anymore is to be flexible in what you can afford. However, the average cost that men pay is five thousand dollars."

Dustin shrugged his shoulders. It would depend more on what he liked rather than settling on her suggested price of five grand. She motioned him to the end of the counter and pulled two diamond rings out and set them on a white velour piece of material. He listened to her sales pitch and noted the differences in the two rings. However, the aching in his chest ramped up and he silently scolded himself for not bringing his next pain pill with him.

The beautiful brunette noticed his discomfort. "Can I get you some water?"

"I have muscle soreness after an accident yesterday, so I can't spend a long time deciding. Just bad timing, that's all."

She smiled like she sealed the deal and made the sale, took a step, and pulled out another ring. "She'll love this 1.3 carat oval diamond set in a gold band. It's a beauty at a little over five thousand dollars and its 4Cs are listed on the tag. You won't need to look at one more."

Dustin turned it around in his hand, held it to the light, and asked her to put it on her own finger. "She has long, trim fingers like yours. Do you think it will fit her?"

"If it doesn't, bring it and your fiancée back in, and we'll adjust it. You won't be sorry. This is one of my favorites."

Dustin doubted if Annabel had the same taste as the woman, but to him, it was a pretty ring. He would never know unless he sprang it on her.

"I'll take it," he said.

The next morning, Annabel ran ten minutes late from a weekend traffic diversion that her driver had not anticipated. As she approached the obstetric nurses' station, heads glanced her way and she made a full stop. Emmett placed his hand behind her and tapped her backpack. She reciprocated and lightly put her hand on his back. They were now bonded because of a hair-raising situation they had handled together.

"Since I've worked here," one of the nurses said, "you are the first medical student to deliver a baby. Which means in the last seven years."

Caleb peered up from a chart and gave her a warm smile. "Did you experience a euphoria with your accomplishment? Maybe you've decided to go into obstetrics?"

She opened her mouth to speak, but Dr. Harvey showed up in the doorway behind the desk.

"It's Annabel Tilson," he said, "baby-catcher extraordinaire."

Kristin walked out from the supply room. "You did it without the benefit of anesthesia for the patient! You're going to put me out of business. How did you perform such a feat anyway?"

Annabel clutched the strap to her backpack and grinned. "You all, I just did what I watched Dr. Gash do. Isn't that how this medical school thing works? Teach one or see one and then *do* it?"

The physicians exchanged glances, leaving Annabel out.

"That refers to a student watching someone start an IV and then trying it themself," Caleb said.

"Or watching someone do an ear exam with an otoscope and then doing it," Kristin said.

"Or watching your new medical team devour a box of donuts and then jumping in yourself," Roosevelt said seriously.

Annabel stood dumbfounded and narrowed her eyes.

Roosevelt thrust his hand to the top of his head and then leaned forward to hide his smile. When he straightened up, his face beamed. "We're yanking your chain."

"Nice work, Annabel," Caleb said. "I couldn't have pulled off what you did."

"And I hope I never have to," Kristin said. "Congratulations."

Annabel shook her head and chuckled. "You are a tough bunch. You had me worried." She glanced at Emmett. "Of course, I couldn't have done it without the excellent help I had in the room."

"I just did what you told me," he said, modestly looking to the floor.

"No. You go beyond your job description, Emmett, and you're an asset on this floor."

"I'll second that," said one of the nurses.

"I think the whole medical staff feels the same way about you, Emmett," Dr. Harvey said. He scanned everyone's faces. "Now let's quit patting ourselves on the back and get this stellar team to work."

CHAPTER 29

When Annabel finished her scut work, and before rounds, she hastened over to the newborn nursery. Thinking about the baby she had delivered, she crossed her fingers. Just because the infant's first few minutes of life had appeared normal, it didn't mean she cleared a thorough evaluation by the pediatricians. Those doctors were wizards at detecting abnormalities. But, hopefully, baby Wilma was just fine and the only baby born the last week with a problem was Bonnie Barker's Samantha.

Annabel felt encouraged by the family dynamics when Bonnie and Tony left the hospital with their baby girl. Although Bonnie had incurred two medical problems during her stay, the two adults' relationship had solidified during her hospitalization. The baby was in suitable and loving hands. With diligent medical care, maybe her life with osteogenesis imperfecta was going to be a minor inconvenience.

Annabel peered through the squeaky clean window at the bassinets. Some babies were asleep, some were squirming in their blankets, and one cried like he wanted to break out of the place. She rapped on the window for the nurse's attention.

A bespectacled RN in vibrant scrubs pushed open the door. "Who are you looking for?"

"Baby Wilma, born yesterday."

"You're not that medical student who delivered her, are you?"

"Yes. Uh-oh, is she okay?"

"She sure is. She's a perky little thing. Dr. Thomas said maybe more medical students should deliver babies. He's not here right now, but he'd probably give you five stars for your accomplishment."

"That is very kind of him, however, the delivery was an emergency and I only acted as an accessory to Mother Nature. Mom was healthy, knowledgeable, and mature about the whole thing." The two women still cluttered the doorway. "May I see her?"

The woman nodded and Annabel followed her in between the back row of infants. Annabel noted the card at the foot of baby Wilma's basket ... her birth weight a hearty 9.7 pounds. Her eyes fell on the swaddled infant, she interlocked her fingers, and put her hands up to her mouth. The baby was precious, with scanty brown hair, vibrant eyes, and full cheeks. Her whole body fidgeted with movement and her feet kicked within the blanket. Because her tiny lips moved as well, it was like she already wanted to form words.

"May I?" Annabel asked, nodding towards Wilma.

"I'm sure her mom wouldn't mind."

Annabel picked her up securely in both arms, stared at her attentive eyes, and lingered while she implanted the memory. Certainly obstetrics has pluses and minuses, she thought, and delivering a baby was a real kick. She had something to do with this little bundle of innocence and the result couldn't have been better. The nurse stepped away and Annabel slid her fingers over the baby's cheek.

"You won't be forgotten, baby Wilma."

With Saturday on the ward over, and the first week of obstetrics behind her, Annabel only had the second final week of obstetrics to finish before her two weeks on gynecology. On Monday, her schedule would change to night call and the most significant event would be her grand rounds presentation, which had been moved up to Monday morning.

With Kristin's help, she was quite prepared for the lecture. Dr. Harvey also promised to be close by, "co-present" with her, and answer any difficult questions that might arise from residents, medical students, or other attendings.

Standing at her front window, Annabel waited to see what dynamics would take place in her favorite tree. Her "buddy" squirrel bolted upright in her nest as she realized a fellow squirrel was darting up the tree. The intruder almost reached the periphery of the nest when her tree rodent decided to face off with him and jumped out of her bedding. The chase was on down the tree. It was fun to witness such entertainment right in front of her, she thought as she watched the silky animal protect her territory. They were hard-working and interesting critters to watch and, unlike most mammals, they could descend a tree head-first.

The builder of the nest succeeded in running off squirrel number two and picked up an extra twig on her way back up. She stuffed it into her bedding and then curled inside. Annabel turned back to her desk and settled on a plan. One more overview of her lecture tonight, and one more sometime tomorrow, and that should take care of it. By Monday, she should be as familiar with it as much as possible. Then, it would be a question of dampening her nerves and getting over the fear of speaking to a large group. In the meantime, she would need to keep that worry out of her mind. No sense in agonizing over it until the presentation time was close at hand.

She read the first half of the lecture and referred to the hidden Power Point notes below each slide, making sure she had the information memorized. For a break, she texted Bob.

"Hey there. Would 8 a.m. be okay for me to pick up Oliver?"

"Sure thing," he responded. "I can bring him to you if you'd like."

"It's up to you. If you bring him here, I'll spring for coffee or breakfast at Pete's."

"I'll be there, at your place first, to drop off his gear."

"Super."

Next, she texted Dustin.

"Hey, Dustin. How about I come over tomorrow late in the morning? However, I plan on going home before dinner. I'm giving a presentation on Monday morning, which is normally given by a resident or an attending."

"Congratulations beforehand. See you then, but I was hoping I could take you to a late dinner. So, instead, why don't we go for an early dinner?"

"Hmm..."

"I'll bribe you. How about the restaurant that bakes that carrot cake you liked?"

"You're on. Don't forget, I'm bringing my new dog Oliver."

"Any dog of yours is a dog of mine. Can't wait to meet him."

She read the other half of her lecture, shut down her computer, and curled up in bed. The next two days would be polar opposites ... fun and terror.

Annabel pulled on cream-colored cargo pants and a summery short-sleeved blouse. Since she was skipping a run, she chose casual sneakers that looked like new. She left small amber earrings in her earlobes, but took extra care with fresh makeup. Lastly, she squeezed a hair shine product on her fingers and massaged it along the front of her hair. It felt great to doll up after being less meticulous about her appearance all week.

As another preparation for Monday, she loaded her lecture on a flash drive and placed it on the kitchen counter. A knock sounded on the door and, wearing an anticipatory smile, she flung the door open for Bob and Oliver.

Like the color of the resin in her earrings, Oliver's big eyes spoke to her with a cheeriness that could not be resisted. His tail swooshed along Bob's leg and his toenails clicked up and down on the landing.

"Oliver, hey, buddy!" She crouched down and wrapped her arms around his neck. "So much for not letting your hair cling to my clothes."

As she let go, Oliver managed to swipe his tongue on her forearm. She peered up at Bob. "He's more than we hoped for, isn't he?"

"I agree. He's something else. And you ..." He stared longer than he should at her.

"Oh, sorry. I took an extra minute on myself this morning."

"And I'm scrubby for a Sunday breakfast."

"No you're not. No one looks as good as you wearing that tapered haircut."

"You're just being nice." He handed her the leash. "You take him inside while I go back to my car and fetch his things."

Annabel unsnapped him from the leash and Oliver bounded inside. When Bob reappeared, his arms were full. Annabel rummaged through a duffel bag, filled a bowl with water, and placed it below the kitchen window. Bob unpacked the rest of the items and stuffed the food bag in the corner.

"I'll buy dog food this week," she said, "then we'll both have our own bags."

"Soon we'll be in a pattern and Oliver's two homes will be second nature."

"And I'll keep him all week, Bob. The situation is perfect. He'll be with me during the day. I can still sleep off my night calls and walk him in the morning, afternoon, and before I leave late in the day. You can finish your week of internal medicine without any distractions."

Oliver lapped up some water and Annabel nodded to the door. "Come on, let's head up the block."

"If it's okay with you, the weather is mild enough to sit outside and we can bring Oliver."

"We both like that plan."

Bob reached into the bag he brought with him. "This is a must have for an Oliver dog mess." He stuffed a small plastic bag into his hip pocket.

Outside, Annabel slowed. "Oliver's peeing on the tree trunk of my pet squirrel, who happens to be my source of entertainment." She pointed upward. "She's made a thick brambly nest and she has a fast reaction to unwanted visitors."

"I rarely enjoy a wildlife view from my place, unless I consider kids."

"Oliver is your obvious entertainment now, as he will be for me." He trotted right alongside her and sniffed at cracks between the sidewalk blocks of cement.

At Pete's, Annabel fastened Oliver's leash handle around the wrought-iron fence and they chose a table.

"What'll you two have this morning?" The waitress spied Oliver and put her hand through two vertical fence spires and petted him.

"Scrambled eggs, orange juice, and two pancakes," Annabel said.

"Make that two." Bob smiled at Annabel. The young woman had put down her notepad and was awestruck with Oliver.

A customer left Pete's and took a double take. "Annabel, is this dog yours?"

Her downstairs neighbor grinned and joined the waitress in petting their dog. Oliver took one step back and sat. His tail brushed slowly on the sidewalk. He loved every minute of the attention.

"Meet my friend Bob," Annabel said. "And Bob, this is Travis."

Travis gripped Bob's hand and then put it back on Oliver.

"Excuse me," the waitress said. "I'll be back with those orders."

"I'm surprised she heard them," Bob said when she left.

"How's your college semester coming along?" Annabel asked her neighbor.

"Not bad. So will I be seeing this furry fellow once in a while?"

"Yup, and his name is Oliver."

The lanky-limbed student shook the dog's paw. "If ever you need a pet sitter ... ."

"Thanks, Travis, I'll remember that."

"Nice meeting you," he said to Bob and glanced back at Oliver after crossing the street.

When the waitress came back and served them, she peeled herself away without petting Oliver. "I must stay away," she mumbled over her shoulder. "No changing my mind that I can't own a dog."

"Who knows?" Annabel said. "With Oliver getting around and causing a stir, there may be an uptick in dog adoptions."

"Wouldn't that be a blessing?"

Annabel nodded and salted the scrambled eggs. "This looks delicious." She took a side glance at Oliver, who clearly wanted a taste test, and peered back at Bob. "Mornings don't get much better than this."

"I agree."

"You feeling up to going back tomorrow?"

"As ready as I can be, I think. However, I sure hope my chief resident does lets me peel away to attend your lecture."

"All you can do is ask. It will be in the OB lecture room at 8 a.m."

"You nervous?"

"Not as much as I'm going to be in the morning. At this late stage, I'm thinking the last best preparation for tomorrow will be to get a full night's sleep. That probably goes for you too."

"So true. And this breakfast, I can't figure which tastes better ... the eggs or the pancakes."

"And I'm treating."

"No you're not. We're Dutch treat, remember."

"That arrangement is not set in marble. I'm paying this morning because my heart's in it. Consider it a gift from Oliver."

Bob turned his head to Oliver. "Do you see how clever she is using you as an excuse? You're going to have to put up with her the next few days."

"We're going to get along today like a butterfly and a wildflower," Annabel said as she let Oliver hop into her SUV. She intermittently glanced in the rearview mirror as she drove to Dustin's. It was one of life's pleasures to watch the glee on a dog's face as it pointed its muzzle towards an open window.

"Oliver and I are almost at your place," Annabel said after reaching Dustin with a hands-free call.

"I'll be outside waiting for you."

She pulled into the driveway, where Dustin popped up from the front step and waved. It was partly cloudy and slightly humid and the curls on Dustin's head were extra tight. She opened the door and quickly fastened Oliver. "Come on, there's another human I want you to meet."

Dustin approached them with a full smile. "Oliver, I've heard all about you. You are one handsome boy!" He let the dog sniff his hand and then ruffled the back of his neck.

He motioned if he could hold Oliver's leash and Annabel handed it over. "I always wanted my own police dog on the job, but many stations can't afford them. They aren't cheap." They began walking absentmindedly along the street curb as Oliver researched the grass.

"Are we going to finish *Gone with the Wind?*" Annabel asked. A sly grin crept over her lips.

"Sure. Nothing like the classics. Plus, weren't you going to get a heads up on Miss Scarlett and her housemaid's delivery of Melanie's baby?"

"Actually, I think I have the characters beat."

"Seriously? Are you telling me that during the last week, you helped out with a delivery?"

Annabel tilted her head and smiled. "I *did* the delivery. It was awesome. I happened to be at the right place at the right time. Now, if I'd had a bad outcome, I would have never wanted to stumble into it. No one was around when this patient's infant was at the doorstep, so to speak, but it all worked out."

"That's crazy. Congratulations. I guess we're so busy that we sometimes don't communicate the most dramatic aspects of our week with phone calls or texting."

"Which is understandable." She faced him. "Don't forget I can't stay over tonight because of the lecture I'm giving in the morning."

"I assumed that. But you're still letting me take you out later, right?"

"I'm wearing Sunday-like clothes for our date."

"Which look great on you, by the way."

She glanced at the front door. "How's Solar going to react to Oliver?"

"Let's go find out."

Dustin swung the door open and they trotted in straight to the kitchen. Oliver wiggled back and forth with his nose to the hardwood floor.

From above, Solar spotted the dog and let out a screech. He bobbed his head like he was going to hammer on Oliver's head with his beak. The parrot screeched again and the dog jumped back and eyed the strange bird, which was inside the house instead of outside where birds belonged.

Oliver rumbled out a low "woof."

Annabel squatted and put his face in her hands. "It's okay, Oliver. It's only a bird."

"Hush, Solar," Dustin said. "Oliver is a dog like you see on television. He's your friend."

Solar stopped bobbing but pranced across his perch. "Friend."

"Oliver. You can call him 'Oliver.'"

"Oliver," Solar mimicked but screeched again.

"That was for good measure, wasn't it, buddy? You're making sure Oliver knows who's boss. You're the top bird. Don't worry."

Annabel laughed and petted Oliver, who finally peeled his eyes away from the parrot and nestled against her.

Dustin kept from laughing. "Can I fix you a sandwich or anything?"

"No thanks. I just had a big breakfast and I'll hold off until we go to this restaurant you're keen on."

"That's a deal." He put his arms around her shoulders and they both kissed. "We've had an exciting week. Want to relax on the couch and resume the movie?"

"Exciting? I wouldn't characterize your concussion as exciting."

"All right then, Dr. Tilson."

"But the relaxing part sounds wonderful."

Dustin dumped a bag of kettle corn popcorn into a bowl and poured two iced teas. Annabel folded her legs beside her and leaned into him on the couch. He pressed the "resume" button on the infamous movie. Scarlett O'Hara and Prissy were still in a state of flux over Melanie's imminent baby. They both put their hands in the popcorn bowl at the same time.

"Last time," Dustin said, "you were worried because you didn't 'know nothin' 'bout birthin' babies.' What a difference a week can make."

Annabel erupted with a smile. "You know, I'm still experiencing an afterglow. It was way cool."

"Are you considering obstetrics as a specialty?"

"I still don't know. So far, I liked each rotation. Well, now I like OB, but I didn't like it at the beginning of the week!"

She glanced back at the kitchen because Oliver had not joined them.

The dog still seemed curious about Solar, who was also interested in the dog. She tapped Dustin to peek at them. Solar flexed his neck at Oliver. "What's your problem?" he said.

As Atlanta still burned and a baby was coming, they both chuckled at the entertainment behind them.

CHAPTER 30

"Table for two," Dustin said.

The maître d' scooped up two menus and led him and Annabel to a table adjacent to a partition. "There's a noisy school reunion on the other side."

Dustin eyed the linen tablecloth and napkins and the fact that there were few people on their side next to the bar. A couple and one woman sat on barstools and were drinking, eating, or watching the muted television screen. On second glance, a tiny vase adorned the table with a single rose.

"This may be perfect," Dustin said with a questioning look at Annabel.

She nodded, didn't wait, and slipped into the chair beside her. Dustin sat across from her facing the front of the restaurant, which was the way he always wanted it. He gathered she remembered that about him and it was now second nature for her to oblige him.

"Your server will be here in a moment," the head waiter said as he handed them the menus. He unfolded Annabel's napkin, extended it to her for her lap, and then turned.

Annabel studied her menu, but Dustin gave his cursory glances. He was nervous. His heart pitter-pattered like a school boy with a first-love crush. This was the first time ever in his life that he was taking the plunge at a huge commitment with a female. One for life. If she would have him, of course.

After being overly analytical at first, trying to make the decision after Sean had initiated the "marriage" conversation, and after buying the engagement ring, he finally let go of his pondering and scrutinizing of details, and was ready to ask her the big question. After all, the worst that could happen was that she said no. But that would be hard to swallow too. He slid his hand into the pocket of his trousers, as if reassuring himself that the time was ripe to pop the question, he let his fingers settle and let go of the smooth box with the diamond ring.

Annabel crossed her legs under the table and bumped into him, causing him to startle.

"You're jumpy," she said. "I hope you're not reliving memories of your recent encounter at the diner or your terrible car accident."

"No. Sorry about that."

She grinned. "I am tickled to death that we're sitting here and left a dog and a parrot together in the same house after they just met. Your house may be full of surprises when we go back and I pick up Oliver."

"Ha. Oliver is still a child in human terms and Solar is a wise ass. You're right. I'd better not think about them and spoil this romantic afternoon."

"It is romantic. Thank you for bringing me to this place."

"I'm your waiter this afternoon. My name is Chris." A man with a black short-sleeved shirt and dark trousers poured ice water into their glasses. He wore a red mustache and one earring. "Are there any questions about the menu?"

"How is the salmon and cheese grits?" Annabel asked.

"Excellent. With grilled asparagus, you won't be disappointed."

She handed him her menu and nodded.

"I'll have a medium cooked ribeye with the same sides," Dustin said.

"And may I bring you anything else to drink?"

"I'm good," Annabel said.

"I'll have one of those Tennessee Calfkiller beers," Dustin said.

The waiter tipped his head and left.

"Glad to see you're patronizing a craft beer from my state," she said.

"Sure thing. I have yet to spend much time there. Maybe you can take me down there and show me the sights."

"That would be fun. We can start with a honky-tonk weekend in Nashville."

Dustin's heart rate and rhythm settled down into a much easier pace. They were talking about plans together and this gave him comfort that she saw at least a near future with him. His proposal, he had decided, should come after dinner, around the time to order or eat the scrumptious dessert she liked.

Annabel was talking about the nightly constant party atmosphere on downtown Broadway in Nashville. He got a kick more with how stunning she looked and the enthusiasm she emanated for her home town. Perhaps it wouldn't be too long before he met her family. The little she mentioned about them ... they sounded like a thoroughly interesting cast of characters.

Chris appeared from Dustin's side of the table and put down their entrees. "Be careful, the plates are hot. Is there anything else I can get either of you?"

Annabel and Dustin shook their heads. "Bon appetit," he said.

After sampling her meal, Annabel rolled her eyes. "I'm glad I didn't order grits at breakfast. I ordered pancakes and eggs. These can't be topped."

"Where'd you go?"

"Just up the block. Bob and I ate there since he brought over Oliver."

Dustin let the tremor of jealousy pass. It would be stupid to react that way, he thought. Jealousy was a trait he saw in many men he booked for domestic abuse. They were the controlling types, domineering and possessive of their girlfriends or wives. He was levelheaded, and as far as he knew, she and Bob were tight friends with their mutual studies in common and a source of support for each other. He would need to totally accept Bob as a part of Annabel's life.

"That was nice of him to bring Oliver over. You two are apparently off to a fine start sharing him."

"Yes, I think so and I hope so."

The maître d' sauntered in for a second and pointed to the bar. A man in his early to mid-thirties with an average build thanked him and, walking with a limp, chose a stool not too far across from their table. He checked out his surroundings and his chin had a noticeable scar. Dustin gave the man a fleeting thought ... his limp and scar might be the result of something innocent, from police work, or perhaps he did military service in Afghanistan.

The man turned his head purposefully a second time, barely giving Dustin a glance. He leaned to the side. Dustin wasn't sure, but the man seemed to show a glint of recognition as he studied Annabel from the side. The bartender handed him a menu and, after he ordered, he peered over at her again with his hand partly covering his face.

Despite the jitters that were starting to resurface in Dustin's stomach, he ate most of his steak.

"I think the two of us brought a healthy appetite," Annabel said to their waiter as he picked up their plates. "But why we're really here is for your carrot cake."

"Then I don't have to ask you if you're having desert," the young man retorted. "Shall I bring two and will you be drinking coffee?"

"Do you want to split a piece of cake?" she asked Dustin.

"Yes. For such an important date, it would be more memorable to share."

"All our dates are important." She looked up. "We'll share one piece and I'll take decaf, please."

"I'll take the real caffeine."

The waiter nodded and strolled off.

Dustin wrapped his fingers around the ring case in his pocket. His pulse quickened and he realized he should use the restroom after the beer and water he drank. He would be a lot more comfortable without a full bladder diverting his attention.

The man at the bar finished his beer as well as an appetizer of shrimp cocktail. Another beer was placed in front of him on the fine wooden counter, but he stepped down and gently limped past their table.

Dustin rose. "Give me a moment to run to the restroom. I do have something important to ask you." He smiled and tilted his head.

"I'll be here." She wondered about his question. "But, no, you can't borrow Oliver to keep Solar company."

Dustin laughed, turned, and headed to the men's room. He pushed the door and stepped in. The man from the bar stood at a middle urinal and Dustin stood two over as he unzipped his fly. An air of hesitancy hung over them, as if they both had something to say.

Dustin was curious why the man gave Annabel a double-take, but he spoke up using a different tactic. "I hope your limp isn't from a war injury."

The man finished his stream. "It's my take-home souvenir from Afghanistan. What about you? Serve any time?"

"That was slightly before my time, so I missed it. Thank you for your service. I do, however, try to give back to society because I'm a police officer."

The man nodded. "I don't do anything near as important now. I'm a financial consultant in Louisville. Come up the Ohio on my boat every couple of weekends. I know the right places to eat." He zipped up his fly.

"The boating sounds like fun. Your job doesn't sound too bad either, especially since you're a bit disabled."

"Yeah, the boat is a blessing. Did you meet your date on the Findar app? I'm pretty sure I know her, so I might stop by and say hello."

Dustin began pulling up his zipper and almost caught his skin. "Really? Are you saying that you met her on the dating app? My date with her isn't over yet today, but how long ago did you date her?"

Both men went to the sink and the man contemplated. "I don't know … six, not more than twelve months ago. Yes, we stumbled on each other through the dating site. As a matter of fact, she did come on board my *Hannah* .. my boat, which I dock on the Kentucky side of the river when I come up here."

"That must have been fun. You gave her a ride?"

"No," he said, looking down for a moment. "We ate at the marina and then she stayed on board. We had a great night. She left early in the morning for her graduate work."

Dustin caught his breath. He wished he had not heard this. No, actually he was glad he did. He was aware when he started dating her that she'd been up to a little risky behavior, but maybe it was more than he ever figured. This was the woman he was about to propose to. He took a big gulp.

The man sensed Dustin's discomfort. "If you're really going to date her, don't get me wrong. She seems smart and like a good person. I can't blame her too much for finding men on the social app because I was using it for a while as well … looking for women. My wife died and it kind of filled a void."

The both men finished washing over the sinks and shook hands. "By the way, I'm Dustin."

"And I'm Jerry."

"If you don't mind," Dustin said, "I'll head out first. Feel free to say hello to her, but I'm staying out of it. I have a lot to think about."

"Good luck, buddy, and be careful with your police work."

Dustin felt absolutely awful. As nervous and as elated he had been over asking Annabel to marry him, he was now despondent and unsure. Each footstep back to their dinner table lingered like an eternity as he tried to grasp her rendezvous one-night stand with Jerry. His own history of sexual encounters was nowhere close to hers. He'd gone to bed in the past with two women he hardly knew, but even then, they had dated once or twice.

And he certainly didn't meet them through swiping left or right on an iPhone.

He dug down into his pocket and put his thumb and index finger around the velvet case with the engagement ring. No. Not today. Not this week. Not this month. He couldn't ask her. He needed to think some more about this.

Why the dichotomy? Hell, her studying medicine and helping people; her fine manners and personality; her thoughtfulness and intelligence; they were in glaring contrast to her risky dating behavior.

Yet, this modern app service was spreading like wild fire and he'd read how common it was, including the quick hook-up sexual flings that were understood beforehand by some of the parties. He arrived at their table, so he had to dismiss his introspection of the situation. His mind was made up … there would be no marriage proposal today. He shoved the box as deep as he could into the recess of his hip pocket.

Annabel looked up at him with a grin and held a fork in her hand. "I couldn't wait, but I only took one bite."

He joined her and she handed him a utensil. He had no appetite now for the carrot cake, but took a bite. "It is as moist and scrumptious as before. You may eat most of it in lieu of my being such a gentleman."

"You are, Dustin. You have many fine qualities and that's one of them." Her eyes took a double take beyond Dustin and Jerry paused beside them.

"I thought I recognized you," Jerry said. "Annabel, correct?"

"Yes," she stumbled, her pulse quickening. "Jerry, right?"

"Yes."

"You gave me your financial consulting business card. I kept it."

"Here." He dug for his wallet in his back pocket. "This is for your friend too. Even if either of you don't need financial planning now, some day you might." He handed Dustin his card. "Nice seeing you again, Annabel."

"You too."

"Thanks," Dustin said.

Jerry went back to his bar stool and Annabel stuck her fork into the icing. It's a small world, she thought. Too small. She watched Dustin. She needed to shake off the close encounter; one which Dustin wouldn't appreciate knowing about and one which she had mixed reservations about. Her time with Jerry was enjoyable the night they met. They ended up sharing personal stories and physical intimacy.

"Jerry lost his wife," she said. "and I think he's still getting over her. He told me when he gave me his business card that he named his boat after her ... *Hannah*."

"That must be a special boat."

"I think so." She savored another piece and she wondered why he was looking at her so intently. "You mentioned you wanted to ask me something important."

Dustin shook a packet of sugar in his coffee. "It was nothing that can't wait or maybe my idea should be tabled indefinitely."

CHAPTER 31

"Oliver," Annabel said, "you are amazing. To think you spent the afternoon with a chatty bird in another new place and were good as gold. After all, you're still a big puppy, and young dogs are known to be unpredictable at times."

Annabel sat on her desk chair after getting home from Dustin's and looked Oliver square in the eyes. The dog stared back at her and then stretched out, ready to settle after the busy day. She went and poured a glass of water from the kitchen sink. Totally full from the wonderful meal, that was all she brought back to her desk.

Dustin's company and the early dinner had been stellar, but she could have done without bumping into Jerry, her previous date with his own boat. He was a fine man, but most women know it's not wise to mix new boyfriends with old ones. Well, she thought, Jerry didn't qualify as a previous boyfriend. He had been a one-night stand. However, he would certainly make a fine partner for someone after the grieving for his deceased wife was behind him.

Thank goodness, she thought, that the short interlude with Jerry at their table had not delved into a more in-depth conversation. She liked Dustin very much and wanted in no way to jeopardize their relationship. After all, she wouldn't be happy if she found out that he had a history of a flurry of one-night interludes in the not-too-distant past.

She showered and put on pajamas and went back to her computer, all the while trying to wipe relationship thoughts out of her head. She opened the desktop; she needed to go through her lecture one more quick and final time.

Satisfied that she knew the presentation as well as she could, she closed down, and bused her glass back to the sink. Now, as importantly, she needed to get a full and perfect night's sleep. It was 9 p.m., so she was on track. She set her alarm for 5:30 a.m., allowing a half hour to walk and feed Oliver, and an hour to dress, drink coffee, and leave.

Oliver followed her over and settled next to the bed. Before getting in, she kneeled down and ruffled his hair. "Good night, buddy." She gave him a kiss and then scrambled under her covers. Within a half hour, she was fast asleep.

Startled right out of her sleep, Annabel woke and tried to figure out what the hell was going on. Oliver walked on top of her, prancing on top of her abdomen from one side of the bed to the other. She extended her arms, barricading him from coming up any closer, and then sat up.

"Oliver, bad dog! Get down." She tried to push him off, but he insisted on staying put and carried on prancing all over her sheets, trying to sidle as close as possible to her. He panted like crazy.

She glanced at the clock on the nightstand. It was only ten o'clock. She swung her legs off the side of the bed. Oliver jumped down. He lowered his head and squeezed past her rolling chair and into the space below the desk. He cowered against the wall but, not satisfied, he slinked back out. Pacing back and forth, he stopped momentarily and clung to her legs.

"Oliver, what's going on with you?"

She turned on her room light, stepped into the bathroom, and sat on the toilet. Oliver tagged along. When she stood and washed her hands, the dog tried to jam himself behind the commode. Now she wondered if she had a mentally disturbed dog on her hands. She said, "What on earth is wrong?"

Back in her big room with Oliver at her heels, she went to the front window and peeked out. Through the heavy clouds, which had built up during the evening, she detected a flash of light … lightning somewhere off in the distance. By the time she tried to settle back in bed, she heard a low rumble of thunder.

"Oh no," she said aloud as Oliver pawed at her closet door. She padded over and opened the accordion door. He hurried in, wanting to bury himself in the back confines of the space behind a pile of shoe boxes. Which lasted a half minute. He weaved himself back out and circled her.

She would have never counted on this in a hundred years. It appeared that she and Bob had a dog who was deathly afraid of thunderstorms; their otherwise well-behaved Oliver was revealing his phobia to her. She'd known about such dogs, but her family never owned one with this problem. If the storm continued, she thought, his behavior would escalate. The thunder and lightning was headed in their direction.

Annabel slumped on the floor, her back to her bed, and coaxed Oliver over. Wrapping her arms around him, she whispered in his ear, "It's okay, boy. The storm won't hurt you."

A significant thunderclap sounded and Oliver broke from her grasp. He panted all the while, his tongue hanging and his chest cycling faster than an athlete's respiratory rate after a hard run. Annabel shook her head. After eleven o'clock, she slid under her covers again, but Oliver jumped up and wasn't satisfied unless he was walking over her chest and up to her face.

She pushed him gently but firmly. Midnight was approaching and she was losing valuable sleep. This was an untimely situation, she thought. The presenter of any fine medical lecture needs to be rested and coherent from a long and halfway decent night's sleep.

The thunderstorm grew more significant, and by 1 a.m., the rain pounded forcefully on the roof above her. Being on the top floor of the house, her place bore the brunt of it. The lightning continued with a light show and the thunder roared with impetuous claps that dwarfed their senses. Her heart wrenched in her chest as she watched her previously calm companion strive to escape and take shelter from the ungodly weather. But there was no escape from Mother Nature and there was no sleep for Annabel.

The hours ticked by and, as the rain tapered off to a trickle and the thunder and lightning ceased, she threw some clothes on and walked Oliver at 5 a.m. When she came back in, she dried his paws and put on a French vanilla Keurig coffee cup. Her bed in the other room was like a magnet trying to snap her over. She placed her elbows on the kitchen counter and dropped her head into her hands.

"What lousy timing," she mumbled and lowered her hands. Oliver, now subdued, cocked his head at her. He no longer panted or paced. "What? You want to eat and, while I'm gone, you're going to catch up on your lost sleep?"

She dressed in tan trousers and a plaid blue blouse and tried to camouflage the circles under her eyes with makeup. When she left the apartment, her thinking was so fuzzy, she almost forgot the flash drive on the kitchen counter.

CHAPTER 32

On Monday morning, a few early medical students dotted the OB/GYN department's auditorium as Annabel made her way down the aisle to the stage. A technical assistant at the podium fiddled with wires from the laptop stationed there and, as she stepped up the stairs, she heard Bob call her name. He approached her from a chair in the front row.

"You made it," she said. "Did your internal medicine chief resident give you a hard time about peeling away from the ward?"

"I really lucked out. My chief resident for this make-up last week is our old chief, Donn Schott. He said your lecture subject matter is extremely important. He even sent another one of the students on the rotation with me." He pointed to a student behind him.

She nodded and followed up with a grimace. "This is going to be awful. My head isn't screwed on this morning to present a lecture. I went to sleep for one hour last night and then that storm blew in. So guess what?"

Bob shook his head.

"Oliver is deathly afraid of thunderstorms. He acted like a cornered jungle cat and didn't know what to do with himself. No matter what I did, I couldn't appease him. The poor boy. However, whenever I tried to go back to bed, he was up and down and all over me. And his panting and trying to get away from the weather was crazy. Ha! Now he can de-stress and sleep and I have to give this lecture."

Her eyes narrowed and her lips trembled. As she stared at the floor, she shook her head. "There's not enough coffee in the world right now to help me sharpen my brain cells."

Bob's expression changed to concern as he reached forward and touched her forearm. "Annabel, I'm so sorry. I had no idea. There were no storms when Oliver was at my place. Had I known, I would have never brought him over to you."

"What happened is not your fault. Besides, you needed to sleep as well before starting back today."

"However, giving your first big lecture to the whole department and then having to be on OB/GYN call tonight is a different ball game."

The technician plugged in a cord on the wall socket and pointed to

Annabel. "If you're the one giving this lecture, we better get ready."

"Yes, I'm coming." She looked at Bob and their eyes held.

"Good luck," he said. "Only focus on the lecture material. You can do this."

She grimaced and, on the top step, she glanced back at him and gave him a faint nod.

Bob took a seat next to his student colleague in the front row and Annabel pulled out the flash drive from her white jacket. The technician plugged it in as Dr. Harvey came strutting down the aisle and joined her on the stage.

"Good morning, Annabel," he said.

"Dr. Harvey, an unfortunate event occurred at my apartment last night during the storm. So not only am I scared to be up here and talk, but I basically didn't sleep all night. I apologize beforehand because, in all honesty, I'm going to blow this talk."

She watched his hands and expected Roosevelt to tuck in his shirt, but he didn't. He sighed and scratched his neck.

"I wish I could recite some significant quote to help you get over your sleepiness, but you have an inner strength that you can pull from, despite your tiredness, and your fear, and your nervousness to present this talk. As a matter of fact, for the next hour, your fight and flight hormones will kick in, and if you know your subject matter, which I know you do, they will pump you with enthusiasm and wakefulness and you will do better than you think.

"Another thing ... a lecture is not about the lecturer, it's about the content. Take yourself out of the picture. It's not about you. Deliver the important subject matter so that each individual sitting here goes away with something they learned. They don't care if you mess up a little bit; they want to know the bulk of what you're enlightening them with."

Although Annabel's heart rate had inched up, her attending's words were like manna from heaven. She gave Bob a second glance.

"I've pulled up your lecture," the technician said and showed her how to use the laser pointer. He pointed out the forward and back buttons for her slides and clipped the wire for the microphone on her lapel. "You're ready to go."

The auditorium had filled up with long-coated attending doctors and residents, short-coated medical students, and some folks without white

jackets at all. Situating themselves on the end of an aisle, Kristin Fleming and Caleb took a seat. Annabel glanced up at the three screens ... one behind her and two to the side ... confirming the title slide to her lecture:
"Medical Errors, Physician Burnout, and Drug Shortages."

Her heart raced like a runaway thoroughbred as she cleared her throat. To stand behind the podium felt too formal, so she stepped to the side, looked at her audience, and then the center screen.

"Most of you know me. I'm Annabel Tilson, an almost-fourth-year-medical student, and I'm about to cover three subjects of importance to physicians in any field of medicine and students on all rotations. Although each subject is important, I'm starting backwards, first with drug shortages. I'll end with medical errors."

With each sentence, Annabel's pulse slowed down and a bit more composure took root. She went to the first slide.

"The FDA, or the Food and Drug Administration, has a strict definition for drug shortages," she said, pointing the laser at the slide. "A period of time when the demand or projected demand for a medically necessary drug in the U.S. exceeds its supply.

"What this means to us is that doctors cannot give the right drugs to patients when needed. I had a first-hand glimpse of this recently when one of our obstetric patients was not able to receive the epidural drug that our astute anesthesiologist wanted to inject.

"This is a problem some of us in training are not aware of, but need to be by the time we're loaded up with more responsibility. At present, our country is short on 182 drugs and medical supplies and the list is insane."

Her arrow scrolled down the list on the slide and she read some of them aloud: "IV bags, injectable morphine, other painkillers, anesthetics, antibiotics, electrolytes, cancer drugs, and much more."

She glanced at her audience; almost all of them were paying strict attention.

"So why is this so important?

"Drug shortages have serious consequences. When a health care provider cannot administer needed drugs, then they are not providing the proper treatment. Shortages endanger patients' lives."

Annabel went on to explain the reasons for shortages, much of what was explained to her by Dr. Fleming, and then discussed the effects the problem had on health care costs.

"Drugs shortages also increase the country's health care costs. Staff must take hours to manage the shortages by tracking inventory and figuring out alternative drugs. Decisions must be made about rationing the scarce resources that exist. And most despicable of all, certain drug vendors then price-gouge the drugs that are in short supply. All told, that alone costs the U.S. several hundred million dollars a year.

"Dr. Kristin Fleming, one of the anesthesiologists, and I would like to mention one more thing. It is important to inform policymakers what is going on in the clinical setting. Without real-time stories of the drug shortages and how they affect our patients, they cannot set policies in place."

Annabel peered over at Dr. Harvey, who flashed her a smile and gave her a thumbs-up. Her composure ramped up. Perhaps her lack of sleep helped to settle her nerves, she thought.

"Dr. Harvey and I will take questions in the end. I'll go on to my second topic of 'Physician Burnout.'" She scrolled to the next heading.

"Presently, this is a *huge* topic for M.D.s," she stressed. "My next three slides list the physical, emotional, and behavioral signs and symptoms of physician burnout. These are important because ..." She focused on her audience and held her gaze. "We should learn to recognize these signs and symptoms in the doctors we're working with and, hopefully, recognize them in ourselves."

The first slide she highlighted by talking about providers feeling tired and drained, having poor appetites or sleeping habits, and other physical signs and symptoms similar to depression.

She thought about Ling Watson when she scrolled ahead. "Look for the emotional signs in your colleagues - things like no motivation, constantly being cynical, and voicing helplessness. Or what if they derive no more pleasure from activities that used to give them joy?"

Annabel pointed to the third slide on the topic. "Here's the third list, which I hate. Behavioral signs can include the physician turning to drugs or alcohol to cope, or snapping at their colleagues, or being nasty to their patients." There were more signs and symptoms and she gave the residents, students, and staff a few moments to process them.

"So, being in training or being an M.D. *is* stressful. Prevention is the first key to avoid burnout. If you haven't learned tricks to lower your stress or create balance in your life, then it's time to learn some. We need to stop being invincible and learn to admit that sometimes we're just not tough enough to handle every responsibility dropped on our plates. We must learn to ask for help and to recommend help for other colleagues. This is where the Psychiatry department is skilled. They have a program for docs, which is stupendous, with different treatments, therapies, and discussion groups.

"Don't forget," she said, "the symptoms we talked about can threaten your career as well as your marriage or relationships. Even your life."

Annabel took a deep breath and glanced down at Bob. He nodded his approval and she gave him a small smile.

"Last but not least, here's a problem that severely affects patients. The next department's M&M meeting, or Morbidity and Mortality lecture, will cover an OB/GYN patient that we just lost because of a medical error." Her face saddened, she scanned the faces in the room, and pressed the forward button on the remote. In bold letters, everyone read "MEDICAL ERRORS."

"Officially, what are the three top causes of death in the United States as reported by the CDC? Most of us know the answer to that and we see patients with these underlying issues daily in primary care, internal medicine, and the sub-specialties." Her next slide listed:

1. Heart disease
2. Cancer
3. Chronic respiratory disease

"But we have to wonder about this; perhaps this list will be amended. Over an eight-year period, researchers at Johns Hopkins calculated something else ... that 250,000 deaths each year are due to medical errors. That would surpass the figure of 150,000 people who die each year from respiratory disease. In that case, medical errors would be the third leading cause of death in the United States!"

The expressions from the audience wore worried looks. Dr. Harvey stood at attention to the side of the stage. She took a step and demonstrated her next slide.

"Yes, appalling, isn't it? Does this mean we are training bad doctors? Does this mean physicians in university teaching situations and those out in private practice are inherently bad?"

Some folks squirmed in their seats. "No," she said, answering her own question. "The researchers say that most errors are represented by systemic problems. Health care workers may poorly coordinate the care of patients; hospitals, other health care facilities, and doctor's offices may lack or underuse safety protocols; there may be physician practice patterns which lack accountability; and insurance networks may be broken down.

"I wonder if medical errors are even underreported because there is always the fear that if a physician or other health care provider reports an error, they will be punished or they will be incriminated by the legal system. As you all are aware, in our training programs, those repercussions are dampened because of the systems we have in place. We should all report errors when we learn about them so that the problems involved can be addressed, allowing us to change some medical schematic that is in need of repair."

Bob nodded in the front row and she glanced quickly at Roosevelt.

"Here are some tips about giving a medication to a patient. Some of us personally deliver drugs more than others, such as anesthesiologists; in other cases, the nursing staff is carrying out doctors' orders.. Remember all the 'R' tips." She turned to a slide with a list of eight bullet points:

"Right medicine

Right dose

Right patient

Right time

Right route

Right documentation

Right reason

Right response."

She paused, giving everyone a chance to read. "Remembering and abiding by these may prevent a medical error. They are self-explanatory, such as … is the right medicine being given or is the medicine you're about to give going to the right patient? What about the correct route? Are you sure whether or not the drug is to be given by mouth, through a vein, or an intramuscular shot? Is the patient exhibiting the correct response from the drug you just gave?

"This last week, a patient died on the obstetrics ward because the correct drug was given but in an accelerated intravenous time frame because of a mix-up when the medication label was incorrectly slapped on the wrong IV bag. In essence, the simple Lactated Ringer's IV solution without the label was the bag that had the magnesium sulfate in it and ran into the patient's vein at a higher rate meant for hydration … causing an overdose."

There was so much more she could tell to all the concerned faces in front of her. "Another thing … we had a patient on the ward mistakenly receive morphine instead of Motrin. Sometimes caregivers have difficulty reading physician's handwriting. If an order is handwritten, it must be legible!"

Next, Annabel highlighted drugs that sound alike when an order is verbally given, cautioning physicians to pronounce them clearly. When she looked over at Dr. Harvey, he pointed to his wrist watch. She looked at the wall clock.

"It's time to wrap this up," she said. "Although we've only touched on these three topics, I hope they leave you with a lasting impression and you will take care to practice the advice or look into these matters further. Dr. Harvey wants me to remind you to attend the next M&M conference."

Roosevelt began clapping as he strolled over and the audience gave her a loud applause, which was more emphatic than most endings to grand rounds.

"Thank you, Dr. Tilson," Roosevelt said. "We appreciated your fine presentation and important topics."

Annabel nodded and put the remote on the podium.

"Are there any questions?" he asked.

No one raised their hand and yet no one seemed to be in a hurry to leave.

"Thanks, Annabel," someone finally said.

"I second that," Bob said from the front seat.

The technician helping with grand rounds stepped over from the sidelines, pulled out Annabel's flash drive, and packed up the wires. Many attendees came forward and complimented Annabel, and soon the majority of people thinned out of the auditorium.

"Nice work," Dr. Harvey said. "You did an excellent job. The residents, students, and staff in this room will especially remember this talk because it was given by you ... an example of a doctor-in-training who is and will be making a difference in health care."

He nodded as she slipped the flash drive in her pocket. All of a sudden, every last morsel of nervousness from before the lecture lifted like a bird in flight and tiredness swept over her. She arched up her eyebrows, trying to fight the feeling.

"Thank you, Dr. Harvey."

"I think you have some sleep to catch up on. You call me late in the afternoon if you don't nap. If that is the case, I'll arrange for you come in later, around 9 p.m., for overnight call."

She took comfort in his words and thoughtfulness. "I don't know what to say."

"You're welcome." He left in a hurry, ready to face the responsibilities of the obstetric ward.

Annabel walked down the short staircase where Bob waited for her.

"You hit that lecture out of the ball field!"

She rolled her eyes. "You're just saying that."

"Really. You didn't bore us with jammed up slides with too much to read like some lecturers do. You were succinct and interesting and educational. Shall I go on?"

"No, but Dr. Fleming and Dr. Harvey did render their help."

"Yes, I'm sure. But you pulled it together and stood on that stage like a champ."

"All right already. That's enough."

"I'm finished, but I'm so sorry again about Oliver. We have to do something about his behavior. You can't not sleep like that."

"Neither can you. Your time will come. I'll ask the vet and search online about dogs with storm phobias. Poor Oliver. He doesn't intend to be so frightened. It must be in his genes."

"Speaking of genes, Oliver's DNA results arrived in an email. But, come on, I need to hustle back to the internal medicine ward. The student who was with me already left. And you ... you must go home and get some sleep and be sure not to tank down coffee from the Keurig machine I gave you."

"His DNA results are back?"

Bob nodded with a mischievous smile.

"Bob Palmer, do I have to squeeze the report out of you? Let's hear it."

They both walked out the back door with their shoulders close together, talking about Oliver the whole way.

End

FROM THE AUTHOR

Barbara Ebel is a physician and an author. Since she practiced anesthesia, she brings credibility to the medical background of her plots. She lives with her husband and pets in a wildlife corridor in Tennessee but has lived up and down the East Coast.

Twitter: @BarbaraEbel
Facebook Author/Reader Group: Medical Suspense Café
Visit or contact the author at her website: http://barbaraebelmd.com

The following (two medical suspense series and other books) are also written by Dr. Barbara and are available as paperbacks and eBooks:

The Dr. Annabel Tilson Series:

Dead Still (Dr. Annabel Tilson Novels Book 1)
Deadly Delusions (Dr. Annabel Tilson Novels Book 2)
Desperate to Die (Dr. Annabel Tilson Novels Book 3)
Death Grip (Dr. Annabel Tilson Novels Book 4)
Downright Dead (Dr. Annabel Tilson Novels Book 5)
Dangerous Doctor (Dr. Annabel Tilson Novels Book 6)

The Dr. Danny Tilson Series:

Operation Neurosurgeon (A Dr. Danny Tilson Novel: Book 1)
Silent Fear: *a Medical Mystery* (A Dr. Danny Tilson Novel: Book 2). Also an Audiobook.
Collateral Circulation: *a Medical Mystery* (A Dr. Danny Tilson Novel: Book 3). Also an Audiobook.
Secondary Impact (A Dr. Danny Tilson Novel: Book 4).

The Outlander Physician Series:

Corruption in the O.R.: A Medical Thriller (The Outlander Physician

Series Book 1)
Wretched Results: A Medical Thriller (The Outlander Physician Series Book 2)

<u>Stand-alone Medical Fiction:</u>

Outcome, A Novel

Her Flawless Disguise

<u>Nonfiction health book:</u>

Younger Next Decade: *After Fifty, the Transitional Decade, and What You Need to Know*

Also written and illustrated by Barbara Ebel: A <u>children's book series</u> about her loveable therapy dog; illustrated with real pictures:
Chester the Chesapeake Book One
Chester the Chesapeake Book Two: Summertime
Chester the Chesapeake Book Three: Wintertime
Chester the Chesapeake Book Four: My Brother Buck
Chester the Chesapeake Book Five: The Three Dogs of Christmas

Made in the USA
Middletown, DE
26 August 2022

72297146R00129